Nothing to Lose

THOMAS WAUGH

"A murderer is regarded by the conventional world as something almost monstrous, but a murderer to himself is only an ordinary man."

Graham Greene, *The Ministry of Fear.*

"Good Lord above, can't you see I'm pining?
Tears all in my eyes
Send down that cloud with a silver lining
Lift me to Paradise
Show me that river, take me across
And wash all my troubles away
Like that lucky old sun, give me nothin' to do
But roll around Heaven all day."

Haven Gillespie, *That Lucky Old Sun*.

Chapter 1

It was late. Cold. But Michael Devlin's heart was colder. Frost dusted the cars, hedges and slate rooftops alike. The moon was dim and sickle-shaped. Pink-grey clouds, like tumours, blotted out the stars. It was a fine night — for killing.

Smoke pirouetted up from Devlin's cigarette as he followed Martin Pound, Conservative Member of Parliament for Wiltshire South, down the quiet street, full of attractive terrace houses, in Chiswick. Pound was heading for his London home (taxpayers had bought the property but the minister intended to pocket the robust profit when he sold it on). Devlin's window of opportunity would close when the MP reached his drive. But it only takes a moment to assassinate someone. Devlin had stalked his prey since the minister had left his club in Piccadilly and got on the tube. Pound liked to use public transport. He liked being recognised by members of the public, especially young women.

The clip-clop of Pound's polished oxford brogues, no doubt purchased in Jermyn Street along with the rest of his wardrobe, sounded like horses' hooves upon the concrete. Devlin's footsteps were quieter and quicker. He carefully pulled out a black-handled kitchen knife from the inside pocket of his dark blue suit. His orders — given to him by Oliver Porter — were to use a knife instead of a gun.

Talking out on the terrace of the National Liberal Club, Porter had briefed Devlin about the contract: *"Make it look like a street crime. A random act. There have, fortunately for us, been a number of stabbings in the area over the past few months. The nature of the crime shouldn't raise too much suspicion."* The two men had been friends, and business associates, for several years now. Oliver Porter had his manicured fingers in several pies and served as a middle-man

1

for all manner of spooks, gangsters and commercial organisations. Porter 'fixed things'. He had encouraged Devlin to continue to use his skill and training after he came out of the army. The well-connected ex-officer was comfortable moving in both the underworld and the upper echelons of society. Business was business.

Porter had explained to Devlin that the politician owed some businessmen a large sum of money. *"Pound lives beyond his means and has a nasty gambling habit. And he has borrowed capital from some even nastier people."* Pound had become embroiled in a business deal for the notorious gangsters, the Parker brothers, and though he had paid off a substantial amount of his debt to them, his creditors were still not happy. Now he was threatening to confess all to the authorities, unless his debt was written off.

Devlin wasn't particularly concerned with his victim's sins or the reasons behind the contract. Everybody sins, and everybody dies. He flicked his cigarette butt into a drain. There were no cameras on the street, and no lights on in the homes which flanked the road they walked down. Devlin's iron-wrought, work-hardened features barely changed as he put his hand over the minister's face and silenced his scream. His other hand curled around him like a snake and buried the knife into his chest, puncturing his lungs. The minister shot out an arm, his hand outstretched, but then he slumped to the floor like a puppet whose strings had been cut. To give credence to the scenario of a street crime Devlin stabbed the politician several more times. The minister's woollen overcoat soaked up the blood, which oozed out of his body. Devlin took the man's wallet and jewellery, as any good mugger would.

Devlin proceeded to calmly walk down the street. He wiped the handle of the kitchen knife, so as not to leave any prints, and tossed the weapon into a bush in the nearby park.

He walked for half a mile — the bitter chill in the air didn't bother him — and then hailed a black taxi to take him to Rotherhithe. Devlin was a polite but forgettable fare. He made a modicum of small talk, but for the most part thumbed his way through the last chapters of Turgenev's *Home of the Gentry*. He got out the cab near Southwark Park and walked half a mile back towards Tower Bridge and his apartment. On his way he sent a brief text message to Oliver Porter: *Job done.*

Chapter 2

Devlin's fifth floor apartment was located off Tooley Street and overlooked both Tower Bridge and an attractive square containing shops, a fountain and a bronze statue of Charles Dickens. Aside from the endless rows of bulging bookcases the apartment had an air of emptiness about it. It looked as if the occupier was either moving out or waiting for someone to move in. There was a leather sofa and widescreen television in the living room, but no ornaments or photographs – and only one framed picture on the wall. The apartment lacked a woman's touch. The bathroom contained a mere half a dozen items and the bedroom was equally spartan – save for more books and a collection of silver-framed photographs of his late wife, Holly, on top of a chest of drawers.

Michael Devlin's build and looks were average. "You have a wonderfully anonymous, forgettable face," Oliver Porter had remarked when he made his pitch for the ex-soldier to become a contract killer five years ago. His hair was shortish and light brown. His hairline was receding and small patches of white hair were creeping into his stubble. If you looked closely at the forty-year-old you would have noticed one eyebrow was slightly shorter, from where a bullet in Afghanistan had struck a piece of masonry and a stone shard had injured him just above the eye. All the other scars he had brought back from the war remained unseen.

Devlin had been born in London, a Bernardo's child. He had lived in a number of foster homes, but never settled. Although he seldom struck the first blow Devlin regularly fought with his classmates and fellow foster children.

Eventually he found a piece of normality when he was fostered out to a couple — Bob and Mary Woodford — who lived just outside of Rochester. His resentment towards the world subsided and he threw himself into his studies. But although Devlin read voraciously, the idea of university never appealed to him. 9-11 happened and Devlin decided to join the army. He wanted to do something. Help someone. Devlin served briefly in Northern Ireland before being posted to Iraq and then Afghanistan. After two tours in Helmand his former commanding officer offered Devlin a job as a security consultant for an investment bank. Devlin left the army and, shortly afterwards, met Holly. Life and love slotted into place. Happiness came – and went, when Holly died in a car accident. It was a hit and run. They never caught the driver.

So now Devlin drank heavily, kept himself to himself, read voraciously and occasionally killed people. Life was lived in the shadow of Holly, of an alternative present where she was alive. Devlin only accepted three or four jobs a year. Each job paid well and he lived relatively frugally. Having bought his apartment, his biggest expenditure was now paying the fees to the care home for Bob and Mary.

Devlin sat, slumped, on the sofa. He worked his way through a pack of cigarettes and turned his stereo to shuffle. Bob Dylan's 'Red River Shore' played in the background…

"Pretty maids all lined up
Outside my cabin door.
I've never wanted any of them wanting me
Except the girl from the Red River shore."

It was now after midnight. Friday, December 13th. Twelve days before Christmas. The blinds to Devlin's balcony window were open and he watched a young couple, in an apartment across the square, start to put up their Christmas decorations. This would be his fifth Christmas without Holly. His first the wrong side of forty.

Rain began to pepper the window. Soon it would sleet. A chill wind whistled through a gap in the warped balcony door. Devlin downed another inch of bourbon. Grief began to well up in his stomach again.

"Well, I can't escape from the memory
Of the one I'll always adore
All those nights when I lay in the arms
Of the girl from the Red River shore."

Devlin gazed up at the large framed print of Holbein's *The Ambassadors* on the wall. Tears moistened his hazel eyes. His hand shook a little as he lit another cigarette. Holly had given the picture to Devlin as a Christmas present. On their first date together she had taken him to the National Gallery. Holly had led him around each floor and exhibition, a whirlwind of enthusiasm and knowledge concerning iconic canvases by Turner, Constable, Gainsborough and the like. The climax of her tour was Holbein's *The Ambassadors*. The self-taught art lover (Holly had read as voraciously as Devlin) decoded some of the painting's messages for him: how the painting represented the spirit of the age — the growing division between church and state and the emergence of science and rationality over the spiritual. Holly had led a captivated Devlin around to the side of the painting to view the counterpane at the centre of the work of art from a different angle. The image of a macabre skull came into focus.

"For some people death lies at the heart of the painting," Holly had remarked, prettily tucking a strand of her long blonde hair behind her ear. "Death casts a shadow over everything and should lie at the forefront of everything. But my favourite part of the painting is this." She had pointed to the top left-hand corner of the canvas. A silver cross could be glimpsed behind the large red curtain, which served as the backdrop to the painting. "Despite the world's growing devotion to science, politics and philosophy I think the artist is saying that God and faith are behind everything."

"Philosophy cannot and should not give faith," Devlin had said, quoting Kierkegaard. The arguments of first cause, the intelligence of design, the scriptures or the divine hand of providence hadn't proven the existence of God for Devlin at that moment — the expression on her face had. Philosophy cannot give birth to faith. Faith gives birth to faith. And faith can give birth to goodness. Devlin believed that the soul was real. That love was real.

The depressed widower raised a corner of his mouth in a gesture towards a smile, recalling the scene. Devlin closed his eyes and tried to re-live the touch and taste of their first kiss, hear the gentle rustle of her silk blouse as it pressed against him and smell her favourite perfume (Chanel's Chance Eau Vive). God, he loved her. Memories of Holly sustained him, and damned him. Devlin poured himself another drink, hoping it would finally usher him off to sleep.

"Well, the sun went down on me a long time ago
I've had to pull back from the door
I wish I could have spent every hour of my life
With the girl from the Red River shore…"

Chapter 3

Martin Pound's body was found by his neighbour, Ernest Holland, who was out walking his wife's black labradoodle, Poppy. Ernest dutifully called the police. The call operator instructed him to wait by the body. Rather than praying for the departed soul of his neighbour Holland pleaded that no one would come along and see him with the unsightly corpse. He dreaded the sheer awkwardness of the scenario. What was one supposed to say? As much as the treasurer of the local rotary club had sympathy for the victim sprawled out before him, he did not want to become a victim of gossip.

Thankfully the murder of a prominent MP prompted a rapid response from the police and a nervy looking Earnest Holland did not have to stand sentry-like for too long before the emergency services arrived. The police ran a background check on the accountant to rule him out of their investigation before letting him go.

Virginia Pound was informed about her husband's murder. She agreed to accompany the police to the station to help with their enquiries. As distraught as she was the politician's wife still had the presence of mind to fix her hair and make-up and put on an appropriate black dress before she left the house, believing that the media would soon be thrusting cameras into her face. Virginia was a former journalist for the *Daily Express* and was as prepared as one could be for the oncoming storm.

The police called the security services and Home Secretary, among others. Their initial thoughts were that the murder was a tragic street crime. To their knowledge the minister was not in possession of any sensitive documents. His wife – and his mistress – had alibis.

*

Later that morning Virginia Pound ventured downstairs, into her husband's study. She opened the safe, concealed behind a large portrait of Disraeli, and went through some papers and files upon a memory stick.

The storm in a teacup was about to boil over...

Chapter 4

Emma Mills sat in her florist shop, at the base of Devlin's apartment block, perched on a wooden stool behind the counter. Her dog, Violet lay curled up, contented, on the floor by her side. The shop, *Rosebuds*, was a festive fiesta of colour and aromas. Frosted wreaths, smelling of pine and cinnamon, filled one of the windows. A tree — decorated with crystal baubles, fairy lights and foil-wrapped chocolates (which the florist gave out to any children accompanying their parents) — was topped off with a gleaming, porcelain angel resembling Grace Kelly. Yet the decorations were the poor cousins, in beauty and life, to the flowers populating the shop. The room teemed with handcrafted bouquets of bluebells, peach blossoms, wild roses, carnations, elegant orchids, lilacs, daisies, tulips and more. Turner and Monet would have envied the shop's palette.

Emma glanced again at the bouquet of lilies which sat waiting by the till. She tapped her foot in impatience. Every fortnight Devlin came into the shop and purchased a bouquet of lilies to place by his late wife's grave. An upturned copy of Graham Greene's *A Burnt-Out Case* lay on the counter. He had mentioned the book and recommended that Emma read it a month ago. She thought he might notice it and appreciate that she had taken on board his recommendation.

God, I'm like a teenage girl with a crush. Have you got so desperate that you're trying to send out signals to a widower whilst he's on his way to the cemetery to pay his respects to his wife? Get real.

Emma gently shook her head, chiding herself, and smirked at her ridiculous behaviour. She resisted taking the copy of the book off the counter though. She still wanted to impress him — and make him think about her.

The thirty year old florist was good natured and good humoured. A Louise Brooks bob framed a sweet, pretty face. A ribbon of scarlet lipstick ran around Emma's mouth and a thin line of black eye shadow accentuated her almond-shaped eyes. For the benefit of Devlin she undid an extra button on her purple polka dot dress (a dress which accentuated her enviable figure).

As per usual he was on time, and, as per usual, he wore the same charcoal grey suit (the suit he had worn to his wedding and also Holly's funeral). Violet scampered out from behind the counter and greeted her favourite customer, wagging her tail with excitement. Violet was as friendly and sweet-tempered as her owner. The black and white dog stood just under knee height. She was part beagle, part hound, part Staffordshire bull terrier. "But all mongrel," Emma would say. "Like me," Devlin had replied, having met the dog and its owner a year or so ago.

Devlin crouched down and scratched Violet behind the ear whilst retrieving a chew from his pocket with his other hand. He looked up at Emma and made a face to ask permission to give the treat to the dog. She smiled and nodded. Devlin smiled back – and not with the mechanical smile he usually offered up to the world. His grin melted his usually frozen features, but Emma couldn't fail to notice his eyes, red-rimmed with sleeplessness.

"Morning. How have you been?" he asked, whilst surveying the new layout of the shop.

"Busy, as you can see. If I have to put up another piece of tinsel I might hang myself with it. Thankfully everything's done now. How have you been?"

"I've been busy doing nothing — working my way through the pub's selection of guest Christmas ales," Devlin (half) joked. The assassin had explained away his lifestyle and lack of a job by saying that he lived off some good investments he made after leaving the army.

The sound was on mute but the news was on a small television at the end of the counter. A rosy-cheeked reporter was standing outside Martin Pound's house in Chiswick. A flurry of scrolling captions – and pictures of a tearful family – told the story.

"It's sad, isn't it?" Emma remarked, her face creased in sympathy.

"I must confess I find it difficult to mourn the death of a politician."

"No, I meant that it's sad for the family. Those children are now going to grow up without a father."

Devlin was going to reply that he had grown up without a father – and that it never did him any harm. But he refrained from saying anything. He felt somehow aggrieved that she was taking his victim's side over him. Violet, having finished her chew, jumped up at Devlin and licked his hand – but he failed to notice or respond. Sensing his awkwardness Emma decided to change the subject.

"Will you be popping in to the Nelson this evening?" she said, making reference to the apartment block's local pub, *The Admiral Nelson*.

"Probably. And you?"

"Definitely. My father's Irish. I'm beginning to think that I've inherited his tolerance – and addiction – to alcohol," Emma joked.

Devlin and Emma had met each other several times in the Nelson before. The first occasion had been on a sort of date, when he had realised that the florist was also a neighbour. They spent a long night together, over several drinks, talking about his time as a soldier, her plans for the shop and their favourite novels. Neither could remember the last time they had laughed so much. He enjoyed her company. But Devlin had made a promise to his dead wife that he would never fall in love or marry again. A sacred promise. Devlin felt guilty, feeling something for Emma. He couldn't just sleep with the florist and creep out before dawn, never to see her again. He didn't want to hurt her, promise something that he could never deliver on. And so they remained just friends, as much as Emma often signalled that she wanted more.

"I've got your flowers ready," Emma said, handing him the bunch of lilies.

"Thanks."

As he cradled the flowers Devlin noticed the copy of the book she had been reading. He wanted to say something. But didn't.

Emma craned her head and stared through a gap in her festive window display in order to watch Devlin walk across the square. Her face was creased in scrutiny. He was a puzzle — and she still couldn't put all the pieces together. Devlin sometimes told funny anecdotes about his time as a soldier, or spoke about military history, but what had he seen and done in the war? Had he killed anyone? She admired Devlin – and was attracted to him all the more – for still being devoted to his wife. He was being faithful to her, even in death. Most men are seldom faithful to their spouses when they are alive. But, even though she knew it was irrational and unkind, Emma resented Devlin's late wife for still having a hold over him.

13

Emma turned up the television in an attempt to stop thinking about him. The victim's wife was speaking."This was no accident. The person behind my husband's murder will be brought to justice," Virginia Pound was declaring. Her face was a picture of disdain and determination as she glared straight down the barrel of the camera lens – and Emma fancied that she wouldn't have liked to be in the shoes of the killer right now.

Chapter 5

"That fuckin' ponce... Stupid fuckin' bitch... We can't be seen to be connected with this," George Parker spat, as he looked up at the television. The career criminal was sitting opposite his younger brother, Byron, in an Italian café they owned in Shoreditch. The café was closed whilst the owners discussed business. Two heavy set men, one white and one black, stood bouncer-like at the door, out of earshot. Jason and Leighton served as bodyguards, as well as drivers, to the Parker brothers.

The ceiling was yellow from the eatery's pre-smoking-ban days. Black and white photos of Sophia Loren, Gina Lollobrigida and Anita Ekberg livened up the sepia-tinged wallpaper. A signed colour photo of Trevor Brooking took pride of place on the counter, next to the flapjacks. The smell of bacon wafted through the establishment from where George Parker had ordered the manager to make him a sandwich. "And I want a proper bacon sandwich, with brown sauce. On white bread. None of your ciabatta or panini shit."

George Parker's flat, triangular face was shaped like an iron. He was a monster of a man, standing over six foot tall. An alloy of muscle and fat. His upper body was all shoulders and no neck. His nose had been broken on numerous occasions and zig-zagged across his face like a bolt of lightning. The fifty year old gangster's left eye was permanently bloodshot. Chubby, scarred fingers dripped with jewellery. A chunky, bejewelled Rolex jangled on his wrist. He was the eldest son of the notorious gangster, Ivan ("The Terrible") Parker, and was part Irish, part Jewish and part Cockney. George Parker had had blood on his hands from an early age. He had broken

15

his first jaw at fifteen and first kneecap at seventeen. At least nobody could accuse the gnarled-faced enforcer of breaking hearts. He liked to dominate women in and out of bed. Sex was an animalistic act for the Viagra-taking ex-boxer. Romance for George Parker was giving his wife or mistress his credit card and telling them to go out and buy something pretty. He demanded his wife remain faithful, whilst she turned a blind eye to his own infidelities – which included bedding his sister-in-law.

George Parker enjoyed having a good time. He called himself a larger than life figure and claimed that the crime writer Martina Cole had based a number of her main characters on him. He wore loud, shiny suits like those of talentless chat show hosts and overpaid footballers. He owned a yellow Rolls Royce, metallic blue Porsche Cayenne and white Jaguar XF. Not to be outdone by any Russian oligarch in Hampstead he had recently added several subterranean floors to his main house in Chislehurst. The property now possessed a snooker room, cinema and space dedicated to various pieces of West Ham memorabilia. George Parker had more money than sense – or taste.

George Parker had stood trial on two charges for murder, but had been acquitted. His first wife had been the bottle blonde actress, Shirley Dobbs, who the *Radio Times* once described as being like 'Barbara Windsor – but without the talent'. He had been shot three separate times over the years, but had survived. The last shooting incident involved his third wife firing a gun at him – but she only shot him in the leg. "God or my old man must be looking after me, bless his wicked soul," George had explained to the cameras outside Old Brompton Road hospital, after the shooting.

George and Byron Parker had business interests in central, east and south-east London. They had inherited a criminal empire from their father which revolved around drugs, prostitution, extortion and racketeering. Intimidation and violence were standard business practises. George Parker longed for the good old days, when he had driven around London with his father in his silver Bentley. There was no high like the adrenalin kick of power and violence – of drawing blood. George could scarce recall a year in his life when he hadn't killed a man, either with his bare hands or with the pearl-handled Browning pistol he carried with him at all times.

George still regularly frequented the clubs and restaurants of his youth (which he now co-owned with his brother). He had any new girl his escort agency hired sent to him first. He liked to test drive them. Drink lubricated his life and the former heavyweight champion of south-east London could never quite deliver a knock-out blow to his cocaine and gambling habits.

Byron Parker on the other hand, felt he needed double the patience and prudence of ordinary mortals to compensate for his elder sibling's foolhardiness. Few would have picked the two men sitting around the table as brothers. They were like chalk and cheese in dress, manner and build. Byron Parker looked like an accountant. His build was slight. His head was narrow, coffin-shaped. An often plaintive expression hung beneath a crop of thick black hair, flecked with grey. His suit was tailored, his nails manicured. He wore an elegant, antique Patek Philippe watch. Oliver Porter thought that his wire-framed glasses made him look like Heinrich Himmler.

Whereas George Parker liked to reminisce and yearned for a lost past Byron Parker focused upon the present and future. He had transformed his father's empire. Bettered it. The old revenue streams were drying up (and the Chinese and Eastern Europeans had cornered some markets due to the use of slave labour). It was now more profitable to rent out rooms in Soho to start-up tech companies than to use the spaces as brothels. Shoreditch had become similarly gentrified. The once grotty corner of London was now filled with Mummy- and Daddy-funded graduates who spent their working day – and leisure time – on Facebook and twitter. Pubs had turned into coffee shops or, equally hideously, gastro pubs. The new residents lauded the diversity of the area. Even after they moved out of London so that they could send their children to schools containing other nice, white, middle-class children they still spoke about their time living in East London as though it were a badge of honour or virtue. George Parker lamented some of the things the area had lost but he was compensated by the rise in rents and house prices. Various nightclubs and restaurants they owned in Shoreditch were proving worthwhile assets, and not just because they could be used to launder money. The Parker brothers made more money, legally, through their investments in the London property market than they did selling drugs nowadays. Their greatest enemy was the taxman and the rise in interest rates.

As Byron Parker grew ever more 'legitimate' his ambition grew to move in different, rarefied, circles. He had contacted Oliver Porter not just to resolve the problem of the loose-lipped politician. Porter could introduce him to the right people, facilitate memberships to the right clubs. He wanted his children to attend the best schools. His son would be a banker, not a criminal. Money could buy the finer things in life. Better food. Better clothes. Better friends. A good life was a prosperous life. He was fiercely loyal to his business partner, but Byron had out-grown the grunts and curses which served as conversation for his brother.

Byron Parker sat with a double espresso, a piece of biscotti and copy of *The Financial Times* in front of him. He obsessively straightened the cutlery on his side of the table. "Let's find out what is happening first, before we react in earnest. We have the necessary contacts with the police in the area to find out what the wife knows or doesn't know."

"We should have never have used that spiv of yours to get rid of Pound. We should have used our own people. I could have fuckin' put a knife in his chest for nothing. Why couldn't he just pay up? Silly bastard thought he was something special, threatening to blackmail us if we didn't write off his debts. Fucking politicians. Whores are more trustworthy. I'm not sure I trust this Porter friend of yours, either. He can use what he knows as leverage over us. And what do we know about the doer he used to take out Pound? Can we trust him? I don't want some bastard crawling out of the woodwork in a week's time, looking to exploit a situation."

Byron Parker subtly moved his plate away from the flecks of spittle which had shot out of his brother's mouth and landed on the table. His expression was pinched. He disapproved of his brother's ignorance and base manner – and he also felt that, behind his criticism of Porter, his business partner was criticising the way he had dealt with things.

"Porter's not to blame. And the job was carried out professionally. If it looks like we might be exposed in any way then we'll cross, or burn, that bridge when we come to it. Let's just find out what the wife knows first."

George Parker grunted in reply. Come what may he would take care of business.

Chapter 6

The cold numbed Devlin's face. He wished that it could numb his thoughts as well. Some of the newer recruits in Helmand had described the paratrooper as having ice in his veins, such was his coolness under fire and lack of remorse in killing the Taliban. But Devlin aspired to have nothing running through him, ice or fire. He envied the marble statues populating the cemetery. They didn't do harm to anyone and no harm came to them.

Low, leaden clouds besmirched the sky. Before him was a sea of grey and black headstones, occasionally pockmarked by the odd bouquet of flowers. Devlin walked quickly along one of the gravel paths in Garrett Lane cemetery, towards his late wife's grave. The army encouraged speed, efficiency – to be better than the enemy and civilians. Devlin had shaved that morning and polished his shoes as if he were attending a parade ground inspection.

Devlin bent down and pulled up the weeds upon the patch of grass around his wife's grave before placing the lilies next to the headstone. He used a handkerchief to wipe away the tiny flecks of mud on the classically-designed black, marble stone. Devlin read again the lines from Coleridge. Love and sorrow welled up in his chest.

"To be beloved is all I need
And whom I love I love indeed."

His loneliness seared, piercing his numbness. He wanted to tilt his head up to heaven and roar, have his body crack and crumble like a statue. The injustice of her death eclipsed any crime he may have committed, he believed. *I'm more sinned against than sinning.* Devlin's heart felt so heavy that he could have sunk into the sodden turf beneath his feet.

The sound of footsteps on the gravel attracted his attention. An old man shuffled by. His hair was snow-white, his expression glum and sunken. His skin seemed so powdery that Devlin feared a strong gust of wind might blow his features away. Both men nodded to one another and forced a perfunctory smile. The old man had put on his best suit too (which was now several sizes too big). Time and life had diminished him. No doubt he was a widower as well. Both men shared a similar haunted gaze, their eyes and souls hollowed out. Devlin experienced a strange presentiment of his future self. The hunched-over old man, wounded by the loss of his wife, was not long for the world. The young widower envied his elder. The thought of death brought a sense of consolation to the soldier. Devlin's face broke out in a sprained smile as he remembered a quote from Walt Whitman: *"To die is different from what any one supposed, and luckier."*

*

Oliver Porter allowed his wife to sleep in. He made breakfast for his children and drove them to school in his recently bought Range Rover. Porter cherished his time with his children. Although not immune to bouts of selfishness and spite they were on the whole good-natured and contented. He was not making the same mistakes his father had made with him (which was not to say he wasn't making his own mistakes). During the thirty minute drive to their ferociously expensive school he asked them about their homework and what they would like to buy their mum and grandparents for Christmas. Porter was relieved – and enthused – to be back home. To be back to some kind of normality. A home cooked dinner by his wife and evening spent playing Risk or chess with his children was worth a hundred dinners at *The Ivy*. The routines of domestic life gave the ex-Guards officer structure. The mundane and familiar enriched his soul.

On his way home Porter stopped off at the village to order the goose and gammon for Christmas, from his local butcher. He also popped into the art shop and picked up two watercolours he had ordered, painted by a young local artist (the daughter of his postman). Porter's final visit was to the parish church, where he made a generous donation to the Christmas fund which provided food parcels for the elderly over the holidays. As much as the fixer liked to make money he also enjoyed spending it – and not necessarily on himself. Wealth is a great enabler of generosity.

The Range Rover crunched across the drive. The vision of his six bedroom Georgian house — its russet brickwork glowing in the pale sunlight — was a sight for sore eyes. The property was one of the most sought after in the area. On more than one occasion Porter had turned down exorbitant sums of money (from agents acting for football players, stand-up comedians and disc jockeys alike – the veritable royalty of the age) in offers to buy the house. They had moved in just over a decade ago. His wife had transformed the garden all by herself — and she, far more than him, was responsible for the much admired décor of the property. A large "shed" at the bottom of the garden served as Porter's office. The wooden outbuilding had its own specially adapted internet and phone connection, and a keypad lock prevented him from being disturbed. The domain was out of bounds to his children and even his wife. Work and family life needed to be kept separate, for various reasons.

A cup of tea and a bacon sandwich were waiting for him in the kitchen, as was his wife, when Porter got back home. Victoria was seven years younger than her husband. She was blonde, statuesque and well-bred but owned a healthy, broad sense of humour which allowed her to laugh at most things, including herself. She enjoyed the finer things in life but had enough character not to be a slave to them. Her family and interests (gardening, painting, charity work, shopping) kept her engaged and contented. Victoria was patient and understanding about Oliver's frequent periods away from home. She rarely asked about his work because, deep down, she didn't want to know the answers. Oliver had first met Victoria at a function for his regiment. She was the daughter of a brigadier. Both believed they had found themselves a catch and, within a year, they were married. Although some fellow officers called their barracks home Porter chose to take early retirement because he wanted to make a real home, with Victoria and his children.

Victoria switched on the news. The breaking story, that Virginia Pound had possible evidence proving that her husband's death was not the result of a mugging which had gone wrong, dominated the headlines. Victoria saw her husband's eyes harden and nostrils flare in what was, for Oliver, a disquieting expression. He pursed his lips — clamping his mouth shut for fear of betraying his raw anger and frustration.

"Is there something wrong, darling? Did you know the man?" Victoria said, her Home Counties accent awash with genuine concern.

"No. I may have met him in passing at a party though," Oliver replied, distracted by his own thoughts rather than his wife's words. The wheels of his mind turned as he tried to hammer out the ramifications of Virginia Pound's outburst. Firstly, it was conceivable that the Parker brothers may well send someone round to visit the widow – and it wouldn't be Santa. They would first interrogate her and retrieve any evidence linking them to her husband – and then they would silence her. Porter had seen a look of steely conviction in his eyes when Byron Parked had paraphrased Stalin to him over lunch: "Seven grams of lead to the head solves any problem." The Parkers may not be viewing the widow as the only loose end though, he thought to himself. Although Porter had an outstanding reputation for discretion he did not have a long-standing history and business relationship with the brothers. *They may consider me expendable.* Similarly Devlin may become a target. Without a shooter or fixer any case against the brothers would prove circumstantial, regardless of any evidence Virginia Pound might possess.

Porter sighed again. His phone felt heavy in his hands, like a gun, as he sent a message to Devlin, instructing him that they needed to meet up. He would have to travel back to London.

No rest for the wicked.

The season of peace and goodwill to all men couldn't start quite yet.

*

Devlin bowed his head before his wife's grave.

You must see everything — or nothing. Like God. If you would have made me promise that I would never kill again I would have kept my word. But that was a promise for another lifetime… Don't think less of me, although I think less of myself, for what I do. I wish I could talk about other, good things in my life. You kept my secrets and forgave me when you were alive. You're still doing it now. Please tell me you forgive me… Killing has become a job, as it was in the army. A doctor saves lives — it's his job. I get paid for taking lives. It's the same but different. Or at least that's what I tell myself. We all tell ourselves lots of things.

None of my victims are innocent. The world is a better place without an IRA brigade commander and corrupt Labour peer and pederast. Although what right do I have to be judge and executioner?

I'm not sure whether the job makes me feel numb or alive. But it makes me forget about you. I'm good at what I do. Porter says I've found my calling. We both know he's flattering me. But I have a moral switch, which I can turn on and off at will. The moral switch was always on when I was with you. But now I'm killer one minute, half decent human being the next.

Work gives me some respite. But then I feel guilty for forgetting about you. And the grief sets in again even more... You probably saw me with Emma today. She's just a friend, if that. I'll keep my promise. It's the only thing meaningful, honourable, I have left in my life.

The promise Devlin made to Holly on the evening of her funeral went bone deep. He swore that he would never marry or love again. He made it late at night, fuelled by love and alcohol. He made it to God as well as his wife, even though he cursed God's name for having taken her. It was a sacred pact, bigger and truer than life itself or his wedding vows. It was more important that any order he had been given as a soldier or any contract he had been offered by Porter, no matter how lucrative. All Devlin had was his grief and promise. If he didn't have those he would have nothing.

Chapter 7

The décor in *The Admiral Nelson* had barely changed over the past thirty years. Traditional pint glasses hung down from the horseshoe bar and a forlorn dartboard hung in the corner. The heavily veneered oak tables and beams were gnarled and cracking and the worn russet-coloured carpet was infused with the smell of tobacco from hundreds of lock-ins. A jukebox, which was seldom switched on, contained music by Fleetwood Mac, The Drifters, The Rolling Stones and Showaddywaddy. There was also a solitary album by Bon Jovi, for the 'younger' crowd. The floor was sticky and a number of planks creaked. But the regulars wouldn't have changed a thing, partly to put off other locals in the area from intruding upon their place of respite – a sanctuary from the modern world. Most of the young professionals in the area put their head in the door, cringed and walked away.

The landlord of the pub was a retired Scottish merchant seaman, Michael Robertson. He had bought the pub ten years ago, after he and his wife had been regulars for five years. The atmosphere was warm (as was the beer most of the time) due to the landlord's affable character. *The Admiral Nelson* had about a twenty-strong crowd of regular patrons. Thankfully they could drink for fifty. Everybody knew everybody else and, so long as you could take a joke and stand a round, it didn't matter who you were or where you came from – you were welcome.

Devlin entered the pub at around nine o-clock. Without a word the barmaid, Kylie, started to pour him a drink. The pint of the new Christmas guest ale was ready for Devlin before he even reached his regular stool at the bar.

"Thanks. Could I also have…"

Before Devlin had finished his sentence Kylie had proceeded to pour him a Jameson's and water. He finished off the round by buying the barmaid and landlord a drink. The latter sat down next to Devlin, one of his favourite regulars. Both men had spent many an evening drinking into the small hours. Michael Robertson was approaching sixty-five but a love of life, and alcohol, kept him young. His nose was as red as his eyes and his pot-belly now protruded out further than his once barrelled chest. His waxy skin sometimes looked as if it might fall off his face, but his smile routinely propped it up. His wife, Maureen, was Scottish Presbyterian. She could curdle her husband's blood with just a look, but still the old sailor had a roving eye for the ladies (fortunately or not for him they rarely gave him a second look). "I had a girl in every port when I was at sea. Luckily I knew where all the venereal clinics were in every port as well," he had joked to Devlin on more than one occasion.

Christmas songs played on a loop in the background, but not too intrusively.

"*I could've been someone.*

But so could anyone."

A couple of patrons swayed a little and mouthed the words. But the pub was quiet. It was the time of year for Christmas parties and work drinks – and Michael Robertson was not keen on hosting either.

"How are you, fella?" the landlord said, genuinely pleased to see the former soldier. Robertson appreciated Devlin's company and the amount of money the paratrooper spent in his pub.

"Fine, thanks. Where's Maureen tonight?"

"She's upstairs, watching one of her blasted soaps. But it could be worse, she could be down here watching me!" Robertson cheerfully explained. The sanguine landlord tipped his head back, laughed and downed his drink in one fluid, well-practised, motion.

After he had Kylie serve him another drink – and line another one up for Devlin – Robertson asked her to retrieve the small Christmas present he had bought his regular. Devlin picked up the wrapped hardback book. He thanked his friend awkwardly. He couldn't remember the last time that someone had bought him a gift. For the first time in a long time Devlin was touched.

"Just a little something, laddie. It's a thank you for all your support and for lending me half your military history library. I'm not sure if you'll like it. The lass Emma gave me some advice on what you might enjoy reading. She's a good sort, that girl. You could do a lot worse. She can hold her liquor too. Although in my past I liked women who could be under the table, or under me, after just half a bottle of wine. It saved time and money."

The landlord tilted his neck back again and let out another burst of laughter. But Devlin barely registered his drinking companion. Emma had walked through the door. She had changed into a black pencil skirt and had put on a new top, made of fine cashmere. She also wore a pair of silver droplet earrings, which had once belonged to her grandmother. Devlin had commented on how pretty they looked, many months ago. Her copy of Graham Greene's *A Burnt-Out Case* could be seen peeking out of her stylish leather handbag. Emma turned more than one head as she stood, slender and elegant, in the middle of the pub. Tinges of shyness highlighted rather than diminished her attractiveness. Devlin thought that she might be going out to a party and was just popping into the Nelson for one or two beforehand, or maybe she was going off on a date? Devlin didn't know quite how to feel about the prospect of Emma dating someone. He knew that he couldn't be with her, but he didn't necessarily want someone else to be with her either. At the very least any prospective date should treat her right, Devlin thought. *She deserves someone special... She deserves to be happy*. Devlin hoped that she could stay – and not just because of the way she was looking tonight.

The two figures smiled across the room as if they were the only ones present. Their eyes locked onto one another, neither quite sure which was most like a deer caught in the headlights. Something fell into place, like tumbler wheels in a vault door. Emma did and didn't want him to look at her in an amorous way. He never behaved in an inappropriate manner with her but there had been times when she wished that he wouldn't always play the gentleman. Sometimes a woman needs a good kiss, as a well as a kind word.

Emma was pleased to see that Devlin had changed his clothes. The suit would have reminded her of his late wife. He had changed into a dark blue polo shirt, jeans and – what with it being Bermondsey – a pair of white Reebok's. A black sports jacket sat on a stool next to him. Some may have judged the ex-soldier's face to be weathered (or even pained), but Emma thought he looked ruggedly handsome. He had a face that told a story – and one which concealed a story, too. It was also a face which reminded Emma of a painting she had received on her confirmation, when she was thirteen. Her aunt had bought her a series of illustrations depicting the story of Christ's crucifixion and resurrection. Devlin resembled the figure of the soldier who pierced the side of Jesus.

*

Devlin and Emma sat at their usual table in the corner, beneath a faded print of Turner's *The Fighting Temeraire*.

Light shone from a teardrop-shaped bulb beneath a nineteen-seventies style lampshade. Devlin took sips from his drink even quicker than normal. His heart was beating a tiny bit faster than usual. He craved the taste of a cigarette in his mouth but he didn't want to rudely get up and abandon his friend.

Devlin was just about to compliment Emma on how nice she looked, but as he opened his mouth Kylie came over, bringing with her a couple of drinks courtesy of their landlord. Robertson raised a glass to his regulars from the bar and (unsubtly) winked at Devlin and nodded his head towards Emma.

The buxom barmaid, who was wearing a tight-fitting silk blouse and tighter-fitting short denim skirt, smiled at the former soldier far more than at the finely dressed florist. Devlin smiled back at the barmaid – but he did so a little cautiously. He hoped that Emma hadn't found out that he had slept with the fun-loving Bermondsey girl six months ago. They had just had sex, after a late night. Devlin knew that Kylie wasn't looking for anything more. And he had nothing else to give. Although Devlin had made a solemn promise to Holly and God that he would neither love nor marry again, he was a widower – not a priest or eunuch. He didn't want Emma to think he had rejected her in favour of the blonde barmaid. But if he had slept with Emma all those months ago he knew that it would've meant something to her. In the world Devlin had created for himself, killing and meaningless sex were no longer sins. But love was.

Devlin was even more embarrassed Kylie stroked him on the back and asked, with a flirtatious gleam in her eye, if she could do anything else for him.

"So do you have any exciting plans for Christmas?" Emma asked, once the barmaid had departed.

"I'm due to meet up with some old friends from the regiment," Devlin replied, lying. He was planning to stay at home on Christmas Day and work his way through a Bernard Cornwell novel and bottle of McClelland's. He didn't particularly care if people thought him lonely, but he felt awkward receiving any feigned sympathy. On the whole most people only really cared about themselves, Devlin believed. Nobody had seemed to genuinely care when Holly died. Everybody moved on easily enough, except Devlin. The cynical explanation for things was all too often the right one. Human beings are mainly selfish animals. "How about you? Where will you be spending Christmas?" he continued.

"I'll be heading back home for a couple of days and suffering my family. My mother will be especially keen to tell me how best to live my life. 'New year, new you,' she'll say. My father should be fine though, after his second glass of port. I'm looking forward to attending midnight mass in my old church. I'll take plenty of money so as to light plenty of penny candles and pray my mum loses her voice over Christmas. Have you ever attended midnight mass?"

"I have, but many years ago now. Even God doesn't have a good enough memory to recall the prayers I offered up back then, I imagine."

The chaplain attached to Devlin's regiment in Helmand had always been encouraging him to attend service. Occasionally they would talk about the Bible – but mostly they chatted about Camus and Chekhov. *The chaplain never gave up on me, even when I gave up on him.* Devlin wryly smiled to himself, recalling how the chaplain had once asked him what he felt when he shot an enemy. "Recoil," Devlin had matter-of-factly answered.

Emma tucked her hair behind her ears, perhaps to show off her silver earrings, and fingered the stem of her wine glass.

"Do you mind if I ask you something? I don't want to offend you though."

"I'm not easily offended."

"Do you believe in God?"

"I believe in God. I'm just not sure if he believes in me."

"He believes in everyone."

"He must be exhausted, believing in everyone for so long a time. It's made him the world's oldest – and greatest – holy fool. But ignore anything I say. I don't want you thinking I'm trying to offend you, Emma. As a soldier I'm just used to having a black sense of humour about things. Especially God."

Devlin's foot tapped the floor in anxiety. He craved a cigarette even more. He couldn't quite meet Emma's probing expression and averted his gaze to look out of the window. Flakes of snow shimmered under the glow of amber streetlamps. The cold called to him, like a siren song.

"I sometimes think God must have a black sense of humour too, given the state of humanity, so you're in good company," Emma said, trying to ease any awkwardness.

"You have a strong enough sense of faith for both of us. The world could use some more good Catholic girls like you."

"Well I'm not so sure about that. What does it mean to be a good Catholic girl nowadays? You need to feel melancholy, guilty and superstitious."

"Catholic girls have got plenty in common with soldiers, it seems," Devlin wryly remarked.

"Do you get to see your old friends from the regiment often?"

"When I can," Devlin answered, lying. Every month or so he received an invitation to a reunion or charity event. He would send his apologies and decline – and also send a cheque if the event was linked to a worthwhile cause. He had attended a few gatherings after Holly's death. One time he was asked to apply for SAS selection, by a former commanding officer. One time he was offered counselling. It was understandable that some blamed Devlin's retreat from the world on the war. But it was grief rather than PTSD which shaped his psyche. Devlin had no desire to trade combat stories with his former comrades. He already looked backwards enough in his life, in regards to Holly. But he couldn't move on either. He was in limbo. Devlin wanted to tell Emma that once you've been to one reunion you've been to them all. They usually ended in a drunken brawls – and that was just the wives and girlfriends.

Devlin wanted to talk to Emma about other things too. But he didn't.

Chapter 8

Midnight approached. The music in the pub was turned off. The snow had failed to settle outside but a frosty wind still howled through the narrow Dickensian alley which ran along one side of the pub. Emma had gone home. She didn't like to leave Violet alone for more than a few hours. There were times when she thought the mood music might be right between her and Devlin. They had laughed enough, drunk enough. But ultimately he only offered up a kind word, rather than a kiss, as they parted at the end of the evening.

Everyone else had called it a night too, bar Devlin and the landlord. Robertson proposed one last drink. He was in the process of locking the doors, so that his friend could smoke whilst they drank, when three late night revellers came into the pub.

They were city boys, derivative traders, who had strayed south of the river after a night celebrating their bonuses. They had wandered over Tower Bridge after cocktails, a curry and an hour or so at a lap dancing club. Cocaine as well as alcohol fuelled their mood. All were former public school boys, the nation's brightest and best. Wealth creators.

"I'm sorry lads but I'm closing up," Michael Robertson said, apologetically.

"We just want one last drink," the self-appointed spokesman for the group said. He spoke in the form of an order rather than request. The former rower stood over six feet tall. His jaw was chiselled and even Hugh Grant would have envied his head of floppy brown hair.

"I'm sorry, we have to close," the landlord reiterated, this time with as much firmness as politeness in his voice.

"C'mon Rupert, let's just go. The place is a fucking dive, fit for plebs, anyway," his compactly-built companion remarked. Justin Dalton lightly clasped his friend on the elbow as he spoke but he was shrugged off. Rupert Spence did not understand, or appreciate, the concept of "no". The gilded youth, whose parents had never refused him anything, was used to getting his own way, especially in the case of procuring women. He had once been accused of raping a woman after a night out in *Boujis*. The case didn't even go to court though, as it was his word against a hairdresser's from Balham. His father had provided the best legal team money could buy. The Spence family were even tempted to sue the girl for vexatious litigation.

"No, I want to stay and be served here."

"Just give us one drink and we'll get out of your hair. It's Christmas. We've got plenty of money. It looks like you could use a few extra quid, from the state of this place," the third young trader in the group, Hector Baring, said. He eyes devoured the bottle of Jägermeister behind the bar. He fingered the small plastic bag of cocaine in his pocket again, paranoid that someone might have stolen it.

The landlord stared with trepidation at the three young men and then at Devlin. His mouth was agape but no words issued forth. He was tempted to call the police but he feared that doing so would stoke rather than put out any fires. He knew from experience that if he served the drunken and belligerent youths one drink then they would ask for one more – and one more after that. They had the devil in them – or just too many units of alcohol.

"You've been asked to leave," Devlin said, evenly, as he got up from his stool next to the bar and walked towards the three men. The landlord edged around the bar and locked the till. Devlin's arms hung down by his side, like a gunslinger ready to draw. But, like a town sheriff, Devlin preferred to end things peaceably. "I can give you the number for a local cab firm if you like."

As much as one might have imagined the former soldier being similar to a coiled spring he appeared tired, or even bored, by proceedings. His brow was creased, as hard as corrugated iron. He scrutinised the trio, making a risk assessment of the situation. He'd had a fair few drinks but a para who was unable to fight drunk was no para at all. All three could pack a punch – but Devlin had no intention of allowing any of them to land a punch. Their unofficial leader, Rupert, looked like he had some conditioning. Perhaps he boxercised or practised a martial art – or more likely he took Zumba classes, Devlin fancied. Ultimately they were amateurs and he was a professional.

"And who the fuck are you?" Rupert asked, raising his voice – incredulous and insulting. The derivatives trader equated volume with authority.

"I'm nobody," Devlin replied.

"Why don't you mind your own business old man and sit back down. Or fuck off altogether," Justin Dalton advised, walking towards Devlin and puffing out his barrel chest.

The former soldier smiled to himself. It was the first time that anyone had ever called him "old".

Perhaps I'm not long for this world after all.

"What do you think you're going to do? Throw us out?" Rupert said, part laughing and part snorting in derision. "There's three of us and one of you. Do you have a death wish?"

Devlin could smell the curry and lager on the young man's breath. He recoiled more from the trader's liberal use of cologne though. The stench was nearly as pronounced as his arrogance and sense of entitlement, the soldier considered. He had encountered more than one Rupert during his time in the army.

"Something like that. You can always call up a few more friends to be on your side if you want to make it a fairer fight."

Devlin stared at the young man with thinly veiled contempt. Goading him. If the would-be alpha male threw the first punch then Devlin could claim self-defence, if the police got involved. Violence doesn't solve everything, but it does resolve some situations.

Man is born to trouble as the sparks fly upwards.

Devlin subtly altered his stance, so his feet were apart, in order to be better prepared to attack or retreat backwards to avoid any initial blow. His opponent would probably look to swing his arm in a right hook. He would have plenty of time to move inside and strike first, if that was the case. Instead, however, Rupert Spence merely tried to force Devlin backwards, out of his space, by shoving him in the shoulder. The former paratrooper stood statue-like. He sighed, in relief, that finally he was justified in drawing blood – and wiping the self-satisfied grin off his antagonist's face.

Devlin whipped his forearm around so that his elbow smashed into the young man's fine, aquiline nose. The sound was somewhere in between a crunch and a crack. Rupert Spence was immediately disorientated. His vision was blurred and his natural reaction was to bring his hands up to his wounded face. He would have lost his feet but Devlin held him up by the lapels of his coat, so that he could whip his right forearm around again and break his nose a second time. Elbows, knees and foreheads were far more useful in a fight than making a fist and throwing a movie-style punch. All too often Devlin had seen men break their hands. The harder they hit the worse it was for them. Amateurs. Blood and cartilage glistened, as the bridge of Rupert's nose opened up. This time the city trader fell to the floor, groaning.

Hector Baring let out a curse and squared up to Devlin. He raised his hands, like a boxer, but couldn't then decide whether to attack or back off. There was nothing he had learned on his business course which applied to his situation. Devlin experienced no such moment of indecision. His arm shot out like a ballista bolt and the hard base of his palm connected with the young man's throat, just beneath his chin. Hector made a slight choking noise. Fear gripped him and the gargling sound he was making turned into a whimper. Hector Baring wished he could be back at the club, with the Estonian dancer whispering sweet nothings and flicking her tongue out, swirling it around his ear. The young man performed his own version of a table dance however as he stumbled backwards and fell in between the gap of one of the pub's booths.

Justin Dalton's eyes bulged in rage. The fearless fly-half lowered his square head, thick neck and rounded shoulders and charged Devlin as if he were a bull. But Devlin moved with the swiftness of a matador. Devlin grabbed the top of the back of the chair nearest too him and swung it round, smashing it against the shins of his powerfully built assailant. The chair broke, falling apart like Lego, but it did its job. Dalton fell to the floor, snarling in pain. He slowly rolled over on his back, to witness a stoical looking Devlin standing over him. The impassive soldier stamped on his opponent's groin – twice. Dalton writhed in agony, twice, before turning his head and retching, ruining the carpet even more.

Devlin grabbed Rupert Spence by his hair and half-dragged him out of the door. The soldier ordered his two friends to follow him. Devlin gave the three men directions to the nearest main road, in order to flag down a taxi. The defeated young men, our brightest and best, were too ashamed and too hurt to fully take in what the brutal stranger said however.

Devlin went back into the pub. The landlord's mouth was agape. He recalled something the former soldier once said to him: "Train hard, fight easy." Robertson was taken aback by his friend's ferocity and efficiency in dealing with the youths. At no point had Devlin appeared to lose control of himself during the fight.

"I'm sorry about the chair. I'll be happy to pay for it."

"No, laddie, it's fine. Thank you," the landlord uttered, his voice somewhat croaky. He needed a drink.

Devlin's brow was still furrowed, in annoyance rather than sorrow. His "work self" had crossed over into the domain of his personal life.

"Please don't tell anyone about what just occurred, especially Emma," Devlin said, with a pained expression on his face.

"Don't worry, I won't," Michael Robertson promised, out of loyalty to his regular or, perhaps more so, out of fear.

Later that evening, as Devlin lay in bed, he wondered if he had performed one of his small acts of kindness by ejecting the unpleasant trio from the pub (God knows what might have happened if he hadn't been there) or had he committed an act of violence — a sin — which he would need to atone for by another thousand acts of kindness? Had he turned his moral switch on or off?

Chapter 9

Morning.

A sterile sun hung in the air, its watery light seeping in between dreary clouds. The view of the back garden was an island of calm compared to the throng of reporters and photographers at the front of the house. Virginia Pound sat in her Victoria Plum kitchen and stared at a photograph of her husband. The photo was of him and their eldest daughter, Beatrice. She was dressed in her graduation gown. It had been a special day for the whole family. Yet still he smiled in the same fake way whenever a camera was in front of him. The same expression on his face could be found in a thousand photographs of him with his constituents. When Virginia had first met Martin Pound, whilst campaigning for a seat on his local council, she had been impressed by his energy and conviction. She fell for him, they got engaged and she proudly composed the copy for some of his campaign literature. He was handsome, eloquent and genuinely wanted to make a difference. Martin Pound was a caring Conservative, a catch. Her friends envied her. She sacrificed a burgeoning career in journalism to play the loyal wife and devoted mother. If only *he* had been so loyal and devoted, she mused. The higher he climbed politically the more of his principles fell by the wayside. In the end he never even tried to reach a compromise with his beliefs. Compromise turned into capitulation. His first affair was with a constituent and his second was with an intern. Virginia lost track of his infidelities after that. She lost track of the money he squandered through bad investments and gambling as well. But still she played the loving wife (having no other role open to her). Virginia hosted dinner parties, pounded the pavement in painful heels on the campaign trail and was a patron of a number of charities which meant little or nothing to her. She was "Mrs Martin Pound". Most of her days were spent shopping and being a domestic goddess. In the evenings she helped her children with their homework and then worked her way through a season of Desperate Housewives and a bottle of mid-priced Rioja. Few of her friends envied her life now. She loved her children dearly, but they were growing up fast and would eventually fly the nest. Virginia Pound wasn't celebrating that her husband was dead – but she realised that she now had the opportunity for a second chance in life.

Virginia looked good – and not even just for her age. Friends said that she looked like Sophie Raworth. She thanked God, and her genes, each month that her long blonde hair was still free from any streaks of grey. A tan from her recent trip to Cyprus had given her complexion a healthy glow and concealed some of the wrinkles lining her forehead and eyes (perhaps she would have Botox, when the life assurance payment came through). Spin classes helped maintain a naturally elegant figure. She still turned the heads of plenty of men her age – but she would now turn the heads of younger men, she vowed to herself. She had taken a younger lover, her daughter's tennis coach, out of revenge for her husband's first affair many years ago. She would take another.

Virginia sat by the kitchen table with a cup of coffee and a half-eaten bran muffin in front of her. The news was on the television and her laptop was open. Worried that it might seem inappropriate for a widow to be out shopping so soon after her husband's death, Virginia had bought a number of new outfits online, in which to appear in front of the cameras. She wanted to look glamorous, yet solemn, like a female news anchor.

Thankfully her local salon would send someone around to the house do her hair and nails.

The ex-*Daily Express* journalist had spent the morning going through articles relating to her husband's death. She needed to know the facts – and fiction – that were being disseminated. The court of public opinion was the highest in the land, for good or ill.

Virginia had also called her lawyer again. She needed to know how she should manage the evidence in her possession, which could expose or compromise a number of people (lobbyists, fellow politicians, property developers etc). She had yet to trawl through all of the documents and emails on the memory stick but her husband had saved everything. Among other things there was a series of emails exposing how a windfarm company had paid her husband to promote the "green" argument for sustaining the massive subsidies and tax exemptions the industry received. She wondered how, such were the frequent payments her husband gleaned for "consultancy" work, he could still be mired in so much debt. But the gambling debts, payment to escorts and keeping his mistresses in clover added up. *Why couldn't he just have kept on screwing his interns? Then we wouldn't be in this financial mess.*

Virginia needed specialist legal advice on how much evidence she was obliged to pass on to the police, and how much she could hold onto, to sell to newspapers or utilise to secure a book deal. She wanted to take advantage of the situation, strike while the iron was hot before she became yesterday's news. Virginia also made a call that morning to Phillip Simmonds, a publicist-cum-media agent. Simmonds had been described as a "young Max Clifford" — but in a good way, if it was humanly possible. Simmonds briefly offered his condolences before running through his terms of business. He agreed with his new client that she should put her story out there immediately (although she should make sure to sell that story to the highest bidder, but Simmonds would happily handle that, for a twenty-five percent commission). Virginia Pound was a wronged woman, a victim of a violent crime and a politician's wife. There were numerous angles to play, he argued enthusiastically. Simmonds promised to make some calls. Virginia argued that she did not want to use any short-term exposure to leverage just one big pay-off however. She wanted the agent to use the tragedy to organise a regular column for her in the *The Times*, *Evening Standard* or *Grazia*. She had been a good, punchy journalist over a decade ago. She could be the same again, or more. The wife and mother had more life experience and could write upon a variety of topics. Her ultimate ambition was to appear as a semi-regular guest on *Loose Women*. Her friends would envy her again then. She would explain to her children how she needed to work more and couldn't spend so much time looking after them. But she would hire a nanny. They would understand, Virginia reasoned. She was doing this for them, to provide for their future, after all.

*

The Parker brothers sat in the back of the blue Porsche Cayenne as it gunned its way towards the centre of town. Byron had just explained to his bleary-eyed sibling that it seemed the politician's wife was indeed in possession of information on a memory stick about some of Pound's business dealings. Byron's contact in the police couldn't be sure about the nature of the information however — or if it incriminated the brothers.

George Parker held his large bald head in his hands — he resembled Marlon Brando's Kurtz in *Apocalypse Now* — and let out a groan. "Fuckin' Pound. We should have tortured the sly bastard to silence him before we had him killed. I'm not having his stupid bitch wife be responsible for me doing time. If it's even just a rumour that this memory stick exists — and our names could be on it — then that's enough to sign her death warrant. We should act quickly too, just in case the police decide to put some protection on her. We don't know what other enemies Pound made. Plenty it seems. We'll kill the wife and retrieve the memory stick. We might even be able to make a few quid out of the memory stick ourselves. She's a looker — and I'd prefer to put something else in her mouth other than a gun barrel — but needs must. We should at least try and sort it so that her kids have no chance of witnessing anything though," Gentleman George stated, in deference to his late father's code of conduct that young children should never be harmed in the name of business.

As George Parker spoke, his voice more guttural than usual, his brother raised an eyebrow and looked askance at the carpeted footwell of the vehicle. It was littered with cigarette butts, fast food packaging, some suspect-looking pills and a small transparent envelope of cocaine. Byron not only disapproved of the mess because of the chance of police pulling them over; he also disliked the fact that his brother's young children used the car. He didn't want his nephew and niece growing up with their father's habits — and IQ.

"I agree," Byron replied, resigned to events. It was a shame to have the wife pay for her husband's indiscretions – but it was also a necessity. The choice between whether he or Virginia Pound suffered was no choice at all. "I've also had an idea as to how we might kill two birds with one stone. I can contract the job out to Porter again. I will try and get the name of his operative out of him when I do so. Once the job is finished I'll suggest that we pay him in cash. When we meet we'll dispose of him. And then catch up with his associate."

The asset of Porter had now become a liability for the accountant-criminal. Byron Parker was confident of finding another fixer who could second him for the Garrick.

"If the prick doesn't give up the name of his man I'll get it out of him."

There was a gleam in his brother's eye and verve in his tone which Byron found unattractive. He recalled the last time George had cause to be violent towards a woman. One of their call girls had been on the take. "Women – and their divorce lawyers – have been torturing me for years. I was due some payback," the brutal, priapic enforcer had grimly joked to Jason and Leighton afterwards.

"I'll make the call to Porter and set things in motion."

"Good. Fingers crossed we won't have to pay the prick any more money before we off 'im. Any other things we need to discuss?" George Parker asked, his mind half-distracted by a ripe looking twenty year old walking along the pavement in stripper heels and a figure hugging dress. She reminded him of a friend of his eldest daughter who he wanted to fuck.

"We've sold the three properties on the new development at Greenwich. We should net half million. A Canadian pension fund has bought the apartments. They may well rent them out, once finished, but they may just leave them empty and sell when the price is right."

George Parker pursed his lips, almost in a kiss, and nodded in appreciation. The thought of making money turned him on as much as the blonde in the stripper heels.

"Gorgeous. Fucking gorgeous."

"One bit of bad news is that we might need to find another manager for The Blue Note. Bobby's wife wants to have him move to Australia, so she can be with her sister. Bobby does a good job at the club. It'll be a loss."

"Australia? It can't be that fuckin' great there. All the bloody Aussies want to come over here. Want me to give Bobby, or his wife, a slap and tell them to stay?"

Byron mulled over the option of his brother intervening — as it would prove an inconvenience finding the right new manager and revenues at the club would dip. But he decided against it. They needed to start running their empire like businessmen rather than thugs, he told himself.

"No, Bobby can go. He's been loyal and hardworking, as much as it seems he's under the thumb of his wife. Our loss can be Australia's gain."

Their driver, Jason, braked suddenly. He spat out a curse at a cyclist and then apologised to his employers.

"Don't worry. The cyclist cunt jumped the light. He's probably late for a meeting with some tofu. Prick!" George Parker exclaimed. He planned to open the window and knock the skinny faggot off his overpriced bike should the car catch up with him.

Byron Parker rolled his eyes and pressed his lips together in mild frustration, preventing him from swearing and sounding like his brother, as the sudden jolt made him misspell a word in the email he was composing to his stockbroker. The traffic was beginning to snarl up, as they headed down Charing Cross Road, towards Shaftesbury Avenue and the Century Club where they were due to have a meeting with the actor, Connor Earle. Connor had been described as a "poor man's Ray Winstone and even poorer man's Michael Caine". Earle was an old school friend of the brothers and had set up a meeting with them in order to discuss a business opportunity. He wanted George and Byron to invest in a gangster movie he was intending to produce. He would give them a credit as producers and the investment could be written off against tax. Byron would tell the actor that he would consider the offer (with every intention of not investing a penny). However, it was worth having a short meeting with the scrounging actor. Earle was friends with a number of the cast of EastEnders and other people in the media. He could push more product out to them.

They can kill even more of the few brain cells they have left between their ears.

Byron craved a coffee, the drug of his choice. He noticed how his brother was increasingly fidgety – and sniffed repeatedly. He was craving something other than coffee. Byron failed to mention the plastic envelope of coke beneath the heel of his left shoe. Instead he gazed out of the window and watched the world go by. A stream of shoppers, tourists, workers and others — most with their heads buried in the screens of their smartphones — snaked up and down the streets. Byron noticed a fair few elderly businessmen turn off to head towards Soho. More than one might be heading to a brothel that he owned.

London was a din of iniquity.

Everyone was a sinner or customer.

Business is good.

Chapter 10

Oliver Porter answered Byron Parker's phone call and told him that he would be happy to take on the additional contract. He also agreed to his fee being paid in cash after the job was completed.

"I'll be paying even less tax on the money than if it went into my Cayman's account. My associate may not be keen on joining us when we meet but I'll speak to him. I just wouldn't want to make any promises. Also, let me take you out to dinner in January. Come to the Garrick and I can introduce you to some people who will support your membership bid."

Byron Parker offered up a laugh in response to Porter's joke about tax and accepted his invitation to dinner — all the time believing that he was talking to a dead man. But for all intents and purposes it was business as usual.

Porter pressed the button and ended the call. Lying came as easily as breathing to the two men. But in truth most people, most of the time, lie to themselves or others. It was the human thing do so.

Never work with children, animals or gangsters.

The fixer exhaled, puffing out his cheeks, and slumped down on the bench where he was sitting. Porter became the most world-weary person in view. For once he hoped that he would be proved wrong in his calculations — in his pessimism — but the Parker brothers intended to betray and murder him. He felt deflated but through an act of habit his body and mind became taut again. The blood returned to his face, as if he were a fresh-faced officer again receiving his first important order. As troubling as the news was that the Parker brothers wished to kill him he was consoled by the argument that they had no idea that he had every intention of killing them.

Porter sat on a bench in St James' Park and waited for Devlin. A number of shopping bags sat next to him from the likes of Hamleys, Boodles and Hatchards. Peace offerings for his wife and children. Porter had promised them he would be at home for the next three weeks —— and he had broken his word. He pictured again how his wife had pursed her lips in response to hearing the news. "I hope it's a matter of life and death," she had said, after taking a breath, with little humour in her voice. Yet she walked out of the room. There were no protests or histrionics. There was no point in trying to question him on his reasons for travelling back to the capital.

The silence had been deafening as his wife drove him to the train station that morning. Most of their silences were comfortable but this one wasn't. But she had still kissed him goodbye and lovingly said "take care". Marriages survive by leaving some things unsaid, rather than said, Porter philosophically thought to himself.

The cold wind chilled Porter's scalp, cutting across it like a razor blade made of ice. The sensation prompted Porter to remember the advert, for hair transplants, he had glanced at in *The Spectator* the previous week. The procedure had worked wonders for Wayne Rooney, the ad pronounced. For a second or two the balding Porter was tempted to check out the company online. But he smiled to himself rather than tapped the name into the browser on his phone. What would be the point of the act of vanity? Would he be doing it to attract a mistress which he had no intention of procuring? And Victoria would love him in the same way, regardless of the state of his hairline. As Porter thought of his wife though he was gripped by a sense of terror, rather than fondness. A shrapnel of despair lodged itself into his breast as he imagined George and

Byron Parker driving through the gates of his house. Porter pictured his wife and children and realised that he had everything to lose. The former soldier didn't want to admit it to anyone, least of all himself, but he was scared. The even cadence of his heart and breathing became discordant, as if someone had swapped all the white keys with the black on a piano. His expression, for a brief moment, became contorted. *A secret life can only remain secret for so long. The truth will always out.* The dark, vile, polluted world of his work life cast a shadow over the veritable paradise of his life at home.

Devlin walked towards his associate, his expression seemingly frozen in the gelid air. The two men had often met at the park. The bench was reasonably secluded and one only needed to turn one's head slightly to catch a view of Buckingham Palace. The two patriotic soldiers had served the crown rather than self-serving politicians. Their hearts swelled in their chests that little bit more at seeing the Union Jack rippling in the breeze on top of the palace.

If Porter wanted him to do another job then Devlin would hear him out, but he would probably turn him down. He didn't need the money and he felt perpetually tired (but still a good night's sleep proved elusive). He certainly wouldn't work on Christmas Day. In a small nod towards some remnants of religion and faith Devlin believed that the twenty-fifth should be given up to God in some way. It would feel too wrong to take someone's life on Christmas Day.

"You're looking well, Michael," Porter remarked, in a spirit of politeness more than honesty, as he shook his old friend's hand. But Devlin immediately recognised that something was wrong. His palm was moist and the lustre in his eye, which could shine in the face of an abhorrent world, was missing.

Devlin was tempted to reply that his liver had been getting plenty of exercise this month. But he decided against it. He remained silent, hoping that it would prove a prompt for Porter to get down to business quickly.

"I have some good news and bad news. The bad news is that the Parker brothers want to kill me. They're only human, some might say. You may have seen the news. Virginia Pound made a statement, implying that she has evidence to suggest that her husband wasn't just the victim of street crime. The brothers are worried that they could be exposed. They consider me — and you — to be loose ends they need to tie up. What is the world coming to when you can't even trust a pair of vicious gangsters?"

Devlin listened on impassively, although he could not help but notice the anxiety which crept into Porter's voice, ousting out his normal jocose disposition.

"And the good news?" Devlin asked, his voice low and neutral.

"The good news is that the Parker brothers think I'm unaware of their intentions — and that I'm not willing and able to kill them first. I'll be doing the world a favour by wiping away their blight. George Parker is little more than an animal. He should have been put down, or at least neutered, years ago. And Byron Parker's sole virtue is that he isn't his brother. When their lights go out the world will be a brighter place. There are poppy growing warlords in Helmand with more scruples that those cretins. I'm worried for my family more than me. They should not have to pay for my sins. I need you to do the deed. You're the best man I've got. I'll pay whatever sum you want. You could make enough to retire. The contract will be for both of them — and it won't be a case of two for the price of one. Seven grams of lead, times two, will solve our problems. The good news is that they spend plenty of time together. Although they will also have bodyguards. I am having an associate hack Scotland Yard for their file. I can provide you with some more intelligence this evening. I am usually the person who fixes things, who is owed a favour. But I now need to ask for one. And I need you to let me know now, either way, whether you can do it. I only have a small window of opportunity. There will be no hard feelings if you want to turn the job down."

Despite the cold a few beads of sweat had formed on Porter's temples. Devlin had never seen the former Guards officer scared or vulnerable before. Porter resented himself for having to nigh on beg someone else to solve problems of his own making. But needs must.

Devlin stared out across the park. Bone dry, withered leaves scraped along the asphalt path. A hotdog vender warmed his hands from the steam coming off his cart. Shoppers walked through the park briskly, looking to get home or out of the cold. Lovers walked hand in hand, more slowly. The gentle clip-clop of horses could be heard in the background.

They don't quite sound like the Four Horseman of the Apocalypse.

Devlin briefly thought how he could disappear. He would be leaving behind next to nothing and he had next to nothing to take with him. The Parker brothers would have more chance of finding Lord Lucan. Porter had dug his own grave. The fixer could fix things himself. He could ask another shooter on his books or, if things became truly desperate, he owned more than one gun himself. But…

I know what I have to do. You wouldn't think much of me if I abandoned a friend in his hour of need. Even if I fail I'll succeed. Because I could be seeing you again soon.

"I'll do it. And you won't have to pay me. Think of it as my Christmas present to you," Devlin said, his brain already ruminating on the possible location of the hit. Killing had not quite become as easy as breathing for the assassin, but the list was growing longer in regards to things which seemed more difficult.

Porter breathed out and his expression softened in gratitude and relief. He closed his eyes and clasped his friend's forearm, offering up a silent prayer of thanks. He Porter made a silent promise — which time might erase the sovereignty of — that he would not be fix any more contracts involving innocent or good men.

I'm saved.

"You're making me feel somewhat deficient. I've only bought you some cufflinks in return. I'd like to invite you over for Christmas though, if you don't have any other plans. I'm sure that you have spent far too many Christmas Days on your own, over the past five years. If your culinary skills are as good as mine then Christmas dinner will be thoroughly unpleasant. I've just ordered a goose that could feed a brigade. I'd welcome a drinking companion, who has no desire to watch Strictly Come Dancing. You could travel down on the twenty fourth and attend midnight mass with us, at our local church, if you want. Or perhaps we should spend time in the confessional — although if the two of us were to confess our sins we might still be there on Boxing Day, or Shrove Tuesday even. You will turn the heads of a few of the young, available women — and ones that are married — in the village too. What do you say?"

The clip-clop of horses grew louder as a brace of attractive horsewomen approached, dressed in riding breeches and scarlet jackets. One looked like Kate Beckinsale and the other resembled a young Julie Christie. Sometimes Devlin's promise to Holly and God was hard to keep.

Devlin was going to reply that he couldn't be sure he'd be free on Christmas Day, as he might well be dead or serving at Her Majesty's pleasure. But he didn't.

"Let me get back to you soon, when I know my plans," he said, committed to being non-committal.

"That's fine. Nice fillies," Porter exclaimed, as the horsewomen rode by.

Devlin wryly smiled to himself. He knew his friend was complimenting the shiny-coated mares rather than the two comely riders. Devlin had never known Porter to even look at another woman in the time he had known him, let alone have an affair. As much as he sometimes reminded Devlin of a modern day Harry Lime he was a good husband and father.

He's worth saving. I'm just not sure I am.

Chapter 11

Fields, buildings and skeletal trees passed by in a blur — and not just because Porter had consumed a bottle of Chianti at the Athenaeum after meeting Devlin. He was now on the train home, being gently rocked from side to side as if he were in the cradle again. Yet he sat in his First Class seat uncomfortably. Any man who communes with his conscience or thinks about death shouldn't feel at peace. For a moment or two the fixer felt dizzy, nauseous, by the fate which hung across his shoulders like a milkmaid's yoke. Life was a blur. All he wanted to do was get home to his family, curl up on the sofa with his wife and experience the light in his children's eyes when they opened their presents. Contentment is so much better than happiness.

He pitied Devlin. He would go home to a black hole, where his wife and unborn children were, at best, spectres. Five years ago Porter had invited his operative over for Christmas out of a fear that the recent widower might put try to put a bullet through his skull and, as much as Devlin was an admirer of Joseph Conrad, the assassin wouldn't miss unlike the melancholy novelist. Five years. So little and so much had changed, for both of them. One could be forgiven for thinking that the soldier's grief was unnatural or unmanly. Porter once mentioned to Devlin how Holly would have wanted him to get on with his life, find someone else. Devlin vaguely nodded in agreement but Porter's words fell on deaf ears. Fathoming the soldier's grief, or love, for his late wife was as difficult as getting blood out of a stone.

Porter had recently woken from a dream, having dozed off shortly after the train left the station. The dream was thoroughly restrained, English and mundane — up to a point. He and his family stood in the passageway by the door, waiting for Devlin to arrive on Christmas day. His wife was wearing her favourite lilac dress. Porter spoke of the soldier's heroic acts in Afghanistan. He told his children that for every classic novel they had read Devlin had read ten — or twenty — more. "He is Meursault, Sharpe and Homer's Hector all rolled into one," Porter remarked in the dream. He also wanted to tell his wife that Devlin had been their guardian — or avenging — angel who had saved them all. But some things must still be kept secret, even in the realm of dreams. And so they waited for him to arrive. And waited. It began to snow heavily outside. The goose sat on the table, and loomed even larger for the fact that Devlin might not eat his share. His children began to complain that they were hungry. His youngest son shivered. "He'll turn up," Porter assured his family more than once. "He's a good man, the best man I know." There was, finally, a knock on the door. The snow stopped falling, his son ceased to shiver. All would be well. But instead of the stoical features of his friend Porter was met by a gnashing George Parker when he opened the door. His demonic eyes were ablaze with violence and cocaine. Stalactites of drool hung down from his mouth, like fangs. He was carrying a meat cleaver. Byron Parker stood behind his brother, fastidiously filing his nails. A picture of cold insouciance. All was lost. Porter woke up with a jolt, just as the meat clever buried itself into his sternum.

Devlin.

The name was tantamount to a prayer. He was the best man that he knew, Porter realised, but that might have had something to do with the company he kept. Devlin was worth a thousand members of the Bullingdon Club.

As Porter watched a man in ill-fitting blue overalls fill up a vending machine at Slough train station he vowed that he would change his ways if Devlin succeeded. Porter had told himself over the years that he was making a difference in the world by accepting certain contracts. But he knew that the only difference he was making was to his bank account. Porter shuddered — and loathed himself — thinking of the similarities he shared with the reptilian Byron Parker.

For years Porter had told himself that he needed to make money, through honest means or otherwise, to provide for his family. The ends justified the means. But he had enjoyed his work too much.

The wheels beneath him screeched along the track as the train left the station. His ears were soon assaulted, however, by a far more unwelcome sound — that of conversation. Three young women, with outfits as loud as their voices, had come into his First Class carriage. One of them put her muddy, Nike-emblazoned feet on the seat opposite to them. Another chewed gum and tapped so incessantly on her phone that Porter wondered how her fingers had not been worn down to mere stumps. He prayed for a ticket inspector to deliver him and point them in the direction of their correct carriage. Porter turned his head to take in the increasingly green scenery but still had to suffer the sound of them. He winced every time they laughed or yelped. He wanted the earth to swallow him — or preferably them — up as they each went through who they'd like to see enter "the jungle" for some ghastly TV programme which pitted vulgar celebrities against each other. When one of the trio of slatterns commenced to talk about the new photos they had uploaded onto something called "Instagram" Porter wryly implored God to return him to his dream.

*

"He sees you when you're sleeping
He knows when you're awake
He knows if you've been bad or good
So be good for goodness sake."

Devlin listened to Bruce Springsteen and a number of other artists with Christmas songs. Cigarette smoke filled the room. Devin was tempted to try and root out Holly's old iPod. She had a couple of playlists devoted to carols, hymns and Christmas hits, which she had played throughout the year. "It's good to feel Christmassy on other days of the year. Although I'm not sure how many people feel Christmassy on any day of the year," his wife had once remarked, her voice tinged with ruefulness rather than anger.

Devlin finished off writing an email to his accountant, listing some instructions for if anything should happen to him. He had also emailed his lawyer. His foster parents would receive the bulk of his estate when he died. He regretted not seeing them. But there wasn't time. He wanted to say goodbye to them, thank them, but without them getting an inkling that he might be seeing them for the last time. He felt guilty — and his money would not wholly compensate for the time he should have spent with them over the years. But there were lots of things — too many things — Devlin had cause to feel guilty about. They were strewn out along his life like beads upon a rosary.

As soon as he got home Porter forwarded on all intelligence he had on the Parker brothers. Scotland Yard were, ironically, an accomplice to murder — such was the wealth of information in the files that the hacker had stolen. The brothers had been subject to police surveillance on more than once occasion, and thankfully their routine seldom changed. Devlin had lots to plan in just one night. The location and timing of the hit would be key. Most of their day was spent travelling around central London. The amount of cameras — and people — littering the streets ruled out a hit in the likes of Shoreditch or Soho. Devlin had enough weighing on his conscience without shooting innocent bystanders. If nothing else it would be unprofessional and inefficient to injure someone in a crossfire. He was also wary of entering their houses to carry out the job. Not only did both men have families but he couldn't be sure who else could be armed and frequenting the sites. Porter was right in that he needed to find a moment to hit both men together. Given that the brothers would be accompanied by their two bodyguards that would mean four hits at one time. Normally Devlin would avoid such a scenario. There were too many variables. The odds were greater on getting away clean. All would be armed, except for perhaps Byron Parker (so plan things as if he would be armed). Fail to prepare, prepare to fail, the soldier in him stolidly remarked.

Aware that he might have to carry out the job the following day, Devlin sipped his whisky. What with not knowing if he would see Christmas in the flat he had opened the bottle of McClelland's. His ashtray was full by the time he decided on his plan of attack.

At the end of each day, at approximately 6pm, Byron Parker was dropped off at his house in Chislehurst, before the car then took his elder brother to his nearby home. The property was gated and there would be a small but significant window of opportunity. The police report was sufficiently detailed enough to note the type of gate and security system and, after some research over the internet, Devlin worked out the timings. Fortunately there was a small park at the location where Devlin could wait and view the car from afar as it came down the street the house was situated on. The report also noted that their vehicle was not bullet-proofed – and that there was an absence of CCTV cameras at the entrance to the drive.

Devlin spent the next hour committing a map of the surrounding area, where the hit would take place, to memory. He needed an element of good fortune for the street to be empty when he approached the car but otherwise the plan was sound.

The wind howled outside. A few revellers could be heard, singing and wending their way through the square below. The soldier cleaned and oiled his gun, a SIG-Sauer P226, before picking out a book for some late night reading. Devlin thought to himself it may well be the last book he would ever read. He wanted it to be special — and needed it to be relatively short in order to finish it in time. He thought about reading some Chekhov or Camus but he picked out a well-thumbed copy of *The Great Gatsby* to take to bed with him. The novel had been the first book he and Holly had read together as a couple.

Chapter 12

Although he could not find the time to travel to his foster parent's care home Devlin ordered a cab the following morning to take him to Garrett Lane cemetery. Before the taxi arrived he popped into the florists. Out of habit and superstition Devlin wanted to pick up another fresh bouquet of lilies. And he also wanted to see Emma. There was a small hole inside him that only she could fill. Her loveliness was a balm. He owed Emma an explanation, a thank you or a goodbye. Devlin rehearsed a few sentences beforehand as he was putting on his grey suit. But some sentences — or sentiments — which seem fine when voiced by the soul are too naïve or brittle to live in the outside world. It's sometimes best that they remain stuck in the throat. When he entered the shop to discover Emma was absent (her part-time assistant, Molly, was looking after things) Devlin felt the butterflies in his stomach expire. He felt the chill December wind on his face and a presentiment that he would never see his good Catholic girl once more. God had somehow cheated him out of saying goodbye to another loved one. Because today might be his last day on earth.

But what of heaven? And hell? As he stood before his wife's grave Devlin believed that he could endure the latter, knowing that Holly was experiencing the former. But he had faith he would see her again, otherwise his life would have been for nothing. During his youth and time as a soldier Devlin considered God to be a cruel or indifferent deity, an abusive or absent father. Most of the time Devlin could laugh along at the joke of life, but in his heart of hearts Devlin knew that God embodied love and forgiveness.

Devlin raised a corner of his mouth, in a gesture towards the tiniest of grins, when he remembered his favourite Churchill quote: *"If you're going through hell, keep going."*

The widower again pulled up any weeds around the grave and also removed a few stray cigarette butts. He bowed his head in remembrance whilst turning his wedding ring, as if screwing something in or out. With each turn his soul seemed to stretch out even more, like he was being tortured upon the rack by the Inquisition.

Devlin turned his stony face up towards the sky. Anyone observing the solitary figure before the grave might have thought he was imploring God. But Devlin had communed enough with God for three lifetimes. In truth he was merely assessing the weather. The forecast was, thankfully, for clear skies later. The temperature would be mild for the time of the year. His heart could afford to be numb but his hands and fingers couldn't be. It would be another fine night for killing.

Many men, from killers to martyrs, often dream of fame after death — as if fame could be equated to eternal life. They imagine the news reports, church services, tweets or obituary pages. But when Devlin thought of his death he didn't want to be mourned, celebrated or even remembered.

I just want to see you again.

*

Oliver Porter's office was one of the most secure and attractively furnished "sheds" in the country. A back massager was seated on top of a black leather Eames lounge chair. Other pieces of furniture were made from the finest mahogany and English oak, including a bookcase containing a complete set of Loeb classics. The "home from home", as Porter sometimes described the out building, was also filled with items from foreign countries he had visited: rugs from Iraq and Afghanistan covered the floor; his coasters were from the famous Armenian pottery shop in Jerusalem; a Browning pistol, which had once belonged to Eisenhower, was mounted in a glass case; and an antique Russian icon of the Holy Mother hung next to the door. Occasionally, after imbibing a few drinks, Porter imagined that the figure in the artwork was staring at him disapprovingly. She was a mother scolding her naughty child. But at other times she appeared to be full of grace rather than condemnation. The office also contained a fridge, safe, Bausch and Lomb stereo and other essentials and luxuries. Accomplished copies of Grimshaw's *Reflections on the Thames* and Goya's portrait of the Duke of Wellington adorned one of the windows. The fixer promised himself that, one day, he would purchase a genuine Grimshaw landscape.

Wagner played in the background — but at a barely audible level. The television was on — but on mute. A steady stream of emails began to pile up on the laptop screen. Many involved invitations to lunch or Christmas drinks. But, unless he was summoned by the Queen or Palmerston, he would politely decline them all.

Porter sat at his desk with his fully charged mobile phone in front of him. Devlin had sent him a message saying that he was intending to carry out the job today. More than anyone else he knew Porter believed that Devlin would try and make good on his word. Yet, as much faith as he had in the former paratrooper, Porter also believed in having a plan B. Money and passports sat on the desk, next to his laptop and bronze busts of David Hume and Talleyrand. Should Devlin fail to carry out the hit properly Porter was ready to whisk his family away on a surprise holiday. He would also pay for a brace of other operatives to carry out hits on the Parker brothers. Money was no object. George and Byron Parker had to die.

But the hit would be difficult, even for a seasoned professional such as Devlin. He had little preparation time.

The intelligence was good but still deficient. Four targets quadrupled the risk. When Porter briefed Devlin however he instructed the assassin to prioritise taking out the brothers: "Cut off the head and the snake will die."

Porter briefly ruminated on the scenario of Devlin succeeding in killing his enemies but being apprehended by the police. He knew the soldier could be trusted not to betray him. The police couldn't threaten or bribe him. How can you condemn someone who has already condemned himself? No man is an island but the soldier came close. Michael Devlin would be able to endure a prison sentence, so long as he had enough books to read, Porter half-jokingly mused. He was a man who could be bound in a nutshell and consider himself a king of infinite space.

The fixer poured himself another small measure of Laphroaig and thought once more about how thoroughly unpleasant the world was. The single malt shone like honey in the midday sun. He recalled a line from Graham Greene, which Devlin had once quoted to him whilst raising his glass in a toast:

"*Whisky – the medicine of despair.*"

*

Devlin felt a small twinge of guilt as he came down into the foyer of his apartment building. It was time to go to work. The smart reception area to the building was an amalgamation of polished oak and marble. He nodded to Derek, the friendly and efficient Pakistani concierge, and realised that he should have got him a Christmas present or end of year tip.

It might now be too late.

The thought was soon swotted away. As Devlin was leaving Emma came into the building, carrying various bags of shopping. Her cheeks were a little flushed. She was wearing a woollen jumper with a colourful Christmas design on it that one of her customers had knitted for her. Devlin noticed Emma was wearing a touch more lipstick than usual. It made her smile wider and more luscious, although perhaps she was also smiling more for seeing him.

Devlin was wearing a padded blue Barbour coat over his grey suit. He was also now wearing his black Sig Sauer P226 beneath his suit jacket, in a shoulder holster. The suppressor sat in his right coat pocket. A copy of *The Great Gatsby* hung out of the left. The pistol was powerful, compact and reliable. People had let him down over the years but the Sig Sauer never did. Devlin had been given the weapon as a present by a US special forces operative in Helmand, after the two men had spent a long, boozy night talking about guns, Hemingway and Ulysses S. Grant. The pistol was the chief tool of his trade and had never let him down. Devlin fancied that, should he ever be stranded on a desert island, it would be the third item he would take with him, alongside a copy of the Bible and the complete works of Shakespeare.

When Emma had first seen Devlin there was a flintiness to his expression. But when he saw her the scowl immediately fell from his face. Wistfulness now shaped his countenance. Emma simultaneously thought how much she liked him and also how much she didn't know him. So much of Michael was below the surface.

"Molly mentioned that you came into the shop this morning. Sorry I missed you. I'm glad I caught you now though. I wanted to say goodbye and happy Christmas. My plans have changed and I'm heading back to Somerset today," Emma said, wishing that she was wearing something more flattering than her festive jumper.

For a moment or two Devlin stood silently before her, entranced. The last time he had felt so nervous had been when he had asked Holly to marry him. He had faith she would say yes but dreaded she would say no. He had clutched the engagement ring's small box so hard that it dug into his hand. But he barely felt any pain. When she said yes his heart had leapt up to the heavens.

The gun weighed heavy on Devlin's shoulder. He wanted a drink. He forced a smile and fingered his wedding ring.

"I'm glad I've caught you too. There's something I wanted to speak to you about."

After missing Emma that morning Devlin had promised himself that, if he saw the florist again, he would offer up his last confession to her. If she knew about his vow to God and Holly then she might understand why he couldn't give himself to her. If she knew what he did for a living then she might be repulsed by him and go to the police — punish him for his crimes. He admired her. He maybe even loved her, as a friend. But love cannot endure the real world for too long. The air that we breathe seems to poison it. Love may even be a complete myth. The existence of love can only be taken on faith.

Devlin shuffled his feet slightly as if he wanted to set himself — or prepare to run away. Emma was one of the kindest souls he had ever known. He suddenly thought how she reminded him of Tolstoy's Natasha Rostova. But was he Andrei or Pierre? He thought, for a splinter of a second, how she could forgive and understand him. Love him. If she consoled him then he might not want to ever leave. But work — duty — called.

"What is it?" Emma said, her voice imbued with more concern than curiosity. She lightly placed her fingertips on his forearm.

"It's nothing. It can wait until January. Sorry, I've got to go. Have a nice Christmas too, Emma."

Devlin quickly kissed her on the cheek and briskly walked out the door. Although he had brushed his lips against her cheek Emma still felt the tingle of when he had kissed her on the lips, all those months ago. She had noticed the copy of *The Great Gatsby* in Devlin's pocket. She wanted to quote from the novel, to let him know that he was special and meant something to her.

"*You're worth the whole damn bunch put together.*"

But the moment was gone. Some things are not meant to be.

Chapter 13

As Devlin wended his way through London in the back of the taxi some of the sights prompted memories (of childhood, drinking holes and courting Holly). Some were good and some were bad. He was unsure whether he would miss the capital or not.

Devlin got out of the cab around a mile from his intended destination. He walked with his head hung down as if he were playing a game of avoiding the cracks on the pavement. Finally he came to the small park, which overlooked the entrance to George Parker's house in Chislehurst. The property was valued at eight million pounds, but anyone buying the house, with any semblance of taste, would have wanted to substantially redecorate it.

Thankfully the park bench that offered the best view of the road leading up to Parker's home was free. Devlin pulled his scarf up to partially cover his face and sat down and read. Night had fallen like a veil, but there was ample street lighting. The shortest day of the year was fast approaching though, for Devlin, time dragged on. A few dog walkers and locals ghosted past yet no one seemed to take notice of him. There was nothing to notice. Devlin calculated the time it would take him to get up and un-assumedly walk towards the house. He believed he could do it in the time it would take the car to reach the gates (given the number of speed humps strewn across the street that the vehicle would have go over, slowly). The only potential variable which could ruin his plan would be the appearance of a passer-by. But so far the road and park were proving to be deathly quiet.

Usually, before a job, Devlin was too focused on the task to suffer any anxiety. But something out of kilter churned in his stomach. He had no qualms about ending the lives of the Parker brothers. Yet still the killer felt uneasy, like the time when he took his first confession. The priest didn't frighten him but the thought of God seeing all did. The boys Devlin knew who were older briefed him on what he should confess to — or rather make-up. He didn't confess anything of importance to the priest that day but that night Devlin confessed to God. Guilt eclipsed any notion of absolution or redemption. Sin was real. No matter how much Nietzsche he read, God wasn't dead.

In between rehearsing the hit in his mind Devlin felt like a condemned man, due to climb the scaffold. He wryly smiled to himself as Chopin's funeral march played in his inner ear, as a soundtrack to his thoughts.

The readiness is all.

*

Byron Parker rolled his eyes. He had just finished talking to Connor Earle on the phone. Although Byron had been careful not to promise the actor anything Earle was behaving like the money was already in the bank. He talked enthusiastically about approaching Craig Fairbrass' agent. Maybe they could even convince Vinny Jones and Tamer Hassan to be in the movie. "They'll add class and bums on seats. I swear on my son's life, we're going to make a million each on this," Earle declared, high on hope — or a more chemical-based drug.

Byron also rolled his eyes on noticing the new tattoo on the back of Jason's neck, as the stolidly built bodyguard drove them home. As well as a strange Celtic symbol brandishing his large bicep — which various football players and popstars had a tattoo of too, believing the mark to be a source of virility or power — Jason had the word "Respect", in a Cyrillic font, written across the back of his neck.

Byron looked across and askance at his elder brother, sitting to the left of him in the metallic blue Porsche Cayenne. George Parker was asleep, although his mouth was still half open. The enforcer had had a long day — taking drugs, eating a long lunch and breaking the jaw of a gay Bulgarian pimp. Gentleman George boasted how he'd had a long night too, having taken one of his daughter's friends out to a club.

"I showed her a good time. I showed her an even better time afterwards, eh? I promised her a part in Connor's movie. Perhaps we should invest in the film after all."

Byron Parker did his best to tune out his brother's conversation and snoring. Despite not liking his elder sibling he was bound to love him. Together they were greater than the sum of their parts — an alloy, forged in the fires of brutality and efficiency. Each administered to the parts of their empire they were proficient at.

Byron continued to work his way through a few emails on his smartphone. He was keen to take care of all urgent business before Christmas. One piece of business was his desire to buy a number of flats in Elephant & Castle. Although the area was depressed at the moment he believed that, given its proximity to both the City and West End, any property he bought couldn't fail to appreciate in value. We need to think long-term, Byron Parker posited — as though he were Goebbels, believing in his own propaganda of building a thousand year Reich.

Byron took off his glasses and, extracting a small, pristine white cloth, cleaned the lenses. For a few seconds everything was a blur and he squinted like a child but then the world came sharply back into focus.

The car travelled over the first speed bump, at the top of the road leading to his brother's mock Tudor mansion. George Parker stirred, a bear waking up from sleeping through the winter. He rubbed his nose and sniffed, hoping to shake lose any vestiges of coke from his nostrils.

*

Devlin calmly stood up and slid the paperback book into his coat pocket. He had now nearly finished the novel, having read up to the part where George Wilson was about to shoot the eponymous hero. As he left the entrance to the park the assassin quickly retrieved his weapon and attached the suppressor. All the time the Porsche continued to draw closer, occasionally slowing to negotiate a speed bump. Devlin could make out that there were four people in the car.

Four targets. Thirteen rounds.

The road was deserted. Devlin was a gunfighter entering a one horse town. His gait was smooth but as he grew closer to the gates his footsteps grew heavier as if he were traveling to a funeral.

The Porsche braked before the large, black steel gates (which resembled two Rolls Royce Silver Shadow grills next to each other). Leighton — the Parker brothers' other bodyguard — retrieved the remote control from the glove compartment. Devlin timed his walk perfectly and stopped by the driver's side of the vehicle. George Parker briefly scrutinized the pedestrian but judged him to be a nobody. Byron Parker's gaze fixated on the small scar above Devlin's eye.

Devlin raised his arm, mechanically and purposefully. His features were relaxed, free from enmity. His moral switch was off — or on, given his targets. The assassin took out the driver first. Two shots zipped through the window, entered the side of Jason's right breast and scythed through his heart and lungs.

He was dead before he knew it. Although the sounds of the suppressed shot and thud as the bullets hit their mark were not music to Devlin's ears there was still something familiar, natural and pleasing about the noise. It meant that someone had been killed and he was still alive.

Byron Parker's hand reached out and clasped his brother's knee, but the rest of his body froze in terror. His last thoughts were for his wife and children. It looked like he might die of fright. But instead Byron Parker died from two nine millimetre parabellum piercing his chest. Blood began to stain his white shirt immediately, as if someone had already placed two red roses on the dead body.

The bodyguard in the passenger seat pulled out a Glock 18. Leighton fired off a curse rather than a round however as he forgot to switch the safety off. The sight of his dead friend in the driver's seat also gave him pause. But Devlin paused not. The first bullet entered the bodyguard's sternum, the second blew away half his neck. Gore splashed against the window behind him. The tintinnabulation of awful dance music could still be heard pouring out from his headphones but Leighton was no longer listening.

A faint smell of blood and cordite filled the air.

One target. Seven rounds.

In order to gain a workable line of sight for his final victim the assassin moved a couple of steps towards the passenger end of the Porsche. But it was Devlin's turn to pause as he found himself staring down the barrel of a chrome-finished Browning pistol. George Parker was just in the process of turning the safety off. As enraged as the gangster was he was also, largely, keeping his head. This wasn't his first gunfight and he didn't want it to be his last. A ringed finger curled around the Browning Hi-Power's trigger.

Devlin refrained from firing his own weapon. Time moved quickly and slowly. Death will compel a man to commune with God. Devlin was resigned to his fate. He would allow George Parker to shoot first. If he died, he died. But should his opponent fire and miss then Devlin believed it would be a sign from God — and Holly — that they wanted him to live. He would be allowed to turn the page. He needed a new covenant to live by. It was absurd but true.

Devlin lowered his gun slightly as George Parker raised his. The gangster couldn't miss. His snarl morphed into a triumphant smirk. Blood from the black bodyguard's neck freckled his face. George licked his lips, enjoying the taste as much as cocaine. But just as he was about to fire his weapon his brother's body slumped forward, onto his arm, and ruined his aim. Perhaps it was an act of God. Perhaps, in his dying moments, Byron Parker deliberately leaned forward. He and his brother had been inseparable for so long, Byron didn't want to go to heaven — or hell — alone. Byron wouldn't want to see his brother survive him and inherit their criminal empire.

"Holly," the widower said softly – but yearningly.

Devlin uttered the word like a prayer. If his final thought in this world was for his wife then she would be the first thing he would see in the next. *Have faith.* Devlin heard the sound of the gun. His eyes were closed. He was expectant more than fearful. He prepared himself to be consumed by darkness or light. But damnation or deliverance failed to arrive. The gangster's bullet struck the inside of the car door.

Whether God had spoken to him or not a survival or killer instinct kicked in again, fitting like a key to a lock. Just as George Parker was about to take his second shot Devlin swiftly moved his own gun into position and emptied the magazine into his target. The Sig Sauer became an extension

73

of his arm, the dark part of his soul. The semi-automatic was a marriage of precision and power — a marriage immune from divorce. Sometimes a gun will fire a man, given its weight and the force of its recoil. But Devlin was in full control of his actions when he shot George Parker. Parker deserved to die.

The contract killer removed the suppressor, holstered his gun, breathed out and surveyed the scene. The street was still deserted. As much as adrenalin coursed through his body he felt a sense of peace wash over his heart.

Devlin pulled out a small Turkish flag from his pocket and tossed it into the back of the vehicle. The flag was a calling card for an increasingly ambitious Turkish crime syndicate who were looking to expand their powerbase in the capital. It wouldn't do any harm for the remnants of the Parker family and the police to focus their response to the shooting on the Turks.

The temperature dropped but the soldier didn't feel cold. The stars seemed dull, as if the angels had failed to polish them for a while, but they still shone in the velvety firmament. Michal Devlin lit a cigarette, walked back through the park and hailed down a black cab to take him back to Rotherhithe.

Job done.

Chapter 14

Oliver Porter looked positively Churchill-like. He puffed on his cigar with one hand and nursed a brandy in the other as he sat, slumped, in his gazebo, having recently finished his Christmas dinner. It had been a long, calorific day. His family had exhausted him, but in a good way. A heater hummed in the background, glowing like the embers of dusk. A gust of wind blew through two silver birch trees, which flanked the elegant, oak gazebo.

Michael Devlin sat next to him, his Christmas party hat still comically askew on his head. He sipped upon a Bushmills and breathed in the cigar smoke in compensation for only now smoking one cigarette an hour. Devlin had travelled down to visit Porter and his family on Christmas Eve. A few drinks on arrival had emboldened him to attend midnight mass. He felt slightly nervous entering the church. Perhaps he had too many memories of dull, overlong sermons in the cold on uncomfortable pews. Sometimes things can get too Catholic. Or he was scared that God and Holly would be present - and grief and despair would take hold of him, trap his heart in a vice. But his fears were unfounded. There was mulled wine, a warm atmosphere and plenty of hymns and carols. Porter introduced his friend to more than one young woman, a slightly older divorcee. Devlin even found himself singing at one point.

Christmas Day had been enjoyable. Porter and his family were welcoming and fun. He occasionally held court as he told some (sanitised) war stories. Occasionally the widower experienced shooting pains, as if he were suffering pangs of angina or gout, as Devlin thought of how in another world he

75

could be have been spending Christmas with Holly and their family in a similarly beautiful house in the country. But that was another world...

"I understand your decision to take a break from things for a while although I hope you don't disappear for too long," Porter remarked, as he swirled the remainder of his brandy around in his glass. The fixer was worried about his friend's state of mind - as well as his own business. There were plenty more politicians who needed a bullet in the head, he darkly or amusedly thought to himself. "Call it what you will – a bonus or sabbatical pay – but I've taken the liberty of depositing some money into your account. Treat yourself. Meet someone. Marriage might compel you to come back to work sooner, as you'll want to get out of the house. Even more so, though divorce will compel you to come back to work, as you'll need the money."

"I'm not sure what my plans are for tomorrow yet, let alone the next six months or so. Man plans, God laughs," Devlin replied, not committing himself to returning to work either way. Death had stalked him enough - or he had stalked death - for more than one lifetime. "You'll be pleased to hear that I've met someone though."

Devlin smiled as he thought of Emma. His expression softened – and not just because of the drink.

"Really? I'm intrigued. Tell me more, if you don't mind me asking."

"She's a good Catholic girl, for my sins ..."

Devlin planned to ask Emma out on a real date. He wanted to be back in London with her. Back in the land of the living.

THIS BOOK IS FULL OF MORE BODIES

BLOOD SPLATTER BOOKS

RICK WOOD

ALSO BY RICK WOOD

Cia Rose

When the World Has Ended
When the End Has Begun
When the Living Have Lost
When the Dead Have Decayed

The Edward King Series

I Have the Sight
Descendant of Hell
An Exorcist Possessed
Blood of Hope
The World Ends Tonight

Anthologies

Twelve Days of Christmas Horror
Twelve Days of Christmas Horror Volume 2
Roses Are Red So Is Your Blood

Standalones

When Liberty Dies
The Death Club

Sean Mallon

The Art of Murder
Redemption of the Hopeless

Chronicles of the Infected

Zombie Attack
Zombie Defence
Zombie World

Non-Fiction

How to Write an Awesome Novel
The Writer's Room

Rick also publishes thrillers under the pseudonym Ed Grace...

Jay Sullivan

Assassin Down

Kill Them Quickly

The Bars That Hold Me

A Deadly Weapon

This book is dedicated to no one.

I would not inflict such depravity on another human being.

CHAPTER ONE

YOU CAN'T BE SERIOUS.

What, you're back again? Not had enough of this shit?

I mean, fucking come on!

As if the first book wasn't bad enough...

As if there wasn't enough death and guts and gore and violence and mayhem to make you reassess the kind of shit you read...

As if you didn't finish that book and sit back like, *Jesus, shit, what is wrong with me, why do I read this stuff...*

As if you didn't just go read Wuthering Heights or Jane Eyre or some other substanceless, pointless croc of shit to convince yourself that your enjoyment of this book is an anomaly. Hell, maybe you decided that you actually like these kind of books, in which case, fuck me you have issues.

I mean, you actually came back to read more of *me*.

What the fuck is wrong with you?

Oh, you don't know? Huh?

Well, I'll tell you.

...

...

...

1

Still there?

…

…

…

You sick fuck….

…

…

…

You asked for it. I am going to tell you what is so severely wrong with you, and then there is no turning back…

…

…

…

Are you ready?

…

…

…

It is this:

Absolutely nothing.

There is NOTHING wrong with you, my friend.

I was testing. I was teasing. You are bloody perfect, and have an exquisite taste in literature. People will scoff at the content of what you enjoy, but just remember—*you* are the normal one. Not *them*.

Those people who flinched at my last book, or squirmed away, or those Karens who purported "Oh I could never read a book like that, it's so awful how could you read it, oh there must be something wrong with you, oh look at me with my white picket fence and manicure and surgically implanted lips, oh la de da de fucking da, I hope you all enjoy the underside of my nose because it's THE DIRECTION I LOOK DOWN AT YOU FROM"—those Karens can kindly FUCK OFF.

They pretend.

They all do.

They put on their masks and sit at their desks and type at their computers and have coffees with friends and go on Tinder dates and eat croissants for breakfast and try to pretend they aren't animals.

They are.

Freud had it right. He said that in dreams, we discover what we repress. But it's not just dreams. It's books too. It's movies. It's music. Why do you think Marilyn Manson is so popular? Why do you think even a 12-rated movie has violence unacceptable to an audience seventy years ago? Why do you think a book like this manages to sell enough copies to justify its existence?

Because the stricter society becomes, the more we repress our true urges, and the more we need an outlet for our true nature.

I'm doing you a service, really.

And that prick who wrote a review on my last book that said, and I quote, "Nothing new, the writing is only shocking to Americans and Brits who haven't really studied life or philosophy"—a prick who I intend to hunt down, gut, and slice into fifty-two pieces so I can send his wife a slab every week of the year (assuming he has a wife and isn't some bored loner ejaculating in front of his computer screen before typing pathetic reviews with his semen stained, crusty hands) —completely missed the point.

This isn't philosophy. This is truth. This is *release.*This is your opportunity to vicariously experience the secret fantasies you so desperately wish you could experience.

And don't tell me you've never fantasised about murder. A man called David M. Buss did a recent study where he found that sixty-something percent of women and seventy-something percent of men have experienced a fantasy about murder. And those are just the ones who admit it. The rest are lying.

Have you never wondered whether you could get away with it?

See, most murderers find that part the most stressful. That's why they go wrong and end up getting caught. They execute the kill, savour the moment, then squirm and squander the proceeding disposal of the body.

You should learn to enjoy those moments. Engage the euphoria and tension and excitement. Relish the disposal of the body as much as you relish the kill.

And how do you dispose of a body without being caught?

Well, there are three ways I've found to be successful:

1/ Feed the body to pigs. I bought a few and keep them in the field next to my mansion. (I'm rich as fuck, remember?) Pigs eat anything, including bones.

2/ Dump the body in acid. Only issue is, you can't buy acid without arousing suspicion, and you can't really explain why you keep a tub in your house.

3/ Chop up the body into separate limbs. Singe off the fingerprints to remove identification. Remove teeth and eyes for the same reason. Keep these limbs in your car and, every time you go to a new area, dump another limb somewhere in the woods, or in a river. If someone discovers the body part, no one will know who it's from, and they won't be able to link it to any local missing person. (This part takes a while though, whereas pigs are much quicker).

If you wish to improve your chances of getting away with murder then choose a stranger, preferably in a different area from where you live, and from where you have not abducted a stranger before. Why? Because police in different counties don't talk to each other. There isn't a country-wide database, it's all based on location—which is fucking stupid, but whatever, it means people like you and I can evade capture far easier.

Oh, and leave your mobile phone at home. They can track that shit everywhere. Honestly, it was far easier to do this in

4

the sixties and seventies. That's why there was a 'serial killer boom.' There wasn't the technology they have nowadays; it's become almost impossible not to leave a trace of your movements. But, however difficult they make it, there's still something I have that they don't:

Money.

Money buys you attorneys who are better than cops.

Money buys you power and a solid reputation.

And, most of all, money makes you untouchable. Look at Epstein, Weinstein, and every other stein. They went for decades without being caught. Why? Because they had stature. If you were going to take on someone white, rich and powerful, you better have some good fucking evidence. If you're poor, then the world doesn't give as much of a shit.

I'm not trying to make a political statement. Just saying.

And as I say such things, I can hear that prick who did that review now, ranting about the lessons I teach—*oh you haven't really studied philosophy, oh this is nothing new, oh I'm a little runt with a tiny cock that I can't even see because of my fat belly*—you, my friend, can go sit on a fence of barbed wire. I will fucking impale you, you cheap, lousy scum, sitting behind your keyboard with your holier-than-thou-self-entitlement, as if your opinion matters just because the internet gives you a platform to share it. That's another problem nowadays—not only has technology made it tougher to evade capture, it also means that every idiot with an opinion thinks it's valid. Well, you little prick, opinions are just like your life—just because we can hear you, it doesn't make it significant. Now go fuck your mother before I kill her, you insipid little scum.

...

...

...

I'm panting. Fuck. Just let me calm down.

...

...

...

What was I talking about?

What the hell was I even talking about?

Let me read back over it.

... study of murder fantasies... feeding bodies to pigs... evading capture...

Ah, yes. Murder. And the getting away with.

Take Lyndsey, for example.

She's lying by my ankles as I write this, beneath my pristine, wooden desk, in one of my seven offices. My MacBook Pro (latest model with the best CPU, thank you very much) sits before me as her bloody face coughs up bile beside my dark brown *Sagan Classic Precious Leather* shoes. I swear, if she coughs blood on those shoes, I will empty the bottle of wine beside my laptop down my throat and stick it up her cunt (a La Sommeliere SLS117; brilliant wine).

Lyndsey is a good example of what I was saying, actually. She comes from Dalcross, a small town near Inverness. I brought her back to the south of England in the boot of my car, drugged on the finest rupees I could buy. I've enjoyed her for the last five days. She's quite tight. And young. Maybe seventeen, eighteen. Similar age to Flora when...

Ah, Flora.

Fucking Flora.

I suppose we had to get to her at some point.

If you don't know who Flora is, that's because you didn't read my last book, or it was too long ago for you to remember. In which case, why are you not repeatedly reading such a fine work of literature—are you an imbecile?—but hey, some people have no taste, so fine if that is you, just sort your fucking life out.

Anyway, Flora.

She was the daughter of the woman I married.

And why did a man such as myself decide to marry, I hear

you ask? Pretence, of course. To give the world the image they desired. In the end, I murdered her and made it look like suicide. (Again, if you have decent taste in books, you will recall this.)

I fucked Flora over and over behind my wife's back, and Flora loved it. Sometimes. Sometimes, she didn't. Who the fuck cares? I still fucked her.

And then she tried to get away from me, so I bound her up, and it felt like she was finally becoming subservient and joining me in a life where I will be rich and she can be my muse, my slave, my hole to aim at when I can't find a better one.

Then she fucked me.

She hid a corkscrew inside of her vagina and seduced me.

Then she escaped.

My penis was saved, don't worry, that's the benefit of having *private* healthcare. I can't imagine how a poorly paid NHS doctor would have handled my privates. I'm sure they could have restored it, but it would have looked more like a squished mango than a glorious weapon.

Anyway, Flora escaped.

My loose end.

Not that she'd tell anyone. I trust that. If she did, she'd give her location away, and I would be fucking her corpse before anyone could even put me in a cell.

But it's not about loose ends.

It's about *pride.*

Who the fuck does she think she is?

No one escapes me.

No one.

So I hunt her, and I know I will find her, and I know I will torture her for as long as it takes for her to beg me to just fuck her and kill her already—then I'll fuck her with a branding iron, then I'll stand back, watching her squirm, and then I'll begin the real pain.

I have spent the last year searching. I thought I was close at one point. I even thought I saw her, but by the time I had my hands on her, it was just another pointless teenage girl (who did, of course, die for the inconvenience.)

But we will find her, dear reader, my ever-present voyeur. We *will* find her.

Anyway, I digress.

Where was I?

Lyndsey. Yes.

For now, she is lying on the floor, and it's time for me to go pound her skull in with a hammer and let the hogs deal with her body.

Then we shall begin.

CHAPTER TWO

I'M HUNGRY FOR WHORES.

I want a professional slut and, with this in mind, I begin to fathom the possibilities of where my evening could go.

I'm always hesitant to murder a high-class call-girl. Why? Practicality, I guess. If they were the only option, they'd do, but I find it preferable to choose a cheap whore off the street; people don't usually raise an eyebrow until at least five or six back-alley whores have gone missing—even then, the press doesn't really care until the killer targets a middle class white girl.

So I cruise through the red-light district, past the seedy bars where men with matted hair and few teeth stumble out of heavy doors, bouncing against a lamppost as if it's starting a fight. I'd pity them if they were worth pitying.

I direct my Mercedes down the side street, where there are no lights and no windows. Just the backsides of shops. The parts of shops where deliveries are made during the day, and drugs are dealt during the night. I find three whores. Each stands away from the other as if they want to distance themselves from the competition, but there's little difference between them—their eyelids droop, they hold cheap cigarettes between fingers with cracked red nail polish, and their fishnet tights are ripped.

I drive slowly past the first one. Pause. Wind down my window. She stumbles up to me. She smells like weed. I hate the smell; it's a child's drug. She has huge cleavage, large hoop earrings, a tight, tiny skirt made of fake leather, and heels she can't walk in. (Very few women can; most women who wear heels look like they are constantly stumbling forward). She leans an arm on my car roof and her fluffy jacket smells like damp. I hate her for touching my car and I make a mental note to tell my cleaner to wash it.

"Youlookingforagoodtime?" Her words slur into one. She hiccups at the end of the sentence. I fucking hate her and I want to watch her scream, but she's too subdued, too lethargic—she's on so many drugs I doubt she'll even feel me impaling her with my screwdriver.

I almost settle with taking her—I'm tired and bored and I had to get out of bed at ten this morning because Lyndsey was shouting and I hate mornings.

Then I see her.

A fourth whore, down the other end of the street.

And, for a brief flicker, I think it's *her.* Sweet seventeen and blow-job lips. The one I've sought for so long. The girl who got away and will soon be found.

Flora.

And I wonder—is it her?

Can it be?

"Heyyouwantagoodtimeornot?"

"Fuck off," I tell her, and drive up the street, quickly, skidding as I brake beside Flora.

But it's not Flora.

Yet she looks so much like her that she could almost be a clone. Even the way she walks belongs to Flora—the small, eager steps, and the arms folded around her cautious body.

She stops and looks at me. You'd probably say this woman

is too young to fuck strangers—but when are you supposed to be old enough?

She smiles at me—not a distant, forced smile like Whore Number One—this is a genuine smile; a cute smile; a make-your-nuts-go-tingly smile.

She even smells like her too.

"Hey you," she says, leaning against the roof of my car. Hopefully she's wiping away the filth left by Whore Number One. "How are you doing tonight?"

She doesn't slur her words, and she doesn't look dead behind the eyes. She looks vibrant. Full of life. Too good for the street corner; she should be in the classy hotels, not the backstreets.

"My name is–"

"No."

I don't want to know. I'll tell her what her name is.

"Your name is Flora," I tell her. "*Flora*. You understand?"

She nods, never stopping that smile. So many women have resting-bitch-face, and it's delightful to meet a woman who actually smiles and doesn't start quoting feminism when you suggest that they should fucking smiling for once.

"Whatever you say, boss," she says, and the way she calls me *boss* makes me rock hard.

"Get in," I tell her.

She nods, saunters around the car, in front of the head-lights, on purpose, so I can see her. Her legs curve, and she's not chubby but not bony either, and her hair is long and she looks JUST LIKE HER, so it's almost as if SHE IS HER.

She opens the door and puts her leg in first, her skirt riding up her thigh enough for me to see the outline of lace on her panties, then places her delicate buttocks on the passenger seat and stares at me.

Just stares.

Oh, that stare.

"So where to know?" Pretend-Flora asks.

"You want to see my mansion?"

"You live in a mansion?"

"I sure do."

"I've never been in a mansion before."

"Would you like to come in mine?"

"Absolutely."

I drive and we pass late-night clubs with young men in shirts following young women in tiny dresses like a fucking animal documentary, snapping and salivating at each other like crocodiles.

After a few minutes of silence, Pretend-Flora turns to me and says, "Have you any music?"

"Yes."

"How about we hear some?"

I flick on the stereo, which resumes Johnny Cash's Ring of Fire halfway through. She frowns like she's just stepped on gum.

"What is this?" she asks.

"What?" What does she mean, *what is this*? It's fucking Johnny Cash. Who doesn't like Johnny Cash?

"This song doesn't make sense."

"Oh, it does."

"I don't–"

"Cash's family claimed for years this song was about him falling in love despite being on booze and drugs. They insisted, and insisted, and insisted that it was all about love despite the shit he had going on."

"And what was it really about?"

I turn to her and grin. "A woman's cunt."

She sniggers. "Are you being serious?"

"He wrote it when he was shit-fried, off his face high, and he wrote it about a flame-filled vagina."

"And what does a flame-filled vagina look like?"

"I guess we'll find out later."

And here it is.

The moment.

Where there is a small sign of discomfort, a distortion between two thoughts, a decision between *That's sick and am I in trouble* or *It's a joke and I should laugh along.*

In the end, she forces out a laugh and turns back to the window. Conversation has ended. Silence resumes. It's perfect.

I glance at her a few times, and the back of her head looks like *hers*, the same hair I grabbed as I pounded *her* from behind, as I used *her* as a hole for my deposits and ensured *she* never believed *she* was a human being.

Oh, Pretend-Flora, tonight is going to be exactly what I need.

CHAPTER THREE

SHE WALKS into my house like she owns it. She saunters through the hallway and into the first kitchen and runs her finger across the pristine cooking surfaces, taps her nails along the Coffeetek Vitro S1 Bean to Cup Coffee Machine, and clops her high heels along the marble floor whilst swaying her butt from side to side. I know she's sexy, but I've yet to decide if Pretend-Flora is also a nuisance. Like Flora, she is probably both.

"This is very impressive," she says, strolling into the living room and gazing at my excessively large driveway from the grand windows. "I don't think I've ever been in such a big house before."

I fold my arms and lean against the wall. I don't need her to tell me how big my house is; I know, I bought it.

She pauses by the futon. Puts one leg on it so her skirt hikes up her thigh and I can see everything. I see a smidgen of mud on the bottom of her heel, and it makes my muscles tense.

"Take your foot off that."

"Excuse me?"

"That's a Darlings of Chelsea sofa. It's very expensive, and you've been walking up and down that backstreet and God knows where else with those heels on all evening."

She remains silent. She wants to be annoyed, but I'm paying her, so she has no right to be perturbed. Instead, she takes her foot off the futon, removes both her heels, slides her fishnets tights down her legs, dumps them on the otherwise spotless floor, places her bare foot on the futon to reveal her bare inner thigh and expose the end of her panties, then whispers, "This better?"

"Not really," I answer, still not satisfied that the sole of her foot is clean.

"What would you like me to do instead?"

I step toward her. Place my hands on her biceps. Her arms are so small I can wrap my fists right around them. She looks a little afraid. I like that she looks afraid.

"I want you to get on your knees."

She lowers herself, slowly, deliberately, placing one knee on the floor, then another, and looks up at me like *she* used to.

"Now what?" she asks, her voice childish and petulant. I love it.

"Put your hands behind your back and look at me."

She places her hands behind her back, pushing her wrists together as if bound by some invisible restraint. She sticks her bottom lip out and looks up at me, so subservient, so naughty.

"And now?"

"I want you to tell me things."

"What would you like me to tell you?"

I hesitate. Look down at the face of the girl I've been tracking for too long. The irritating mess that still evades my capture. The insult to my ego that is out there, somewhere, living a life she doesn't deserve.

"Tell me that your mum will never know."

"What?"

"Say it."

She hesitates. "Mum will never know," she says.

"Tell me you enjoyed school today."

"I enjoyed school today."

"Tell me you'll never touch another cock as long as you live."

"I'll never touch another cock as long as I live."

"Now tell me you're sorry."

She frowns.

"Say it," I demand, my voice dry. I struggle to hide my contempt for what she's done.

"I'm sorry."

"For what?"

"For... I don't know..."

"For tricking me."

"For tricking you."

"For running away."

"For running away."

"For hiding the corkscrew up your cunt."

She looks confused.

I grab her chin and squeeze her cheeks. *"Say it."*

"I'm sorry for hiding the corkscrew up my cunt," she says, and I can feel the concern mounting, the terror in her voice.

"Say it again."

"What?"

"I said say it again."

She glances at the door.

I squeeze her cheeks harder.

"Say it."

"I'm sorry for hiding the corkscrew up my—"

I lower my hand to her throat, lean my body weight against her, and shove her to the floor. She winces as her back slams against the floor. She glances at the door again.

"Listen, I—"

"Shut up."

"I think—"

"I said shut up, Flora."

My spare hand grabs her crotch. I squeeze it like it's a stress ball. She cries out.

"Get off me!" she says.

I squeeze harder, until I can feel her flesh poking between my fingers, until my nails dig into her arsehole, until she's screaming and begging me to stop.

"I said no! I didn't agree to this!"

"I don't remember asking."

"Please, you don't have to pay me, just let me–"

I smother her mouth with one hand and pull her panties down with the other. She tries to argue, but only mumbles come out. I spread her legs and she bites my fingers as I enter her.

"Ow!"

"I said to–"

I punch her in the face. Her nose bleeds. I force the back of her skull against the floor and her eyelids lower, only for a second, enough grogginess to make her compliant.

And I fuck her.

"How'd you like that, Flora?"

I fuck her hard.

"Hey, Flora? Hey? What do you think of that?"

Harder.

Until she's not a body, just a hole.

Until she's no longer a human, but a vessel I wish to destroy.

Until she weeps.

"I fucking told you, Flora, I fucking told you, we could be happy, you bitch, we could be happy!"

She tries to say something. It's hazy, but there are words.

"What?"

She tries again, but can't quite push them out.

"What is it, huh?"

Then those words emerge: "I'm... not... Flora..."

I stop.

Fury fills my body, surging through my muscles, until I am shaking, all of me, shaking, desperately trembling, and the rage comes over me and I cannot fight it any longer, I truly cannot; but why should I fight the rage when it is so beautiful?

"You will be who I want you to be, and today, you will be Flora."

"I'm not..."

I rest my thumbs against her eyelids. I push them. She screams. She fights, her body thrashing, kicking, fighting me off, but it's useless, I am strong and she is not, and I am pushing down with all my body weight until my thumbs feel like they are sinking into mushy peas.

Her eyes sink deeper into her skull until they are no longer part of her face, and as my thumbs become submerged in her blood, her eyeballs burst and puss dribbles down her cheek.

I stand.

She moans and squirms, clawing at two sockets she used to see out of, feeling for her eyes, crying that she cannot feel them, where have they gone, oh where have they gone.

As she struggles, I stride into the kitchen, take hold of the Coffeetek Vitro S1 Bean to Cup Coffee Machine, and rip it from the wall (it's okay, I have three others). I return to the living room, lift the machine high above my head, place my knees on either side of her waist, and slam it down upon her head. Her skull makes an audible crack, like I've snapped a large twig, and pieces of brain splatter across the floor.

I bring the machine down a second time, but I really needn't. Her body has stopped struggling. There's no breath wheezing out from between her lips. Her face has sunk into the rest of her head, and the top of her skull has collapsed with it.

She looks fucking ugly, and is nothing like Flora anymore.

I'm glad this was over quickly, as it means I have more time to hunt Flora; to search Google for a likeness to her photo; to search for her on social media; to search for her in the media; the same things I do every day.

I shove Pretend-Flora out of the backdoor so I can wipe the blood off the carpet with soapy water and disinfect it without her dirtying it again. Then I put her in a wheelbarrow and wheel her to the field behind my grand house.

It's time to feed the pigs.

NEVER AGAIN

I bet you still search for me, don't you, Gerald?

I bet you sit there, night after night, staring at the computer screen with a whisky in your hand and anger in your eyes, as if Google will have an answer for you. You won't find me there, Gerald.

I'm not on Facebook. Or Twitter. Or Instagram or TikTok or SnapChat or LinkedIn or any other social media site.

Because that would be too easy for you.

And I will not make it easy like before.

Because it was easy, Gerald.

I was there. All the time. When I arrived home from school, when you arrived home from wherever you went during the day, I was there—ready for you to bend me over the kitchen sink, hike up my skirt, fuck me from behind and ask me if I liked it, as if enjoyment was a choice.

I thought I loved you. For the longest time, I thought we'd spend our lives together. I lived in a world where Mum would forgive me for being with her husband, and we would live together, and you would fuck me every night because that's what it meant to be loved; you taught me that; that fucking and loving are the same thing.

But I'm not sure you're even capable of love, are you?

I was deluded.

And then you killed Mum. And everything changed.

But that wasn't enough for you, was it?

Hey, Gerald.

Hey…

If you don't mind my asking…

How's your penis?

Oh, if you could hear my sniggers. I can just see your face. I know you'll never hear this, but I can imagine that snarl, that curl of your lip, that insult to your pathetic male pride as I utter the question.

Your ego is bigger than your narcissism, and that's saying something.

So no, you will not find me. I am somewhere you will never go. You cannot expect your search to reach this location.

Am I in school? College? Work? A psychiatric ward? On an island somewhere? Married, even?

You'll never know, Gerald, because I'll never tell.

I was a child, and you treated me like a receptacle for your cum. Like I was just a hole to take your load.

I stuffed a corkscrew up my vagina to get you, Gerald, and I don't regret it for a moment.

I will never, ever, ever be yours.

Not then, not now, and never again.

Never again, Gerald. Never again.

I want you to listen to those words. They each have two syllables and have been uttered by many women; but I mean them, I really do.

Never again.

Never.

Again.

I will die before you touch me. Before I allow myself to feel those coarse hands again, feel them grabbing at me, seizing my breasts like you were unscrewing a jar, grasping my crotch like you were squeezing an apple, shoving my face against the wall and pummelling your dick up me like you were trying to smother me.

Never again will you bite my clitoris until it bled; like you needed to take it away; like I didn't deserve something that gave me pleasure.

Never again will your hands feel the contours of my neck; stroke the adolescent skin around my gullet; feel what it would be like to choke me until I'm even emptier than you made me.

Never again will you make me feel like I deserve it; like it's how my life should be; like it's all I am; like you're the centre of my world; like you're the only man who'll ever love me; like fucking is something I don't have a choice about; like I'm a vessel to be used; like I'm a pathetic, insignificant, meaningless, pointless vacant entity that is owed to you like property or possessions or a belonging that you can pick up and put down when you feel like a quick orgasm.

I hate you.

I hate you so much.

I hate you so much that I have little left in me for anyone else. With my mind, my heart, my lungs, my legs, my gut, I hate you.

What is there left to give?

You've taken that from me, Gerald. You've taken it all.

And the most painful part?

You will never see that. You will never understand what you've taken from me. Even if we came face-to-face and I explained it in minute detail, I still do not believe you would be capable of understanding.

So keep searching for me. Go ahead. Think you're making progress if you must. Spend your money on it if you think it will help. You have enough of it.

Never again will I submit to you.

Never again will you hurt me.

And never again will I let you make me feel what you made me feel.

With my life, I swear it.

I swear it, Gerald.
With every piece of me, I swear it.
Never again.

CHAPTER FOUR

WHERE ARE YOU?

I never thought it would be this difficult. You're not some ninja or assassin or spy. You're a pathetic little teenage girl. You're not taking up army training or joining the marines, you're watching Twilight on your own whilst strumming yourself over a werewolf wannabe. How the fuck are you so hard to find?

I sit back. Sigh. Stare at the computer like it's going to puke up the answers. Google knows fuckall. Facebook, the detestable site for idiots with no lives to make other idiots think they have lives, is coming up with nothing. As is every other avenue I try. So I sit here, glaring at the screen, with no idea how I'm supposed to find you.

And I stop searching for you, and I try a new search.

Private investigators.

I hesitate. Amend the search.

Discreet private investigators.

I don't want any PI going back to the police with information once the person they find ends up dead. I want someone who knows when to shut the fuck up.

I scroll through the pages until I find a man with

promising credentials. Most of them have testimonies from past clients, but not this man—he refuses to give anything away about who his clients are. I like this. Then I look over his history. He is a former police officer. As adept as he may be, I do not trust him. In fact, I don't trust any of those fuckers. Which leaves me with one option.

I close the browser. Open the VPN and ensure it is encrypted, and unable to stop me from accessing what I wish to access. I search my computer programs for *Tor*. Open it. Then open a password-protected word document I keep hidden on my computer that contains links to various websites, each URL consisting of jumbled letters and numbers. This document cost thousands. The cost made no difference to me. Within it, I find websites with contact information for private investigators, and I try a few links.

Within minutes, I have found a private investigator on the dark web, and we have arranged to meet.

He chooses the location: a small, dark bar in the part of town where Pretend-Flora hung around. I don't particularly like the look of the bar, but I suppose I need to be accommodating. If he does the job competently, then I can accept the inconvenience. He asks me to bring photographs of the target, along with any other relevant documents. I have a box in one of my many spare rooms containing her birth certificate, provisional driving license, photo albums my (deceased) wife used to keep, her diaries (which are highly entertaining; she really doted upon me), her old mobile phone, and a few of her clothes I didn't throw out because I occasionally like to smell them whilst whores suck me off.

I consider leaving my car across town from the bar and getting a taxi for fear of what might happen to my car, but I don't want a record of my movements. I mustn't let my repulsion make me sloppy. So I take the cheapest car I own, a Mercedes-Benz Sedan, and park it on a side street, resentful of the hobos who meander past it, occasionally brushing their dark, dank coats over the immaculate paint job, infecting it with their pointlessness.

I know I have many more cars at home, and I can buy more whenever I wish, but I still rue having to expose such a beautiful vehicle to the dregs of society. I detest that such vermin even steal the same air I breathe, and I often wonder how long it will take evolution to kill them off, and I resent Darwin for not coming up with a theory about a faster version of survival-of-the-fittest.

The bar itself doesn't stand out. I imagine this is why the man chose it. The sign above the dusty window reads *Al's* in black with white lettering and is almost impossible to notice in the darkness. I place my hand on the doorknob and it's sticky and I hate that I must contaminate my hand with the filth of the kind of people who frequent such a place. The inside is small, with stained tiled floors and tables hidden in tenebrosity. There are a few lights above the bar, and a few lamps in a few corners, but otherwise the place is in permanent night-time. It's feels like the kind of place people come to weep or die, and where smiles are seen as suspicious.

As I enter, a barman nods at me. He's probably in his forties. He's short and stocky and missing teeth. He doesn't smile, but doesn't frown either—just stands there idly, like his head is empty of thoughts. A man sits at the bar nursing a dusty pint glass with the last remnants of beer. He wears a trench coat and a hat. He sits over his beer glass like it's his dying wife, in despair over its depleting life. I don't believe in souls, but if I did, I would imagine this man doesn't have one.

"What can I get you?" the barman asks as I walk past.

I do not want to touch any of their glasses, so I ask for a bottle of beer out of the fridge, hoping it is not quite as contaminated.

The barman takes the top off a bottle and hands it to me. We briefly make eye contact. His grim face doesn't flinch. I've fucked corpses with more life behind their eyes.

I take the glass and step further into the bar. In the far corner, a man sits among the shadows. He holds a hand up, his open palm facing me, in what I assume is an indication to join him. I look around, nervous about prying eyes, but no one gives a shit about what we're doing—which makes this place ideal—and I join him at the table. He wears a trilby hat, and I snort at the cliché, like he's dressing up for a film noir— but the hat keeps most of his facial features hidden. I reckon he's mid-forties, but it's hard to tell.

He takes a sip from his glass of whisky. His fingers leave fingerprints in the dust that clouds the glass.

"So what do I call you?" I ask.

He pauses. He's probably trying to be mysterious, but he's just pissing me off. "Dick."

"What?"

"Call me Dick."

"Is that your name?" It must be; who would intentionally choose to be called Dick?

Then it occurs to me he's trying to imitate Dick Tracy. His whole look emanates the character. I don't know whether to walk out and rethink this whole thing, or laugh in his face.

"Right…" I say instead.

"Did you bring what I asked for?"

I pass a bag over the table. He opens it. Peers inside. His movements are smooth yet jilted, like he's trying to be cool but cannot hide an awkwardness that betrays him.

He closes the bag and looks at me.

"I'll find her."

The words hang between us. I wait for more, but that seems it's all there is.

"And money?" he asks.

"What about it?"

"I'm not doing this for free."

"You find her, then you'll get it."

"I will find her."

"Okay, then I'll–"

"I *will* find her."

My arms shake. I want to pound his head against the table for interrupting me, kick his face against the floor, smash his whiskey glass and used the shards to decorate his face in anarchy.

"I am not going to ask what you want this girl for," Dick continues. "I am not going to pretend to care. I am not bothered about consequences or laws or what's right and wrong— but I *do* care about money."

I hesitate. His advert did say twenty percent up front. The amount makes no difference to me, but I don't like giving money for a job that hasn't been done yet.

Still, I take the wad of fifties out of my pocket and place it on the table.

"If you fail to find her after I've given this to you, I will gut you."

He takes the money. Flicks a thumb over the edge as if to count it, then adds, "I told you I won't fail."

He stands. Finishes his whisky. Says, "I'll be back in touch within a week," then leaves.

CHAPTER FIVE

AND SO I have a week to kill. I have to quell the anticipation, and the possibly disillusioned optimism I have in this man achieving the results I couldn't, and find something to occupy my time.

I could practice what I'll do to Flora when I find her. Then again, it's often a good idea to lie low after I've disposed of one insufferable wench, and Pretend-Flora is still only three-quarters eaten. A high frequency of missing women attracts attention.

So I decide to avoid killing for a week.

And what a monotonous week it is.

Day one.

I watch television, and grow to despise the poor delinquents who choose to share their trivial problems on poorly-made daytime shows. I should enjoy them, as they are shows manufactured on anger, and that is something in which I am an expert, but the anger is so… uncontrolled. You need to harness it, not reveal it to the world like a tiny cock for everyone to judge. These people do not know how to channel their fury against each other in a healthy way, such are the restrictions of society imposed upon them, and for that reason, I find the shows too tedious to watch, even if I do find their guests' unsightly appearances quite startling (there were very few guests with all their teeth, most couldn't produce words with more than two syllables, and all of them were too thick to recognise that they were being exploited so the host could shout at them. If he shouted at me like that, I'd show him his liver before I choked him on it.)

I grow bored and resist getting a whore for fear that I will end up killing them. I watch old home movies of Flora and masturbate instead. I feel pathetic for doing so, and end up throwing my computer against the wall. I have six others, who gives a shit?

Day two.

I go to the library, and holy moly I did not realise how many sacks of shit come here during the day. It's mostly older ladies with nothing better to do. I despise older people; they have nothing they can offer me. They think they are full of wisdom because they've lived a long time, but there's a reason that food decays as it grows older: because it's no longer tasty and delicious, but has lost its purpose and is covered in mould. If you no longer work, how do you find purpose?

And before you say it, yes, I do not work either, but I own several businesses that I pay other people to run, thus providing employment, therefore fulfilling a purpose. In fact, I allow myself a tasty bonus from the company's profits every year as a reward for giving so many people employment. It is the closest I get to willingly serving as a functioning member of society. (Though if it weren't for the wealth it provides me, I wouldn't offer this world such a thing; it doesn't deserve it. I would rather society rid itself of everyone who denies their true nature—except for a handful of people for me to hunt.)

Anyway, I digress. I am in the library. It feels like *Night of the Living Dead.* There's a woman hobbling around on crutches with a colostomy pouch tied around her hairy leg.

She doesn't even cover it up, just lets it hang free beneath her beige skirt. Every now and then, a few bubbles rise to the surface. It's sickening.

I go straight to the true crime section. It's my favourite, and it's where I find the least amount of pensioners, and the smell isn't quite as strong. I can even convince myself I'm somewhere else. I look through the books, but they are all dogeared and tatty. It repulses me. A book should be immaculate, and even the tiniest crease on the spine should be met with a severe beating.

A woman stands in the aisle with me. She smiles at me. She has brown hair and sodomise-me-eyes. I remind myself I'm trying to abstain from such activity. Even so, I really want to see what her face looks like with my cock in it as mascara runs down her cheeks and she begs for her life. I can see her naked in my mind; it's a talent I have; any time I look at a woman, my imagination is able to instantly reveal what they look like unclothed. This particular woman has big nipples and a hairy muff. I don't like it. She can fuck off back to her book about bank heists of the 1950s; no thank you, you disgusting bitch.

I choose a book on serial killers. It's always good to develop craft. I sit in a small armchair in the corner. I've never placed my buttocks on such an uncomfortable seat before. The cushion doesn't even sink, it's stiff and hard and rough, and I imagine this is what it's like to sit on sandpaper. I try to ignore it as I read about how Andrei Chikatilo used to take a photo of the last thing his victims saw and about how he chewed off noses and eviscerated stomachs and cut out tongues and cut off genitals, and it makes me think about how my art is really just building on what has come before. Then I realise a child is staring at me.

This revolting child has one finger up his nose, uses his other arm to hold a book about some obscure children's character, and wears a vacant expression that is focussed entirely on me. He's dead behind the eyes, like roadkill. If he doesn't stop staring at me, I'm going to impale him.

I leave the library, disgruntled at my experience, and perturbed that I still have another five days to wait.

Day three.

I go to a matinee at the theatre. An independent theatre company is doing their interpretation of Antonin Artaud's *Spurt of Blood* (also known as *Jet of Blood*). I am fascinated by his theories on the theatre of cruelty and find this company's interpretation quite intriguing. It is a visceral experience that makes everyone feel uncomfortable, but I am fascinated by the nonsensical nature to the script, the lack of narrative, and the expanding clitoris the company creates with a large piece of cloth and cream coloured paint (think I'm making this up? Read the play—the expanding clitoris is in there). They also have masks. Nudity. Costumes decorated in fake blood. It makes me quite excited, and I am happy to have had the experience as I leave.

I do, however, find it frustrating how uncomfortable the rest of the audience appears. I even hear one woman say on the way out, "That was like after a one-night stand where you're grubby and feel all wrong and dirty." I imagine showing her exactly what it's like to feel wrong and dirty.

Day four.

Is it really only day four?

After my excursion to the theatre yesterday, I fear that my week has already peaked, and no one will have created anything in this world sufficient enough to satisfy me. I consider the cinema, but don't want to be trapped in a room with overweight imbeciles rustling their sweets. Honestly, they did it in the theatre yesterday, and it took every ounce of restraint not to shove their packet of sweets down their throat until my fist met their lungs.

I decide to beat the shit out of a homeless guy. I'm getting bored, and knowing I can't satisfy my cravings means they are only growing stronger. I've gone months before. And before you ridicule me for my withdrawal, let's give an example that applies to you and your mundane existence to show just how difficult the power of suggestion is: Right now, I imagine you are not necessarily craving chocolate. But, should it be declared that chocolate is now banned and you cannot have any for the foreseeable future, chocolate will become all you can desire.

So I sit outside a coffee shop, nursing a latte that the barista has drawn a leaf in with foamy milk, (and by barista, I mean the acne-ridden teenager with the voice that broke when he asked me what I'd like to order; honestly, there was a time when a tradesman's title meant something, now everyone's dodgy uncle who can put up a shelf calls himself a fucking builder), and I watch a man across the street. He sits on a blanket. His beard is large—he reminds me of Mr Twit from Roald Dahl's book *The Twits.* Mother used to read me that book when I was a child. When she wasn't fucking everything that moved, that is.

Every now and then someone drops some change in his hat. He's too starved to thank them. A woman walks by and gives him an umbrella as the rain starts to dribble. Her kindness is unsettling. Eventually, he gets up, and he meanders across the street, and I follow him across town, wondering if this is like moving house for him. He looks both ways as he heads down a back alley. I follow him down there to find him pissing against the large brick wall. The alley smells like damp. It's dark and hidden. I hate that he's pissing in public, but I don't know where else he's supposed to piss. At least he's doing it in an alley, I guess. Makes it easier for me. I grab the back of his head and I ram his forehead into the wall.

He falls to his knees and presses the palm of his fingerless gloves against the wound I just created. I wonder whether they are fingerless because he's trying to do his best Fagin impression, or whether the fingers frayed away and he can't afford another pair.

I kick him in the belly. And the chest. He grabs his heart like it matters. I kick him in the jaw and he rolls over. I stomp on his face with my boot.

Day five.

I drive to London and meet Tony and Marcus in Westminster. We eat in The Throne Lounge. I hate these two imbeciles, but they help me keep up the pretence that I'm one of you, even though I'm not. I'm so much better.

Tony works in finance and cheats on his wife with his secretary. Marcus is a marketing executive for a large corporation and thinks we don't know he's a closeted transexual, and I hate that he hides it. You should never hide who you are because you fear this pathetic society might judge you.

I have the Tuna Empanadillas to start, though I'm a little envious of Tony's Sweet Fried Saganaki when it arrives. For my main I have the caviar omelette—a mix that really shouldn't work, and I am hesitant to order it for fear that it may remind me of the repugnant omelettes my deceased wife used to feed me—but turns out to be delightful. For dessert, I have a Snowflake Luxury Gelato that I worry is essentially ice cream, but turns out to be so much more.

Day six.

The day I anticipate draws closer, and I am wet with enthusiasm. The thought of finding Flora fills me with endless possibilities. I almost don't want her to die, as I don't want the torture to end. I want to prolong the pain as much as possible. I want to degrade her until she cannot be degraded anymore. I want to do to her with a corkscrew what she did to me. I want to humiliate her with sexual subservience and make sure she knows unequivocally, undoubtedly, undeniably, that she is worth shit, and that I will forever be superior to her.

God, I want to fuck something. The idea turns me on.

I call a call girl then cancel it. I really can't trust myself.

I go for a walk, hoping to quell my appetite, but spend the time doing nothing but fantasising about what I will do to Flora's naked, brutalised body.

Day seven.

I await his phone call.

It does not arrive.

I get irritated. Then perturbed. Then angry. Then furious. Then I am so full of wrath that I cannot prevent myself from trashing one of my spare rooms. Even my cleaner comments on the mess, and I tell her to fuck off and mind her own business, but she barely speaks English, so just smiles like I offered her a sweet.

I wait until midnight, and I wait longer. I stay awake, awaiting the phone call that doesn't arrive.

I want the advance back that I paid.

I want to find him.

I want to ring his throat out for fucking me around.

I have no number. No way of contacting. He said he'll contact me. I regret this. Severely. I am furious with myself. And with him. This is fucking annoying.

I fall asleep, then wake up late.

Day eight.

I look at my phone as my eyes adjust to the morning light.

He is ringing me.

I answer it.

He's found her.

CHAPTER SIX

TODAY, we meet on a park bench, and he wears sunglasses and a trench coat, and honestly, you cannot make this shit up. He looks like someone trying to be inconspicuous and failing miserably. I almost don't quite know what to say. In the end I go with, "What the fuck are you wearing?"

He glares at me. Or he might not. Who knows, he's wearing sunglasses.

"I mean, you think no one notices you in this shit? This makes you even more noticeable."

A mother and a few children walk past. They point and giggle. I consider leaving right now, deterred by his unprofessionalism, but I'm too determined to find Flora.

He shakes his head and mutters something. I think he calls me a jack-off. I consider breaking his face against the bench.

Then he hands me an A4 envelope, and my mind is distracted. I take it, full of wonder, not wanting to open it yet, wanting to make it last, like a child at Christmas eager for it to go on forever.

"Money?" Dick asks.

"Huh?"

"The rest of my money."

"Oh, yeah."

I take out an envelope. He looks back and forth, like he's checking the coast is clear. I wonder if this is a hidden camera show, and some minor celebrity is going to jump out of a bush and announce I'm caught. He takes the envelope gently, opens it slightly, counts it quickly, then shoves it in his pocket and stands. Puts his hands in his pockets. Looks around.

"It was good doing business with you."

I don't say the same. Honestly, I found the guy annoying, and I am relieved when he finally trots off.

I sit on the bench, still cradling the envelope, and consider whether I should have checked it before I paid him. But I want to be alone for this. I want to saviour it. I want to relish the discovery and bask in the summer sun as I hatch a plan to reclaim what has always been mine.

I place a finger in the flap and drag it across, ripping it like I'm tearing apart loose flesh. I open it. There are roughly ten A4 pieces of paper. The first gives all the details I require. He redacts most information that could mean someone could track him, but the vital parts are there:

Target: Flora [Last Name Redacted]

Age: 17-18

Target was located at 11.57 on Saturday [Full Date Redacted] in a park, pushing a female aged approximately 8-10 on the swings.

The park was located in Tewkesbury, Gloucestershire, in a field off Gander Lane, behind the Tewkesbury Abbey.

She was followed to a home, with this child, to the nearby village of Northway on Hardwick Bank Road.

She lives in this home with a foster family:
  - Shane [Male, late forties]
  - Mariam [Female, late thirties]
  - Claire [Female, 8-10]

She attends college sixth form at the local comprehensive. She currently does A Levels in Philosophy and Ethics, Theatre Studies, and English Literature.

She has a mobile phone that she spends a lot of time on, but no online presence.

She has a group of friends called Ava, Isabella and Eleanor [social media pages attached] who she frequently talks on the phone to and spends her lunch times with. In the three days that she was pursued, she spent time indoors with these friends in the evenings, but never went to an outside event.

She also has counselling with a local trauma psychiatrist called Jason Hawes [credentials and experience attached].

She is very alert when walking alone, and turned her head quickly when she thought she was being pursued.

This is beautiful.

Absolutely beautiful.

Thorough and well-produced. Turns out this guy was a genius.

Beneath the top sheet with the basic information, there are few sheets of paper with photographs on—all of them featuring Flora. Sometimes she is with these friends, sometimes she's on her own looking over her shoulder, sometimes she's behind the window to the dining room of a pleasant middle-class home, having tea with her pretend family.

Everything else I need is there. Printouts of her friends' Facebook accounts. Twitter pages. Screenshots of stupid TikTok videos where they dance, poorly I imagine, and to the abhorrent music of their generation. Her friend's Instagram accounts with several pictures of duck-face and poses in the mirror. These girls are as vain as they are stupid. Flora might have avoided having her own social media, but her friends feature her frequently in theirs.

The next page features details of the house she lives in. The deeds, the value, the homeowners.

The next page features her psychiatrist's credentials, experience, and picture. He is a bearded man in his late thirties with what a young, impressionable girl like flora would call *a kind face*, but an honest man like me calls *deceptive*. He has a PhD from the University of Manchester. He worked in a practice in Leeds for three years before opening his own in Gloucester. Flora gets the bus to him every Friday afternoon so he can listen to her awful, awful life. Poor guy. Hope he gets paid a lot.

She doesn't need a man to listen. She needs a man to fuck her. She needs a cock in her cunt and a hand on her mouth, and to be told to shut up when she objects.

Her school information is printed on the next sheet. Her exam entries, her previous exam grades, her college entry application. I find her UCAS application on the next page. Aw, little girl wants to go to university. I look at what she's applied to do, curious. She wants to study Traumatology and PTSD. The opening paragraph on her personal statement tells us how she wants to help others who have had similar experiences of abuse.

I snort back a laugh.

Abuse?

Is that what they call it now?

She loved being a receptacle for my cum. She loved begging me to stop. She loved being on her knees, sucking on my cock whilst her wide eyes stared up at me, surrounded by smudged mascara, pleading—for what, I don't know, but pleading nonetheless.

And now she wants to tell everyone she was abused?

Oh, no, no, no, no, Flora—this won't do. This really won't.

I lift my head and grin. A child smiles back from beside a nearby pond, as if it thinks I'm aiming my pleasure at them. I've been so excited that I forgot I'm in public, or that there's anyone else here. I look away from the irritating child and return to the documents.

This is beautiful. Glorious. I am so happy I think I might float into the air and start flying over the world.

I need to rent a house in Tewkesbury. I will miss my house, with its shutters and its size, but I need somewhere to stay whilst I'm plotting. And I need a fake name to do it under. It's okay, I already bought some fake identities a few years ago, just in case I need them.

Within half an hour, I have put in an offer to rent a house in Northway, a few streets over from Flora's. It's not quite as large as I'm used to, and that's disappointing, but it's all I can find. I make a generous offer, and offer the estate agent a substantial financial incentive if they can push through the solicitor's nonsense and all the other pointless paperwork and have the house ready for me within a few days.

The offer is accepted, and upon receiving the transfer of the substantial financial incentive, they vow to have it ready for me immediately. It's amazing what a little money can do. An amount that is insignificant to me, but wonderful to them.

And I sit back, and I relish the heat, and I bask in the sun, and I ignore the child's laughter and the rage it sparks inside of me and just enjoy this moment—they come so rarely that, when they do come, you need to soak every second up.

Then I realise—there's a page I haven't looked at yet. The last page. I take it out. It features nothing but thirteen digits. That is all. I wonder what they are, at first. Then it's obvious.

It's her mobile phone number.

And, as I wait for my house to be ready, I decide it's the perfect way to start.

So I buy a new phone. Enter the number. Sit back and begin.

Oh, Flora, you truly do not know how fucked you are.

Hello Flora

Hi

Sorry who is this?

Don't you have my number?

No

Sorry

Oh well that's good to know!

Would have thought you'd have stored it after I gave it to you

Is this Liam?

 iMessage

Yes

Yes it is

It is Liam

Im so sorry

I did add your number but my phone goes funny sumtimes

How are you

I am well Flora

How are you?

Fine lol

 iMessage

You sound weird in text messages

Like all formal and stuff

wud yu rather i talked lik this

Oh god no

I hate people who text like that

Formal is fine with me

Wonderful

Did you want help on that assignment?

Sure

iMessage

> Isnt that why you messaged me?

Yes

And no

I thought it would be fun just to chat

> Oh really?

I like you

> Really?

> Cuz you seem like you don't

I don't talk to you much at school

 iMessage

I know

I'm shy

You don't really talk to anyone

From what I can see

Just hang around by yourself

I know

I have to tell you something

What?

You promise not to tell?

iMessage

Fine

Promise?

I promise

Cross your heart?

Cross my heart

And hope to die?

Er sure

Great

See the thing is

I'm going to run away

 iMessage

What?

Where?

Dunno yet

But I want to keep talking to you

Just please don't tell anyone where I've gone

I will come back eventually

I just need to go

Like now

Why?

 iFakeTextMessage.com

Whats the matter?

I'll tell you some other time

I just need to go

Okay

I trust you

Do you trust me?

Yes

Thank you

I mean it Flora

Thank you

 iFakeTextMessage.com

Xx

Xxxxxxxx

CHAPTER SEVEN

WELL I'M OBVIOUSLY GOING to need to find this Liam guy and kill him now.

I ponder over this as I stroll home, ignoring the insufferable fools who pass me on the street. One old woman walking her dog even tries to say *how are you*. I tell her to mind her own fucking business.

People, eh? They infuriate me!

I try not to let it distract me as I begin plotting. Liam's absence is crucial to my forming this connection with Flora; I cannot have her talking to him at college to find that she's not really been talking to him by text message. And if he's reported missing—which he will be—then that's covered. She won't say anything. She won't want to be noticed. I mean, yes she is an attention-seeking whore—she's studying Theatre Studies after all, meaning she can join with all the other irritatingly extroverted, outgoing people who like to be loud and don't understand when others don't like to be loud—but she is in hiding. She will not want her name linked to anything; she will not want to leave any trace I could pick up on. She would be too worried I'd access police information—which, via the wonderful convenience of the dark web, I have done a few times in my pursuit of her.

But it doesn't matter anymore, because I have found you, you little harlot.

And how stupid are you, by the way? Giving me an opening like that?

'Is this Liam?'

I mean, you're in hiding, you imbecile—don't give an anonymous person the ability to assume an identity you provide. You're such an amateur that I wonder how I didn't catch you sooner, and how I had to buy a seedy-yet-stupid-yet-as-it-turns-out-relatively-competent private investigator to find you.

Right, anyway. Liam. I'm picking up the keys to my house tomorrow afternoon. And I don't want this Liam fellow to arrive at school in the morning—I cannot risk you conversing —which means it needs to be done now. It doesn't sound like many people will miss this repugnant adolescent, anyway.

I sigh. Open Facebook on the new phone. Sign into one of my dummy accounts. Find the profile for one of Flora's friends. Ava seems to be the easiest. She has no privacy settings, and I can easily access her statuses, and her information, and her 'it's complicated' relationship status (a status that I assume means he dumped you then gave you false hope of getting back together? Idiot!), and her photographs. She has long, blond hair, wears a lot of foundation, and likes to eat phallic shaped objects in her photographs—honestly, there's an éclair in one, an iced bun in another; it's like she's asking for someone to ram a cock in her mouth. There are also some wonderful photographs of her with her family in Marbella last summer. She wears a purple bikini, and I must say, her body has formed well for a sixteen-seventeen-ish-year-old. Cellulite on her buttocks, but I don't mind that. A few marks on her arm—self-harm, maybe? The little masochist. Honestly, I'm tempted to bypass Flora and find Ava instead.

But no—this is not about sexual satisfaction (though that will inevitably be a part of it)—this is about vengeance. About justice. About ruining that bitch until she's nothing but guts and juices.

So I regretfully navigate away from the pictures—if I want the live version, I could take it, but I need to prioritise—and I go to Ava's friends list. I search for Liam. He's not on there.

I try Flora's other friend. Isabella. I open her profile to see if I can find access to Liam's through her friend list—and what a surprise Isabella turns out to be! You know how insecure, pretty women often keep an obese, unattractive friend around so they feel better about themselves? Well, Isabella is that perfect friend. She has acne scars down her cheeks and a nice, round belly. Whilst Ava wears too much makeup, this girl could do with wearing more. She has a smaller friends list, too. But still no Liam.

It really does seem like no one cares for this stupid boy.

I find Flora's last friend on Isabella's list. Eleanor. Thick black glasses and ponytail. No cleavage in any photo; she wears blouses or jumpers. Shame, as she looks like she has a nice body. She has selfies of her in the library with a sepia filter. Many of them. It seems she's quite the bookworm.

It makes me chuckle. These four could form a girl band. The hot one, the fat one, the geeky one, and the fucked-up-kinda-kinky one.

I search Eleanor's friends' list. She appears to be a kinder and more intelligent girl, and I hold out hope that this means she'd offer her friendship to charity cases such as this Liam boy.

Aha, I am in luck!

There he is. Liam Tucker. His profile picture is in black and white. He's painted his fingernails black. He quotes Marilyn Manson lyrics on his profile as if it makes him profound. He never smiles. He dyes his hair black, wears black hoodies with band names like *Godsmack* or *Korn* or *Slipknot* (I didn't know they were still a thing?), and occasionally wears a long leather jacket. Perhaps he saw Keanu Reeves wearing it in *Matrix* and thought it would make him look cool, but in truth, I've never seen someone who looks less cool. In between Marilyn Manson lyrics, he posts links about suicide and self-harm, and occasionally quotes Edgar Allan Poe. He wears rings with skulls on. I thought goths died out in the nineties, but apparently they are still in existence.

Unfortunately, nothing gives away where he lives. No picture in front of his house, no tagging locations, nothing. But he does have his family connections on his profile. I click on his father, who has a picture of himself, his wife, Liam, and a young girl as his cover photo. He's included his job in his 'about me' information. He works as a warehouse manager for a local glass manufacturer called *Fine Glass Supplies*. I Google them and check their opening hours. They are open until six. Which means I have plenty of time to get to *Fine Glass Supplies*, wait for Daddy to leave, and follow him home.

Normally I hate the internet, but at times like this, I love it. It makes it so much easier than it could have been.

CHAPTER EIGHT

THE *FINE GLASS Supplies* warehouse is full of men with working class swagger and laddish banter and grubby hands and it's exactly the kind of place I avoid. Even being in the same vicinity as these ingrates is making my flesh prick.

Liam's daddy looks different, though. While everyone else is joking around, he's busy working, and it seems like he does twice as much work as everyone else. His hands look delicate, like they don't belong here. His mannerisms are jilted, more careful than his colleagues. He's evidently tired, and worn down, and I'm not surprised when he has a teenage goth at home jacking off to the Satanic Bible and hacking away at his arm with a broken piece of glass.

Not that I have much against the Satanic Bible, actually. In fact, it is the religious text that infuriates me the least. Its philosophies are beautiful. It isn't about the celebration of evil —evil doesn't exist, it's something you make up to explain what you deny—instead, it is a celebration of liberty. It encourages you to follow your desires, to cease your restraint, and to pursue what arouses you rather than succumbing to societal lessons to rein it in.

At the same time, it's an attention-seeking croc of shit, just like every other book created by a religion. You can have those philosophies without Satan being involved. They deny Christianity in an attempt to appear non-conformist by conforming to something else. It's a fucked up logic, and I have no interest in it.

Anyway, I digress.

Daddy is still there after seven. He stays longer than is required, and is still packing stuff away when the other blokes get into their BMWs and zoom down the road like bellends. It's dark by the time he gets into his people carrier and checks both ways over and over and over again before pulling onto the road. He drives at the speed limit; never a single mile per hour over. It's infuriating to drive behind, and I struggle to maintain distance.

When he finally arrives home at a small, two-bedroom terrace house, I park across the street and watch through the windows as Daddy enters and greets his wife with a kiss on the cheek. She has dinner prepared for him like we are living in the 1950s patriarchy. She wears an apron with a floral pattern on it and calls her children for tea. Liam comes down-stairs with his little brother. I assume they share a room. How disgusting. Imagine being a teenage boy who just wants to have a wank and having to contend with an annoying child staring at you. I'm not sure how I'd suffer through such an ordeal without murdering the little scrote.

Then again, by the look of Liam, he's on the edge of what society might term insanity, and all he needs is time. I only wish I could give it to him.

They sit around the table and Daddy asks questions and Mummy prompts her sons to answer. He earns the corn, and they eat that corn, yet they don't respect him for providing said corn. Family logic baffles me. If I made someone preg-nant, I'd cut their belly open with a serrated knife, pull the foetus out, and rub it over her face until she concedes that she'll never have the audacity to fall pregnant again.

The younger son seems eager to talk. He must be about five or six. Lucky kid, soon he'll have a bedroom to himself.

Liam, however, has a permanent frown on his face. Like a smacked arse. So ungrateful for the life he's been given. I wonder how much he'll beg to keep it once faced with his own mortality. I look forward to finding out.

Daddy occasionally glances at Liam's nails. He says nothing, but I can see the conundrum in his eyes. He must allow his son to explore his identity and explore his sexuality and explore who he is, but *fuck* does he hope Liam isn't gay.

He won't say it. He can't say it. And I resent him for it—if a guy wants to put another guy's dick in his arse, then I'm right behind them (figuratively speaking).

But this guy is from a different generation.

I'm not sure why that matters, but it's always the excuse. Like when a grandparent is racist. Daddy comes from a time when dicks in the arse weren't so widely accepted, and he's failed to adjust.

But Daddy keeps all this frustration inside.

And if the homophobia didn't make me hate him enough, his self-restraint makes me hate him even more. It's bad enough that you hate who your son is becoming; it's even worse not to unleash that hate.

After dinner, Mummy gives the youngest a bath whilst Daddy and Liam watch television. Liam remains engrossed in his phone, and Daddy looks at him occasionally, trying to come up with something to say. But there is nothing. He cannot relate to his son. He has no conversation starters that would interest the teenage boy. So he remains silent, happy he doesn't have to sustain his performance as the perfect father while his wife is out the room.

Later on, I reckon he'll cry. Maybe once Mummy is asleep. Maybe in another room. Somewhere he can't be seen. He'll hate who he's become, and he believes that being strong means telling no one. With the amount this man is bottling up, I'm surprised he hasn't combusted yet.

It reaches half past ten and Mummy and Daddy go to bed. They say something to Liam. I'm assuming they are trying to force a bedtime on him. He grunts, not taking his eyes away from his electronic device. Mummy says something to Daddy, *leave it* or something along those lines, and walks upstairs.

Daddy stays where he is.

Watching his son.

Wanting to say something. Wanting to force authority. Wanting to connect. Wanting to be a better father than the father he had.

And he fails, and gives up, and he reminds his son to lock the doors when he goes to bed. Liam remains in the living room, so absorbed in his screen that he doesn't notice when I walk by the garden window behind him.

I wait in the shadows until all the lights upstairs are off. Unseen and unknown. Then I wait a few more minutes.

I try the backdoor, pressing silently on the handle. It opens, and I move it slightly, aware that it might creak. It doesn't. I open it completely and slip inside, into the kitchen.

I enter the hallway that leads to the living room and pass a small coffee table. There is a statue on it. A Jamaican fertility statue. The fellow with the massive cock. I pick it up and creep into the living room, where Liam sits in a chair with his back to me.

As I approach, I look at what he's doing on his phone, curious. He's reading an article about Marilyn Manson. Learning that his idol is a domestic abuser. I wonder whether this will change his interest in his hero, or whether he'll be one of those superfans who abuses Evan Rachel Wood on the internet for the audacity of speaking the truth, as if idolising someone means never allowing the illusion to be shattered.

I swing the fertility statue at his head, and it knocks him out straight away—which is a relief, as I didn't want him to scream—and he falls from the chair and slumps onto the floor.

I pocket his phone, then pick him up, put him over my shoulder, and tiptoe to the front door. He's lighter than I thought he'd be. He's a scrawny little teenage boy, yes, but I still imagined he'd be heavier than the women I carry. As it is, I may as well be carrying a whore over my shoulder, such is the lightness of this inbred, disillusioned delinquent.

Within ten minutes, I have placed him in the boot of my car, and done so without so much as a flicker of a curtain from a neighbour. Being noticed was a risk I had to take— which is why I covered the license plate on my car and stuck to the darkness to conceal my face.

I drive for a minute then stop to remove the license plate coverings. I don't want to be pulled over.

After another ten minutes or so, the shouting starts, the pounding against the inside of the boot, and I know he's feeling panicked, but he better not wreck my car.

I turn on some music to drown it out. It doesn't take long for us to reach the woods.

CHAPTER NINE

THE MOON IS FULL. They say it brings out the crazies. I say it just gives them a spotlight.

I drive down roads with no CCTV, then into a rural car park with no marked spaces. I bring the car to a stop and look around. I am met by the kind of silence you only find in the countryside. I get out of the car and piss on a bush. I love the woods at night—everything you do here is a secret. The trees hide your movements as the breeze conceals your voice. There is no living soul around to witness your indiscretions, and there will be no evidence of your presence left here. It is a perfect location for an animal to commit their deadly deeds.

I step across the moist gravel surface, pausing to stretch. I look around the absent space surrounded by tall, lingering trees. Brown branches appear black without sun to light them. The floor is covered in leaves, and the shadows take away their colour. Darkness creates its hidden path, and all I need to do is take it.

I tap the boot. He screams. He shouts. He demands to be let out. I sigh. It's the most words he's said since I started watching him. This boy is tiresome.

I return to my glove compartment, take out a knife, and

pause by the boot. This needs to be quick. It needs to be swift. This boy is undoubtedly going to attempt to runaway, and I need to plunge the knife down before he manages.

I lift the boot. He shouts obscenities and tries to push himself up, but I swing the knife down so rapidly that he is screaming at the pain in his thigh before he's able to put up a fight.

I stab his thigh again. And again. Then his calf. Then the other leg. Then I slice the back of the ankles, twice, then a third time, until there is a definite slit, and I do it all so quickly that he cannot adjust to the pain in time to push my hands away.

Then I step back, and I let him weep, let him swear at me over the torment, and I let him push himself out of the boot and onto the floor.

His face lands on the gravel, leaving dirt across his cheek. He tries to get up, but it hurts too much. Still he perseveres, and he straightens his legs, and as he just about withstands the pain enough to push himself to his feet, the slits in the back of his ankles open and he falls to the ground, screaming once again.

I let him scream. Why not? There are no houses nearby. There's a country road, but I parked at the far end of the car park, just next to the labyrinth of trees, so even if a car went by and they happened to hear a faint shriek, they'd think it was a distant animal.

"–fucking prick you fucking arsehole you fucking bastard get off me why do you do this let me go get off me fuck's sake ow it hurts fuck you–"

He lacks coherence. His words are jumbled, leaping from one thought to another before the previous one is finished. Silly boy, he needs to save his energy.

Well, I can't wait around all day.

I check his pockets—I don't want any evidence falling out —and they are empty. I turn my back to him, pick up one bloody leg in one hand and his other bloody leg in the other, and drag him toward the trees, away from the muddy path created for ramblers. I'd forgotten how light he is. I worry about the slight smear of blood he's leaving, but we're due a thunderstorm in a few hours, and I am confident the elements will destroy his trail.

As I pull him through the leaves, his abuse toward me turns to begging. He no longer thinks he can fight me, and is determined to be my friend.

He's never made a friend in his life, and it's going to end that way.

Eventually, we are so far among the trees that I don't think we need to go any further. I stop dragging him, and I clean a few loose leaves off a thick branch that sits along the ground then place my posterior upon it. I really don't want to sit anywhere that will damage my dark grey *Zegna Trofeo Wool Suit*—it's worth more than this boy's entire wardrobe—but I suppose if I damage this one, I still have several more in my cupboard.

He tries clawing himself along the ground to get away from me, but stops as he realises there is nowhere to go.

"What—why—who are you?" he says between pants of breath.

"Which question would you like me to answer first?"

"Who are you?"

"My name is Gerald."

"Why are you doing this?"

I consider explaining, but cannot be arsed. "It would take too much time to tell you." I take his phone out of my pocket. "What's your passcode?"

"If I tell you, will you let me go?"

"What's your passcode?"

"But if I tell you, you—"

I swing the knife to his thigh, just beneath the buttocks, stick it in, twist it, relish his screams, then pull it out again.

"What. Is. Your. Passcode."

"Five four seven two!" I love the effect a little forceful persuasion has. At this point he'd tell me if he wanks over gay porn. (I suspect he does.)

I unlock his phone. Open the settings. Turn off all location services and the GPS. I want to use his phone for things I do not wish to be tracked doing.

Out of curiosity, I open his photos. There are no pictures of friends. Not even family. Just selfies. Him pouting with black lipstick on; giving the peace sign at the camera; looking dark and mysterious (whilst actually looking vacant and uninteresting); staring wide-eyed; applying mascara in the mirror. This boy is *vain*. He probably thinks he looks cool in all these photos, but he just looks alone.

"You are a very, very sad boy," I tell him.

He tries to get up, but his feet give way. He pushes himself up again, determined, relying on adrenaline, but the adrenaline is not strong enough, and he falls once more.

It makes me laugh.

"Even if you did get up, do you think I wouldn't catch you?"

He rolls onto his back. Stares up at the moon. Groans. Then cries.

"I want my mum…" he whimpers.

I stick out a bottom lip. "Poor boy."

I place the phone in my pocket and consider how I'm going to do this. I'd like to do it slowly. I'd like to chop off pieces of his body then show them to him.

I get an alert message from my other phone.

It's Flora.

Liam? You there?

I'm worried.

I don't like how we ended our conversation earlier.

Why are u running away?

I sigh. I need to answer these messages. If she's texting me/Liam, then it's a perfect opportunity to engage with her.

"Sorry," I tell Liam. "I don't really have time."

I stick the knife into the front of his throat, hold it there, then push it harder until it penetrates the windpipe, then drag it around the side of his throat. This takes a lot more muscle than it does in the movies. Human flesh and human muscle are tough things to get through. I manage, though, and he bleeds to death at my feet.

I reply to Flora before I hack his body into pieces.

> Liam? You there?

> I'm worried

> I don't like how we ended our convo earlier

> Why are u running away?

What does it matter to you

> Because people don't just run away

> There must be a reason

No one cares what the reason is

 iMessage

I do

You don't

You just feel guilty

You don't really want to know

I do

And I think you want to tell me

Hows that?

Because you wouldn't have told me you were running away

If you didn't want to

 iMessage

I don't want to

So why did you tell me you were running away then

Because I like you

If you like me tell me why

You wouldn't understand

Seriously?

Yeah

What do you know about it

You have like the perfect parents

iMessage

They are not my actual parents

Whatever

Have you met my dad

He doesn't give a shit about me

He just works all the time

At least you have an actual dad

Did you never have a dad

Kinda

Well

 iMessage

Yes

No

He wasn't

He wasn't a real dad

Who was he

Stop it

I know what you're doing

Diverting my attention

Just tell me why

At least give me that

iMessage

You wont understand

Its not like youve been through any trauma

Not like you know what its like

You being serious?

I have trauma counselling!!!!

And even I cant tell my counsellor the truth

Even I have to hide things from him

Think I don't know what its like to have trauma?

 iMessage 🎤

You have no idea

Why do you have trauma counselling

What happened

A bad man hurt me

Thats all I want to say bout it

Your dad?

He wasn't my dad

Who was he

Why are you running away Liam

 iMessage

Tell me who he was and
ill tell you why

I don't like talking about it

Neither do i

Fine

He was an asshole

I hated him

What did he do

Not buy you your barbies

How about raping me

How did he rape you

 iMessage

All the time

I said how

What do you want a picture

Did you not like it

Want it

Just because he was your stepdad doesn't mean you didn't desire him

Fuck you liam

He was an adult

Should know better

iMessage

Fuck me?

Fuck off then

Fine

Sorry

I just been dealing with this shit for ages

Alone

Its not easy

No one knows anything

Id like to know

I thought you said I should have liked it

 iMessage

Think ill tell you anything now?

My stepdad touched me too

What?

He did

When I was a kid

He used to pretend it was a game

Why didn't you tell anyone

I was scared

And I kind of liked it

 iMessage

But mostly scared

I know what you mean

Like you felt like he loved you

And this was part of love

But you hated what he did

And you realised it was wrong

And you feel awful admitting that

Exactly

You should tell someone

 iMessage

No

Why don't you tell someone about yours?

Fine

I get it

But there are other places you can go

People you could ask for help

I just want to be alone

I just want to be alone
For a while

Ill come back

 iMessage

I promise

Why would you ever come back

For you

Why

Because I like you flora

You understand

I like you too

I really like you

I always thought when you stared at me it was cause you hated me

 iMessage

It was cause I was scared

I wanted you

Im damaged liam

Im not good for you

Im not good for anyone

I don't even know if I can love

Then ill love for both of us

That's sweet liam

Really sweet

I need to go

My bus is coming to a stop

Stay safe liam

I really do care about you

Maybe we can go out sometime

When youre back I mean

Ok

Xxxxxxxxxxxxxxxxxx

Xxxxxxxxxxxxxxxxxx

iMessage

CHAPTER TEN

OH, God, Flora, please don't make me gag.

I mean, really, you were abused?

You wanted it.

Every damn time.

It turned you on.

Being used as just a hole; being bent over and fucked; being told what to do; never being asked – that's what aroused you.

So fuck off, you disgusting piece of shit.

Trauma counselling? Fucking trauma counselling? ARE YOU KIDDING ME FLORA?

Whose dick was impaled on a fucking corkscrew, you self-righteous bitch?

I SHOULD BE THE ONE in trauma counselling. Not YOU Flora—ME.

How dare you?

How fucking dare you?

I cannot wait to break your body apart. I'll show you what it's like to be abused. I'll fucking show you, you ungrateful LITTLE FUCKING WRETCH YOU FUCKING WHORE I HATE YOU.

I hate you.

Oh shit, I hate you.

Fuck you.

FUCK YOU.

I try to rein myself in, but I can't. I've stripped Liam of his clothes and I'm hacking at his body with too much energy. I need to hit the limbs with the right amount of force not to get any blood on my suit, but I'm covered, I'm completely fucking covered in his gross FUCKING DISGUSTING juices.

Fuck it. I'll get a new suit. I've got plenty. I'll replace it. A few grand is nothing. I need this. I need this catharsis. I need this spurt of anger, this unleashing of fury, this beautiful act of wrath, and I will hack his body up into so many pieces that no one will ever know it once resembled a human.

Fucking Flora fucking abuse fucking claims fucking stepdad fucking me knowing better fucking touching her fucking just a kid FUCKING BULLSHIT absolute FUCKING BULLSHIT how dare you Flora HOW FUCKING DARE YOU I did nothing wrong NOTHING you hid something up your cunt you trapped me you conned me you seduced me and stuck the pointed end of a corkscrew down my jap's eye YOU FUCKING DID THAT so fuck you FUCK OFF how dare you Flora HOW FUCKING DARE YOU!

I rub blood out of my eyes. I can't tell what colour my suit used to be anymore. The boy stinks like shit from where he emptied his bowels and it's on the leaves and among the blood and I've made a bloody mess with this one.

I look up. Grey clouds approach. Rain will take care of any mess I've left. If not, it's off the path, and it's just blood. No one will report it. And if they do, they won't link it back to me. I'm fine. I'm absolutely fine.

I'M FINE.

I pile all the loose limbs and fingers and various body parts on top of the boy's t-shirt and wrap them up, then wrap them more up in his trousers, and then my ruined suit jacket, making his limbs easier to carry. It doesn't all fit, and I have to stick a foot and a thigh under my arm. I walk the way I came, no idea if it's the right way, feeling stupid and pathetic as I stumble across wet leaves in the rain, but I find my car eventually.

I open the boot. Take out a large bin bag. Put the remnants of the body in there. Strip off. Put everything I'm wearing in the bag. It's all tainted, it all has his DNA, it all must go. I double bag it with another bin bag. Triple bag it. Put it in the boot. Then stand naked beneath the rain. It gets harder and harder, and it soaks my skin and wets my hair until I am as wet as I can be. Then I get into the car, annoyed that I'm getting the upholstery wet, and search for the nearest farm on Google Maps; it's too late for me to go back to my house, feed my pigs, and return to observe Flora at school.

It takes twenty-five minutes to get to the farm.

By the time I arrive, the car's heater has mostly dried me off. I take a spare outfit I bought for my trip from the suitcase behind the backseat and put it on. I sweep my hair to the side and check my reflection in the rear-view mirror. I look exquisite in a clean navy-blue Alexander Amosu Vanquish II Bespoke suit.

It is still dark, but I can smell early morning moisture in the air. I don't have long. So I park at the edge of the farm and wait for movement. The farm's cottage is across another few fields, and I wait for a light to turn on, or some reaction to my presence.

Nothing.

I step out of the car. Open the boot. Drag the bin bag onto the ground and lock the car. Their pigs are in the next field over. I wait for a light to come on in the house, a sign that someone's heard or seen me, but there isn't one, so I drag the bag across the side of the field, using the shadows of the hedge to conceal my movement.

When I reach the field, I check for lights again—nothing—

and I drag the bin bags to the trough and spill the boy's body into it, along with my bloody suit. The pigs emerge from their den and begin feeding. I count eight pigs. It should be more than enough. A pig can consume 200 pounds in eight minutes, though they'd need to pause to shit as they can't break down bone. It could take four to eight hours for a single pig, but there are enough here that Liam will be gone by the time the hour is up.

I return to the shadows of the hedges and, as I wait for the pigs to finish eating, I use Facebook to find out more about Flora's foster parents. As expected, it is fairly easy—although they have private accounts, they evidently haven't realised that you still need to actively set all your information to private, and the occupations section of their personal information is visible to everyone.

The father, a Mr Shane Warner, is a primary school teacher, and he looks like one too. He wears tank tops over smart white shirts, has a neatly trimmed hippy beard, and eyes that say *you can trust me* whilst also saying *I touch kids.*

The mother, Mrs Mariam Warner, however, is a revelation. I could not make it up! I mean, get this, right—she is a sex therapist. An actual sex therapist. She's even published a book called *Healing Your Sexual Self.* I look it up online. It's about recovering from past sexual trauma that, apparently, all women experience in some form because of men being pushy or giving unwanted touches or catcalls or raping them with their eyes.

(I call bullshit—if a woman makes herself attractive, she makes herself available—you never get an ugly woman moaning about being fancied like good-looking women do.)

(Actually, I stand corrected, most ugly women are feminists. Apparently, they get mad on behalf of attractive women. It's a real mind-fuck.)

The book teaches women to reclaim their sexuality, take

ownership of it, and make sure they get what they want with it.

And, by the look of this woman's photograph on her website, I would love to RECLAIM her sexuality if you know what I mean. She is older than most of the women I fuck, but has that aged dignity to her, and knows how to dress—do not underestimate the power of a woman who knows how to dress.

But that, my friends, is just the first impression. The second is not so convincing.

I look at more pictures of her on Facebook and realise that the photograph on her website must have been done by a fucking brilliant photographer. She dresses all hippy and frumpy and looks like a bloated mother who misses the days her husband found her attractive.

I scrutinise her website further, surveying the services she provides. She gives one-on-one sex therapy sessions. And she gives group therapy. It costs eighty pounds a session. Oh, and there's one tomorrow (/today). In the afternoon. And there are still spaces.

I sign up.

Then I check on the progress of the pigs. There's nothing of Liam left. The lights have not come on in the house.

I return to my car and leave. I should be able to get to school before the morning bell.

I NEVER KNEW

I never knew I could still feel.

I never knew another man could bring it out in me.

I never knew just a text message could make me feel things I've never felt, or that there was still love in me to give.

I thought you'd drained all emotions out of me, Gerald.

I thought you'd killed any feelings I had left.

I thought that numbness you'd left in me was a defence that no one could break through.

I chose not to feel; when I felt all I could feel was hate; and humiliation; and disgrace; and pitifulness; and like I let you take ownership of my body; like I ever actually had a choice.

But now.

I never knew there was a future. I never knew love was something I'd feel.

If it's love.

I don't know.

Can I love?

Is it in me?

Or did you rip that away too?

Because I struggle to tell the difference between love, hate, and what you did to me.

But Liam feels fresh. Untainted. Full of potential. Like he could be something I've never known.

Maybe it's because I don't have to see him or touch him. And he doesn't have to touch me. And his hands on my body won't remind me of all those times you touched me, Gerald. All it takes is a brush on my skin as I pass a stranger on the bus and suddenly I'm back in that kitchen, on the floor, your fists around my arms, crying as you ram yourself as far inside of me as you can get.

Could I ever let Liam touch me?

If he runs away, does that mean I don't have to physically love him? Is that why I feel this way—because his absence makes it safe?

And if I've never spoken to him before, does it make it easier to love someone I'll never know?

I'm scared. If I allow myself to feel affection, then what else will I allow myself to feel?

I hate you.

Oh God, I hate you.

So much.

You have no idea what you took from me. What you wrongly felt entitled to. What you damaged.

And I bet you still feel entitled.

I bet you still feel I am a part of your property that has gone missing and you are still owed it back.

I belong to no one, Gerald. I don't even belong to myself.

I never knew how much hate I'd harness.

I never knew how it would all come out the minute I let myself care about someone.

I never knew a boy called Liam, who wears black nail varnish, who listens to music that sounds like screaming, who isolates himself from everyone at school, would end up being the one to penetrate what I have done so well to hide.

I cried last night. It was the first time I've cried since I escaped. It felt brilliant. Then it felt awful.

I used to stare at the ceiling every night. I used to lie there, wide-eyed, with nothing but white noise stopping me from thinking.

Because if I think, then that's when…

That's when I can no longer control the words in my mind…

See, Gerald.

I don't think because the only thoughts I can think are bad thoughts

And now there's a thought that could be good. Just one. A boy.

What if he's like you?

What if they are all like you?

That's what everyone keeps saying. I've listened to podcasts about abuse where the women say they are wary of every man they pass, that they clutch their keys as they pass men in the street, that they avoid being alone with men for fear of what they might do.

I don't want to let myself believe that all men are like that. Like you. But what if they are, Gerald? What if they are?

Then again, what if there are anomalies? What if that's why Liam's always alone; because he's different, and he doesn't want to be near people like you.

I never knew I could think this deeply. That I am this emotionally aware. That I can consider with such scrutiny what I'm feeling. I guess all that trauma counselling has helped. Except, I don't know. I told my counsellor that you were someone I trusted. I don't tell him anything else about you.

He never knows how far you went.

He never knows how far I went.

And Liam will never know what I did to you. What I'm capable of doing. The extremes that I went to.

Would he still want me if he did?

I never knew that I never knew that…

That…

That I…

I…

I don't know.

I'm fed up with thinking. I'm fed up with debating. I want to go to bed. I want to sleep.

Except, I don't sleep. I can't sleep.

Because if I sit still, even for a moment, or lay there without distraction, then I think and when I think it all comes back and all I can see is you and your face heaving over me and inside of me and the corkscrew lodged so far up it hurts me and I have to pretend it doesn't hurt me and I have to pretend I want you just so I can stop you.

I should have killed you after you passed out.

But I couldn't.

I couldn't kill you, Gerald.

I'm not like you.

I think.

I don't know.

I'm thinking again, and now I'm doubting myself, and now I'm debating, and now it's going around my mind over and over until it's just a whirlwind of negativity and I'm reminding myself that I'm worthless and I'm used and Liam will see that I'm damaged and he won't want me because no one will want me and I won't want anyone because then they may touch me and when a boy touches me it reminds me of when you touched me and I'm right back there again in the kitchen bent over the sink trying not to cry as you fuck me until I bleed and you laugh as you wash me off your cock.

I'm crying now.

I haven't cried for so long, and now I'm feeling, and it's because of Liam, and it's because of you.

Stop thinking.

Stop it.

Because I never knew how painful thinking can be.

My mind hates me. It's the one bully I cannot get away from.

All the time, it's there, thinking these things.

And I never knew how much it would hurt.

CHAPTER ELEVEN

I MAKE it to a local bookshop before school begins and purchase a copy of *Healing Your Sexual Self.* I get a coffee to go from a drive-through, make my way to Flora's school and park across the street, then read a few passages as I wait for the morning hustle to begin.

It is fucking hilarious.

The whole introduction is basically this woman rattling on about trauma from past experience in a way she probably intends to sound spiritual, but sounds like nonsensical bullshit.

Here is my favourite passage:

Once a man hurts you, you learn to distrust all men. Once a man catcalls you, or follows you, or harasses you in the street, you judge all men by this. As hard as it is, you need to learn to forgive those men—not for them, but for *you.* Only then can you enter a relationship with an open heart—only then can you hope that a new man is not as you have judged all men to be.

I snort laughter into my coffee, unintentionally blowing bubbles.

Distrust all men?

Gender has nothing to do with it, love—we're all fucking animals! We all want to fuck and kill and fuck then kill again, only society has taught men that fucking is their burden, thus allowing women to be a lot subtler about the way they hurt the opposite sex. When they act submissively, it is only so we remain blissfully unaware; all women require the need to feel in control, and when she lets you take control, trust me, it's only for a temporary respite from the constant need to regulate everything about their lives. This is why *all* women wish to be bound and fucked—yet only *some* women admit to themselves that they have such a fantasy. Flora's mother was the worst. She used to pretend she didn't want it; used to struggle; used to push me off then tell me to keep going. It turned her on to make her think she didn't have a choice.

I mean, these fucking women…

They wear high heels and low-cut tops and short skirts and do their hair all nice and flowy and claim it's for them.

For them?

Fuck off. If that was the case, then you would dress in such a way when you were alone. But you don't. You spend a day in front of the TV in your pyjamas, not giving a shit for how you smell or look, not dressing in such a way until you leave the house. You need people to see you. You need *men* to see you.

And, most of all, you *need* men to *want* you.

It is how you determine your worth.

Tell you what, wait until you reach forty and have a baby body and saggy tits and fading skin that even layers of foundation won't cover up—I bet you'll miss the catcalls then. When your worth is diminished, and you no longer warrant unwanted attention, you'll miss how good it made you feel.

And harassment in the street?

Hey, bitch, what's the difference between a man who's harassing you and a man who's flirting with you?

I'll tell you.

The guy who flirts with you is good looking, and the guy who harasses you is not. The man who harasses you has been friend-zoned so many times he doesn't know how to attract a woman. Perhaps being nice no longer works, so he's forceful. Because, whether or not you stupid women want to admit it, that is what works. Women date alpha males, then get annoyed there aren't any good men. You date pricks and judge all the non-pricks by their actions.

So go to hell with this shit, Mariam Warner. Go to hell with it. You pretend you're all virtuous; pretend you're all nice and spiritual. This book is just catering for femininazis who hate men because they refuse to admit that dickheads turn them on.

Oh, how I CANNOT wait until the session this afternoon! I still haven't decided what my sexual malady will be, but I'll be sure to make it a good one.

Meanwhile, traffic has grown thicker, and there are teenagers in school uniform walking past me, and it's time to watch.

I want to see her.

Not to do anything. Not yet. I want to destroy her life before I take it from her.

I just need to see her.

I need to know it's real.

I need to see what she looks like. See how she walks, what she does.

All these kids walking by my car are so pathetic. You have the little twelve-year-olds in the first year of senior school with backpacks as big as their torso, and blazers their parents insist they'll grow into so they don't have to spend even more money on their disgusting little children.

What is fascinating, however, is how the skirt length of

these girls decreases as their age increases. Those little twelve-year-olds have skirts down to their calves and high socks, and I bet each of them gets bullied, and I bet each of them deserves it. Then, as you get to the fourteen or fifteen-year-olds, the skirts start rising above the knee. Then you get the sixteen-year-olds and the sixth form girls who are no longer required to wear a uniform and can choose their own slaggy clothes and their skirts ride up their thighs and FUCK I'd love to ruin them all!

One of them sits down on the bench to tie their laces. You can see their white little panties, and this is exactly what I mean, Mariam Warner. Why would a girl dress like this for herself? Why would you ever assume it's not all for attention?

She wants me to see those panties. She doesn't cross her legs when she sits down; she doesn't wear a skirt that covers it; she doesn't give a shit that everyone can see the inside of her upper thighs. They love it when guys ask them to sit on their laps and when guys tell them they are fit and when guys text them pictures of their cock.

I bet these girls send pictures back. They're young enough and stupid enough to keep their faces in the pictures too. As if a guy would keep such a photograph private, and not share it with every fucker he knows.

The road gets busier and the legs keep coming past and I wait, wait for her, wait to see if it's true.

I recognise one girl as she approaches. It's one of Flora's friends. The one with the bikini pictures. Ava. She's with the fat one (Isabella?). Behind them, the geeky one (Eleanor—honestly, their personalities fulfil the criteria of a bad sitcom), and next to Eleanor…

FUCK.

There she is.

My dick tingles at the sight.

Despite everything, it tingles, and my arms shake and adrenaline makes my knees bounce.

Her hair is different. She's cut it to shoulder length. I always liked it long, and she's probably changed it to defy me, the little slut. Her skirt is short. She has opted to wear a t-shirt with a picture of a teddy bear on it, like she's five. Her backpack is fake leather with a vintage design, and she carries a folder under her arm. She walks with the same weariness she always has, each step concealing another hidden struggle. She never takes long strides; she shuffles to keep up with her friends. Occasionally, she tucks a strand of hair behind her ear that instantly flops back into its original place.

And, from the way her friends look at her, none of them have any idea who she is, or what she's done, or where she's come from. Her past is hidden, unlike the scars on her arms. There's a few of them that could easily be passed off as an accident, but if they knew, Flora, if they knew what you were capable of, then fuck, Flora, fuck—imagine how they'd treat someone who hid a corkscrew up their cunt to impale the cock of a man who cared dearly for her.

And I cared for you, in my own way, there is no denying it. I don't love; I obsess; it's just who I am. But please know that what's about to happen has nothing to do with love, Flora. This is entirely about pride, and the damage you did to mine.

She enters the school, her dainty buttocks outlined by her skirt, her backpack bouncing with her tiny strides, and I am so fascinated by the sight of her that I cannot take my eyes away. She felt so elusive, so hard to catch, yet all it took was a little money and now I know everything about her new life.

She follows her friends inside.

Then she pauses.

Looks over her shoulder. Like she senses something. Like she knows I'm watching her.

Her eyes scan the surroundings, passing my car and searching down the street.

There's no one there, she decides, and she walks inside, making sure to shut the door behind her.

You have no idea I'm watching you, Flora, and you have no idea I'm about to dismantle and disfuck everything in your life. You will be a wreck by the time you beg for your life, Flora. *A wreck.*

And it starts with sex therapy.

CHAPTER TWELVE

APPARENTLY, Mariam Warner has a small office that can only fit one client (insert a witty remark relating her office to her vagina here), so we must meet in the village hall a hundred yards from her office.

As I enter, I see the notice board by the entrance that advertises the various groups that meet here. A youth drama club meets here on a Wednesday, the scouts meet here on a Thursday, and Sunday school takes place here on, well, a Sunday. Funnily enough, I don't see any advertisement for sex therapy. I imagine it's not aimed at the same clientele that might look for Sunday school.

I follow the corridor into a large hall with uncomfortable-looking plastic chairs stacked at the side and a small stage at the front. The hall is cold, despite having huge radiators that make a horrible grinding sound every five minutes.

I am the first one here aside from Mariam, who stands at the other end, going through a wad of papers on the desk.

She looks as ridiculous in person as she sounds in the book. As if she was a hippy as a teenager and never grew out of it. She has curly hair that I assume has been recently dyed purple, as it's different to her Facebook profile, and hides the strands of grey she is unable to stop appearing around her ears. She wears a long beaded necklace that protrudes down to her navel; a multi-coloured scarf that sits over her arms rather than her shoulders; a white blouse with purple flowers covered in a knitted waistcoat; a long, flowing light-brown skirt that billows around her wrinkled ankles; and thick leather sandals. That's right, she wears sandals, as if it's a normal thing to wear when you're not a middle-aged man at the beach.

"Hello," she says, and her voice is wishy-washy and meek and I want to cum in her mouth and watch her choke to death on it.

"Hi," I say, edging in, feigning nervousness.

"Are you here for the group? I'm not sure we've met."

"Yes. I am."

She offers a hand. I take it. Her loose grasp feels like a wilting flower. Only her fingers meet my fist, and her arm barely moves. It is quite literally the definition of a dead fish handshake. I want to grab her fist and shake it until I pull her arm off so I can use her own dead fish handshake to slap her across the face.

"And what's your name, darling?"

Darling? *Yuck.*

"Tony." Of course I didn't give my real name. I'm not a fucking idiot.

"Well, Tony, please take a seat, everyone else will arrive shortly."

She smiles at me, and even her smile is annoying. It's so friendly and genuine, like she finds pleasure in other people, and it makes me want to vomit in her mouth.

I take a chair and sit down. She takes another five chairs and places them in a circle beside me.

Within ten minutes, another four people have arrived—two men and two women. Each of them says hello to Mariam with I'm-a-sad-sack-of-shit-smiles, takes a seat, and offers the same I'm-a-sad-sack-of-shit-smile at me. I try to give one back. They buy it. I want to set them all on fire.

"Shall we begin, seeing as everyone is here," Mariam says, her voice still just as annoying. She takes a seat, resting a pad of lined A4 paper on her lap with one hand as the other presses down her skirt (as if anyone would want to look at those veiny legs). She keeps a pen behind her ear and I want to use it to jab her in the throat.

"We have a new person today," she says, indicating me with an open palm. "So if everyone could welcome Tony."

"Hi, Tony," everyone says in almost perfect unison.

I raise a hand and nod. I don't know whether to laugh at these morons, or whether to despair that such sad bastards exist.

"Perhaps we'll let Tony speak after everyone else, give him a chance to make himself more comfortable."

I couldn't give a fuck, you stupid cunt.

"Okay, Barney, shall we start with you?"

She turns to the man to her right. I say man—he looks more like a boy. Maybe early twenties, and by far the youngest one here, yet he looks like one of the most confident. His hair is slicked back, he wears a smart shirt and jeans, and sits with his legs open like he's displaying his cock to the group. He's actually quite a good-looking, charming guy, and I wonder what could be wrong with him.

"How much porn would you say you've consumed this week?" she asks.

Barney looks down. "I'm not sure."

"I thought you were logging the minutes?"

"I was."

"And how many minutes did it come to?"

He hesitates. "794 minutes."

Fuuuuuuuuuuck. That's over thirteen hours. I mean, I enjoy watching a woman get rammed up her snatch by thirty blokes as much as the next guy, but doesn't he want to try some real pussy?

"It's a little bit more than last week, I know," he says. "But I tried, I really did."

"And have you tried having sex with an actual woman this week?"

"Yes. Twice."

Ah, so he did try some real pussy.

"And how did that go?"

He shrugs. "Nothing."

"Were you able to get an erection?"

"Yeah."

"And how long did it last?"

He shrugs again. "A minute, maybe a minute and a half."

"And do you think porn is the reason for this?"

"See, the sex, it was just… sex, that's all. She doesn't let me do any of the things they do in porn. It's just boring."

"But is porn real, Barney?"

He shrugs again. He needs to stop shrugging, this bellend.

"I said, is porn real, Barney?"

He drops his head and shakes it. "No."

Mariam pushes him a little more, then tries to offer encouragement, as if to quell the sadness caused by her pushing. He looks more ashamed than he did when he started talking. Poor guy. She's wrong too. It is quite easy to re-enact the horrible shit you see in porn. I do it all the time. If he was just a little more honest that he wanted to hardfuck a girl then kill her as she screamed, then he might find himself able to keep his erection longer.

We continue onto the other members of the group, and they are all just as pathetic.

Erlinda is next. She's fifty-eight, has huge tits, and ever since her husband died six years ago, her sex addiction has spiralled out of control. She has gone through three different guys in one day on several occasions. Often, they are young men she meets through a milf fetish site, where she enacts their milf fantasy. Mariam tells her she has an unhealthy relationship with sex. I think Mariam's full of shit. She has a brilliant relationship with sex—if you want to fuck three young men in one day, then good for you. Have fun. Don't listen to this insipid hypocrite.

Clyde is next. He's in his forties, wears huge glasses, and flattens his hair to his head with too much hair gel. He looks like he plays a lot of *World of Warcraft*. His wife has no libido, and he's been compensating by having an extramarital affair with another nerd he met on the internet. Mariam asks him why he thinks this is. That's a stupid question. If a guy who looks like him can find a woman who wishes to fuck him, then he must take advantage of it. And whilst he claims his wife has lost her libido because of birth trauma, he doesn't seem to realise that she's lying to him—she's lost her libido because he's ugly as fuck and she can't bear that having a child means she's now bound to this hideous nerd for life.

Finally, the last one before me is Siobhan, mid-forties, has a bit of a stutter, and dresses like a daytime stripper. I can tell everyone here is pretending that they haven't noticed her huge cleavage, but it's the only thing you can notice when you look at her. Honestly, it's the worst thing she could put on display when sitting in a room with people who have what society has determined an 'unhealthy relationship with sex.'

Siobhan has a tremendous problem: she has a persistent fantasy about fucking her twelve-year-old son. Everyone nods and acts understanding, but if this was a man saying this, they'd be calling the police, thus proving what hypocrites there are in this world. Mariam insists we are in a safe space where we can share without judgement, but that's just bullshit she makes up so she can gossip about these people later.

Siobhan lists the things she's done to avoid the fantasy:

focussed on other stimulus, had sex with people without thinking about her child, drunk more water, eaten as a diversion tactic (which is ridiculous as it will inevitably make her fat, and the only thing worse than a thin woman denying her sexuality is a fat woman with a sexuality).

Then it comes to me.

"Tony," Mariam says, and I forget that's my name for a moment, and wonder why everyone's staring at me. "Would you like to share?"

"Share?" I pretend to be shy. Honestly, I can't wait to see how far I can push this.

"Yes. Would you like to tell the group what's brought you here?"

"Of course. See, well, I, er… I can't get a boner."

"Well, that's not a pro–"

"I haven't finished."

"Okay, sorry."

I take a moment to pretend to compose myself. "I can't get a boner unless I fantasise that I'm fucking a corpse."

"O… kay." I can tell she's taken aback. I can tell she is mulling this over in her mind. Honestly, it can't be that bad considering Siobhan wants to fuck a kid who probably doesn't even have pubes yet. "And how long have you—"

"I tell her to play dead, and if she doesn't, I punch her until she's unconscious so I can pretend she's a corpse."

"That's, erm, that's, is she okay with that?"

I ignore the question. "It all comes from this one time I did fuck a corpse."

"I–"

"She had a heart attack whilst I was fucking her, so I just carried on, then phoned the paramedics. She died later at the hospital. They said her heart had stopped for too long. But, since it happened, it's the only thing I can think about. Am I weird?"

Stunned silence answers my question. Mariam leans

forward, passing her pen between her hands, her mouth slightly open as it searches for which syllables to produce.

"It's… an interesting situation," she says. "And have you told anyone about this before?"

"No. But your website said there was strict confidentiality. That we are in a safe space where we can be honest. That you won't repeat anything."

"That's true, but I still–"

"I really want to kill a woman so I can fuck her. Is that normal?"

Again, the question hangs there. I wonder what would happen if I actually told them the things I *have* done to corpses. Their fucking heads would blow off.

"Obviously, I suggest you don't," Mariam eventually says.

"Obviously."

"There are things we keep as fantasies, and that's okay, so long as we understand that it's important they stay as fantasies. Isn't that right?"

I don't answer. She stares expectantly.

"Isn't that right, Tony?" she prompts.

I smile. "A fantasy is a fantasy."

"Excellent. Of course, if you are having these fantasies, and they are persistent—"

"They are."

"Well then–"

"I just find it impossible to meet a woman without imagining her dead whilst I fuck her."

I maintain my eye contact with Mariam. She holds mine. She tries not to break, but it's there, the discomfort, the awareness that this statement applies to her, and that it may very well apply at this very moment.

"And you struggle to stop these thoughts?" she asks.

"Every. Damn. Time."

"Right. Okay, well, erm… We can help, I'm sure, if we give you some tools to block out negative thoughts."

Negative thoughts? I love how she imposes her perspective on it. Like her point of view is gospel. Like she finds the thoughts strange, therefore they must be negative. That's what I hate about therapists, they are always so sure their judgement is correct because someone pays them to give it.

"That would be wonderful," I tell her, and she moves onto someone else, discussing some other problem.

I don't stop staring at her.

For the entire time, I don't stop.

Occasionally, she glances my way, meets my eyes, and forces a fake smile, then carries on talking, denying that voice in the back of her head that tells her I'm picturing her dead and naked and with my jizz all over her.

Which I am. It's method acting.

When the session finishes, she says goodbye to everyone, walks over to the stage and organises her notes.

I stay, and I approach her.

"Mariam?"

She jumps, then turns around. "Oh, Tony, you scared me."

She glances over my shoulder, watching everyone else leave. She doesn't want to be alone with me.

"I found that really useful today," I tell her. "Thank you. It's just good to hear I'm not strange, and there are other people with, what did you call it—a dysfu… dysfan…"

"A dysfunctional relationship with sex."

"Yes. Exactly."

"Well, I'm pleased I could help you."

"I was wondering whether I could book a one-on-one session with you? I think it would really help me."

She hesitates. Stares at me. Looking so vulnerable. So scared. So aware of how much danger she is in, but unable to stop herself from being so profusely nice. I've met people like her, and they are so easy to take advantage of; if she was a prick like me, she'd just say no, but her need to help people is a compulsion.

Honestly, it's not healthy.

"Well, it's very expensive," she says.

"I can afford it."

"It's seventy pounds a session, and they must be weekly–"

"I could pay you for ten sessions in advance, right now."

Oh, how she regrets that. Saying they must be weekly to put me off the cost, only to set herself up for several weeks of this. I cannot wait to destroy this woman.

"Well, I'm sure that we can figure something out."

"This Thursday?"

"I'll have to check my–"

"I already rang your secretary. She said you have space in the afternoon." I didn't ring her secretary; I'm just calling Mariam out on her bullshit.

"Okay, then."

"What would be the best time?'

"Say, two?"

"Perfect."

I step away, going to leave, then pause, hovering my eyes over her, picturing her bloody corpse under my heaving, naked, sweaty body one more time.

Then I smile.

And I go.

And I get in the car and drive away to pick up the keys to my new temporary home.

Oh, that was so much fun!

CHAPTER THIRTEEN

AFTER PICKING up the keys and signing documents and handing over money that is a pittance to me but appears to be a fucking goldmine to these poor fucks, I use Liam's phone once again to learn more about Flora's foster family.

This time, the foster father. Shane Warner.

He loves a black and white filter, this guy. His Facebook is photo after photo of him with his (actual biological) child and his wife, smiling or amid laughter or sitting on a bench or being all happy and cute and making me want to vomit. Everything is staged happiness with this guy. Most of his status updates are links to various petitions and articles. He's desperate to make a difference in a world where no one matters. Pitiful, really.

I scan the first few links:

Petition: *We need 100,000 signatures to get parliament to discuss the need for free milk in schools.* (Who gives a shit about free milk? When I was a child, all I received was a kick in the shins and a reminder not to be a fuck-up, and I turned out superbly.)

Petition: *Stop Female Genital Mutilation in the UK.* (Just the

UK, Shane? I love how your good deeds are limited to this solitary island.)

Article: *Why Vocational Subjects Should Be More Prominent in Education.* (I actually agree with this one. Why force a kid to take English when he can't read, and would be much better at learning how to clean our toilets to a high standard?)

Petition: *Make it Compulsory for Premier League Footballers to Give to Charity.* (There are so many things wrong with this I don't know where to start. First, it's their money, they earned it, so fuck off and let them spend it as they wish. Second, most of them do charity, it just doesn't make good press. Third, and I reiterate, it's their money, it's capitalism; supply and demand; business; and you don't have a right to tell them what to do with it because you're a jealous little shit.)

Article: *Improve Teaching of Consent in Sex Education.* (I actually laughed out loud at this one. We are the only animal who requests permission to take another's body. It's unnatural. And if society deems it natural, then tell them to watch a nature documentary. Lions can fuck up to fifty times a day; do you think they give a shit about whether the other party is okay with it?)

I am yet to meet you, Shane, but I have already decided you are insufferable, and I wish to see what you get up to once the children leave your classroom. There is a photograph of you helping some cheery-eyed students on the school website (I assume the more realistic dead-eyed students didn't make good propaganda), and I have no doubt that this is not who you really are. No one is that perfect, and the pretence must drop at some point.

Within twenty minutes, I am outside the school you work at, looking into your classroom as you tidy up the mess created by thirty insufferable bags of flesh. You wear a tank top that makes you look like a pansy, and grey trousers that were clearly bought at a cheap clothes store. I'd buy you better trousers if I thought it would make me look good, but I'm not sure anyone cares about you enough to appreciate my charity.

You stay in your classroom for a few hours. I get a little bored. I organise the glove compartment. I wonder if you are hanging around for so long because you have a lot of work, or whether it's because you hate the family who smile so well in your pictures and are delaying having to go home to them.

Eventually, after seven in the evening, you walk out of the school with a mobile phone attached to your ear. I open the window a smidge to catch a few words of what you're saying.

"Yeah... Me and Gary are going to watch the football tonight... I should be back later... How's Flora doing, she better?... And Claire, she okay?... Wonderful... Well, don't wait up, it may be a late one... Okay, I love you too... Bye... bye bye bye bye bye..."

He does that annoying thing all British people do where they must keep saying bye until the line goes dead. Just say it once you knobhead, you don't need to make a song about it.

He gets into his car. A Citroën with 2002 plates. It's an old car that makes a rattling noise when the engine comes on. He turns the car onto the road, and I follow him.

As I suspected, he does not go to this Gary's house— instead, he drives around town for twenty minutes, trying to find a free parking space. There are plenty of car parks, but he's determined to find somewhere on the road where he does not have to pay. Once he finds a space, he backs into it carefully, whilst I go to the car park opposite and pay the few quid it costs.

He steps out of the car and walks down the street. I follow. He wraps his arms around himself even though it's not cold. I don't see the smiles from his photos on his face; I only see hesitation and caution. There is something wrong with what-ever he's doing. He feels guilty about it.

When he finally approaches a gay bar, he looks both ways to see if anyone sees him before he enters, and I cannot fucking believe it.

This is beautiful.

I follow him in. I'm not afraid of a little cock-on-cock action, and have no issue sitting at the bar with a whisky (though the whisky is cheap and sticky), and watching Shane from afar as he approaches various men. He's keen, I give him that. And he's evidently not fussy, as he approaches most of the men in here. He starts with a young man with a baby face who looks barely old enough to be in here, then a middle-aged balding man with a potbelly and severe baldness, then a short man wearing bright purple lipstick and a t-shirt that reads *Born to Swing*.

After a few attempts, he finally finds a bloke willing to engage with him—an overzealous Greek camp man who seems enthusiastic about every little intricate detail of everyone else's life. Someone nearby mentions that they are tired, and this man gesticulates wildly about sleep patterns and the usefulness of meditation and his own incurable insomnia. Shane clearly wants to fuck this eager beaver—but, then again, he looked quite willing to fuck anyone in here. The man seems eager too, leaning toward Shane, playing with his hair, showing all the signs. They have a drink (Shane has a vodka lemonade and his new friend drinks a grapefruit flavoured alcopop out of a straw) and talk for half an hour before leaving together.

Oh, Shane, you dirty dog.

The barman has a conversation with Shane before he goes, and they seem to know each other pretty well. How often does Shane come in here? Before Shane leaves, the barman asks if he's coming back tomorrow, and he says probably. I log this, hoping that we can bump into each other, then Shane leaves with his new companion.

I consider following, but I don't, as I have received another text from Flora, and I intend to pursue Shane's bum-fun further tomorrow.

It was weird at school today

People are talking

They say your parents have reported you missing

Where are you?

Just away

Away where

Why do you need to know?

Cuz I'm freaking out

Everyone is saying you killed yourself or somethin

 iMessage

Theres rumours going around

Rumours lol

What rumours

Some say you cut your wrists and bled to death in the woods

Others saying you jumped off Bristol suspension bridge

Keith Smith told everyone a tranny choked you during sex and accidentally killed you

Lol

 iMessage

Keith is a dick

They can say what they want

I'm absolutely fine

I'm worried

I don't like knowing this and not being able to tell anyone

But I thought I could trust you

You can

I havent told anyone

I just dont think its fair

 iMessage

Whats not fair

Me knowing youre fine

When everyone is being so weird

Im surprised anyone actually cares

Youd be surprised

Im just the hot news story

But im worried about you

Its nice that you care

I do care

iMessage

I actually do

I think I really like you

I like you too

So come back

We can get ice cream or something

Ice cream

Are we five

Whatever

We can get a coffee

You can come over watch a movie

 iMessage

Itll be fun

But you cant do that if you dont come back

We will do that

I look forward to it

For now this is something I need to do

I dont like it

Enough about me flora

How are you

Hows life at home

 iMessage

With your foster parents

How did you know they were my foster parents

I only told you they weren't my parents

I never told you they were foster parents

Er

Everyone knows that

Was it a secret

I didn't know everyone knew

Where are your real parents

 iMessage

I don't want to talk about them

Whats it like living with foster parents

Are they nice

They are super nice

Mariam (foster mum) is really caring

Listens to me

Lets me talk

Shane (foster dad) is really sensitive

And they love each other so much

 iMessage

And my little sister has such a character

Then whats wrong

What do you mean

I see you when no ones looking

I see your face

You frown

You look down

You look sad

Why

 iMessage

Why

What are you so sad about when everythings perfect

You don't need to know

Why wont you tell me

You think I wont understand

You wont

Is it your stepdad?

Kinda

Is he still hurting you?

In a way

He hurt me a lot

And it isn't simple

maybe he isnt such a
bad guy

maybe what he did
wasn't so bad

I don't mean to be rude

But what the fuck do you
know

Sorry I didn't mean to
upset you

My bad

 iMessage

Flora?

Flora are you there?

Im sorry

I just say these stupid things

I didn't mean to upset you

Its obviously tough

Its fine

Do you accept my apology

Yes fine

iMessage

But don't ever do it again

Okay

K

I don't want to upset you Flora

You mean so much to me

I cant wait to see you

Me too

You have no idea what it will be like when we are finally together

No idea

iMessage

It's going to be epic

Think quite highly of
yourself don't you

You just wait Flora

It will be magnificent

I can't wait

Me neither

Xxxxxxxxxx

Xxxxxxxxxxxxxxxxxxxxxx

CHAPTER FOURTEEN

MARIAM'S OFFICE is quaint and pointless. She may as well save the money and use her living room. It's about the same size, and is along a corridor of various other ridiculous businesses, such as *Barry's Baldness Hair Loss Treatment,* and *Michael's Maladies Eastern Medicine,* and *Dorothy's Dildo Sales* (I'm tempted to pop in and meet Dorothy—I see her through the window, and she is a small woman who appears to be in her eighties and can barely pick up her phone; she seems like a far more fascinating character than Mariam—but, alas, tardiness is the only deadly sin I despise, and I refuse to be late to my appointment, even if it is with a sycophantic wench.)

Mariam is sitting at her desk when I enter. Her desktop computer makes a lot of noise, and she doesn't even have a flat screen monitor. Her walls are full of posters with images of couples in various sex positions. Many of them have captions, such as *Sex is Good Therapy,* and *Sex Therapy How Hard Can It Be,* and a sign saying *Staring is Intrusive and Sexual Harassment and Should Not Be Tolerated.* I mean, fuck me, are we not even allowed to look at a woman without her getting all sensitive? Next thing you know, they'll have us walking around with blackout sunglasses so we can't see any of their flesh, such is the offensive nature of the direction our eyes are aimed. These kinds of women do my fucking nut in.

Mariam forces a smile and indicates a chair in the corner. It is a large armchair with many cushions on it, most of them fluffy. I sit in it. I sink quite low, and I hate this chair already. She types a few things on her keyboard, then walks from behind her desk and sits on a normal chair beside me. She's slightly higher than me, and I wonder if this is intentional.

She is wearing the kind of ridiculous hippy clothes people full of spiritual crap do, just as she did the other day. A long, billowing brown skirt, and a vest with the peace sign in a tie-dyed style. Her tits sag beneath it and I wonder if she doesn't wear a bra because she's a feminazi and believes women's breasts should not be contained inside boob prisons, or whether it's part of her style. She notices me looking and takes a multicoloured poncho from the back of the chair and puts it on to cover herself up.

That's right, she wears a poncho. And it looks like a rainbow puked it up. It's strange how a sex therapist can be so extremely unsexual in appearance.

"And how are you, Tony?"

I wonder why she's calling me Tony, then remember that's the name I gave her. Phew. If I'd given my real name, then I'd have given myself away, and I would have had to kill her before I was intending to, and it would have ruined everything.

"I'm fine," I tell her.

"Is there anything you particularly wish to discuss in this session?"

"I was hoping to find out more about you."

She hesitates, then gives me a can't-be-arsed-with-this-shit-but-too-nice-to-say-it smile. "I was more thinking we spend these sessions discussing you. It's what you're here for, after all."

"Oh, please don't take any offence." My performance as a pathetic, repressed individual already makes me feel sick. "I just wanted to know more about you before I spill all my darkest secrets to a stranger."

"Does it not help that I'm a stranger?"

"I guess I wanted to know what makes you qualified."

I suppress a smile as I notice a glimmer of resentment pass across her face.

"My credentials are all listed on my website, Tony. If you would like to look now, then please feel free to get out your phone and—"

"That's not what I meant."

"And what did you mean, then?"

"I know you are qualified in the educational sense—more than qualified, even." I haven't looked at her qualifications and don't give enough of a shit to do so. "I just wanted to know what makes you care."

"I just believe in the importance of a healthy sexual life, that's all."

"Did someone hurt you? Is that why?"

"Excuse me?"

"Was it your husband? A friend? A stranger?"

"Look, Tony–"

"It was your daddy, wasn't it?"

She glares at the floor.

"What did he do?"

"Tony, we are here to discuss you, and you only."

"I know. It's just that… My daddy…"

"What about your daddy?"

"He… He liked little boys… Like I was…" My dad didn't give enough of a shit to feel me up even if he wanted to. "He liked to get into bed with me. He said he wanted to teach me what it was like to be a grownup."

"That must have been hard."

"Oh, very."

"And how did that make you feel?"

She waits for the answer: sad; traumatised; devastated; guilty. Instead, I go for, "Aroused."

She frowns. Again, she suppresses her true thoughts.

"It is common," she says, trying so desperately to be understanding, "to feel like you enjoyed the experience, only to realise you were abused when you were much, much older."

"Oh, I was never abused. In fact, sometimes we still..."

"Still what, Tony?"

"Well, he's eighty now, and he has dementia. I guess it's my turn to do it to him."

She frowns again. She's trying to decide whether to call me on my bullshit; whether it's worth the risk. After all, what if she accused me of lying, and I was telling the truth? It would be a disgraceful thing for a therapist to do.

"I think it's why I get aroused by corpses," I say. "Because I like it when they can't fight back."

"Is it important to you that they can't fight back?"

I grin. "Always."

"And do you have a sexual partner?"

"Right now?"

"Yes."

"No. But I did."

"And how did she feel about this fantasy?"

"Oh, she never fought back."

"Was this something you agreed?"

"We didn't need to."

"Then how do you know it was consensual?"

"I couldn't care less if it was consensual to Flora."

"I beg your pardon?"

She stares at me. Not sure if she heard correctly.

"I said I couldn't care less if it was consensual too, for her."

She stares at me. So intently, I'm tempted to direct her

toward that poster about staring. She can't figure out if she heard me correctly. She tries to convince herself she thought she heard her foster daughter's name because the brain often attaches familiarity to words that we don't hear properly. Our brains are fascinating things, really—more often than not, they will show us what they think we perceive, rather than actually what's there.

But there's that niggling doubt. The one that won't escape the back of her mind. The fluttering in her belly. The alarms ringing that she tries to quell.

She wants to go on, but the silence lingers, and eventually I ask, "Is everything okay?"

She wants to ask if I'm playing games. I can see it. She's desperate to know if this is all a performance. She wants to know who I am. Thing is, Flora won't have been completely honest about what happened to her—I'd have been arrested if she had—and so would she with her corkscrew escapades—even if her actions were determined as self-defence, she would still be arrested and investigated; my lawyers would see damn sure of that. But I am a free man. She is a free girl (for now). Mariam evidently does not know about Gerald Brittle and the glorious life he lived with Flora.

But she will know that *something* happened to Flora.

And this concerns her.

Eventually, she shakes it off, and carries on. "Yes. I'm fine. Shall we proceed?"

This entire ordeal gives me one hell of an erection.

"Yes," I say. "Let's."

CHAPTER FIFTEEN

I RETURN to Flora's school in time for the final lesson. I wait outside, staying in my car, careful not to arouse suspicion. It's hard to blend in when you're dressed as impeccably as I am, with an expensive haircut and a gloriously handsome face. It's a burden I'm happy to bear if it means I don't look like any of these cretins.

The first onslaught of students departing the school occurs, and I don't see Flora among any of them. Parents pause in their cars and drive away with their children, streams of kids in uniform exit the school, being rowdy with each other in that repugnant way teenagers usually are, and within ten minutes the school gates are quiet again, and she is not there, and I wonder if I've missed her.

But I can't have missed her. I'm too astute. Too observant. I miss nothing.

So I wait longer, determined to prove to myself that I did not let this ungrateful bitch leave without my noticing. After over an hour of waiting, I finally see her leave, and I am relieved. She wears a PE kit, and I assume she has done some kind of extracurricular sporting activity. Probably netball or something.

Her friends are with her too. Ava also wears a PE kit, and watching the both of them walk down the street in those frilly skirts is enough to make any man shake with arousal. Isabella and Eleanor follow in their own clothes, the supportive spectators following their sporty friends—the fatty and the nerd walking behind their two athletic chums.

I step out of my car and follow them from a distance. I know it's risky, but my legs are cramping from sitting through that intense session with Mariam, and I need to stretch them. I still chuckle at the amount she fidgeted in her seat, and crossed and uncrossed her legs, and bit the end of her pen. She hated every minute of that session, and that only made me love it more.

I keep as much distance as I can whilst keeping the group in sight. I keep my head down, ensuring I never give any CCTV the chance to see my face, even carrying Liam's phone in front of me to make it seem like I'm engrossed in something else. The girls are completely unaware of their surroundings and predators that might lurk behind them. Except Flora. She looks around all the time. Checks every face she walks past, looks in every shop window, in every car that slows down. It's hard to evade her gaze, and I am forced to drop back even further.

Eventually, they start to depart from each other. Eleanor first, who enters the library as they pass it. She is evidently obsessed, this girl. Then Isabella waddles up the path to a tiny house with an overgrown lawn. Then Flora arrives at a bus stop, where she gives Ava a hug and waits for her bus.

I am tempted to follow Flora further. But I don't. I know where she is going. There is nothing else I will gain by following her onto the bus, and the risk of being seen is too high.

But I am entranced by Ava.

The way her backside wobbles. The way her legs sway. The way she just oozes a more mature sexuality than her peers. There is no innocence there; you can tell she has already been with several guys, and that each of them has destroyed her.

I want her.

I know I shouldn't. That it isn't in the plan. So I tell myself, fine, I'll just follow her. It'll be okay. I don't have to do anything.

Even though I want to.

I walk quicker. Until I'm right behind her. Until I can smell her. And I tell myself to stop. I can't take her. I can't. I have a plan I need to follow, and this is not part of it, and risks fucking it all up.

So I stop. Watch those godly legs leave, and I go a different route back to my car, popping into a newsagent to get a can of Diet Coke as I do. I don't need the can, but if I'm seen on CCTV following them then turning back, then when Flora eventually goes missing, I'll be a person of interest—even if they can't see my face, they will go to all efforts to find out who I am—so I make it seem like the newsagent was the target of my route. All the time, I cannot stop thinking of Ava, and how easy it would be just to have her.

But I can't, so stop it.

I return to my car, and I get in, and I drive, and I rue how close I came to fucking this all up.

Silly man, Gerald. Silly man.

Still, I find myself driving around aimlessly, in no particular direction, trying to convince myself that I am not searching for Ava.

Go home, Gerald. Go home before you do something stupid.

Fine, I tell myself, I will.

I drive around the streets, past happy couples holding hands and angry parents shouting at children and an old man hobbling down the street with a walking stick.

Eventually, my libido subsides, and I can think clearly again.

That was close.

That could have been stupid.

And I park the car down a side road. A dark one, where there are no cameras, and think about how perfect this street would be to abduct someone.

And there she is.

Walking toward me.

Ava.

Fuck.

Is she just wandering around? How has she not arrived home yet?

Hang on—is she crying?

It's hard to tell, but I think she is. Perhaps she's going for a walk where she won't be found, not wanting to return home to her nasty parents. Her hips still sway from side to side, like she can't help being erotic even when she's upset.

She covers her face because she doesn't even want strangers seeing her ugly tears, but don't worry, Ava, you could never be ugly.

You are sex itself, Ava. You are the definition of the word.

And I *want* you.

I sigh.

Don't do this, Gerald. Don't do it.

She passes my car.

What are you doing, Gerald? Don't, dammit. Don't!

But that skirt… those legs… that body…

If she didn't want me to be enticed, then why would she entice me?

I burst out of the car and punch her in the back of the head. She falls to the ground, groggy, semi-conscious. I open the boot of my car, pick her up, shove her in, then close the boot and ensure it's locked.

I get back in the driver's seat.
Stare at the steering wheel.
I only went and fucking did it, didn't I?
I just cannot help myself.

CHAPTER SIXTEEN

SHE IS SO light that it takes little energy to get her from the car to the basement. I don't have restraints fixed to the wall like in my mansion's basement, but I do have my suitcase of bondage equipment ready. Luckily, she's still unconscious, and I have time to tie her up, and even have a little fun afterward.

When her eyes do eventually open, her arms are above her head, her wrists bound to a chain I fixed to the wall, and I am sitting on a stool, scrolling through her phone. (It was easy to unlock—I just lifted her head and unlocked it with face ID, then turned off all security features; mobiles are too easy to get into nowadays.)

She looks around. Feels the moisture. The coldness. She screams.

I haven't soundproofed this basement. For fuck's sake, I am so unprepared. Why did I do this?

FUCK.

I leap to my feet and press my hand against her mouth. She tries to bite it and I slam her head into the brick wall. She shuts up and doesn't try to bite it again.

"You shout and I will gut you, do you understand?"

She peers up at me and nods. There are tears in her eyes. Girls are always so emotional.

I return to my stool and carry on scrolling through her text messages. I need to get a feel for the language she uses in her texts if I am going to cover up her disappearance.

Again, I am so PISSED OFF with myself. I was not prepared for this. She was just so delectable, so enticing…

"This is all your fault, you know," I tell her.

"What?" she gasps between her weeps.

"I said this is all your fault. I have a plan and you've gone and fucked it all up."

She really has, you know. If it weren't for her and her legs and her bikini pictures and her sexy strut and her sad tears, she wouldn't have made me so fucking horny that I can't control myself.

"What do you want with me?"

I grin. Nod toward her thighs. It is only now that she realises her underwear has been removed and my cum is dribbling down her legs.

Honestly, for the brief few seconds of pleasure she gave me, it was really not worth it.

"Please let me go," she says. "Please. I'll do anything. Please."

I try to tune her out, but she is rather persistent.

"Please, I won't tell anyone, I just want to go home, I just want—"

"Shut the fuck up, or I will ram my fist up your cunt." This seems to shut her up. I might do that anyway.

I continue scrolling through her texts. She talks like a fucking idiot. Every other word is lol, she says totes way too much, and seems unable to use vowels, condensing words like could to cud and would to wud. It's so fucking childish that I can't believe how much it contrasts with her womanly appeal. She calls Flora Flee—and, even worse than that, Flora seems to use stupid language when she texts back, like she's matching Ava's dumb sociolect.

"Who are you…"

I sigh. I can already tell she's a talker. Those are the most annoying.

Women always fall into four different categories when they are abducted:

1/ The shocked: they can barely say anything as the situation they find themselves in flummoxes them to the point where they are too overwhelmed by shock to speak. They normally snap out of it after a few days, if they last that long.

2/ The warrior: also known as the 'forever feminist.' She refuses to beg and refuses to cooperate and says she'll never give in to a man. She screams for help all night. These are quite rare, as people are usually cowards when faced with their own mortality. I do enjoy these women though, as it's particularly funny to watch them try to be strong and defiant when they are being sodomised.

3/ The inconsolable: the emotional women who can't control their despair at the situation they find themselves in. These are the most common. They cry and weep and never stop.

4/ The talkers: the women who try to humanise themselves to you. They ask you who you are, tell you about themselves, about their family, try to find out what my name is so they can use it. They are oddly calm, but this normally breaks eventually, and they turn hysterical.

"Please, we can pay you, my dad can pay you, he's a lawyer, he has lots of money, whatever you want he can give you…"

I laugh. The talkers always think it's about money. Honestly, I truly do not think her dad can give me what it is I want.

"What's your name?" she asks. "Mine's Ava… Please… Just talk to me… I'm a nice person…"

I sigh. Lean my head against the brick wall. It's not comfortable.

I check my watch. It's getting late, and I need to text Flora to give Ava an alibi for the next few days, and I need to do this before getting to the gay bar in time to intercept Shane before he hooks up with someone else.

Fuck, this bitch has made things difficult.

Still, I enjoy the sight of her, and I'm tempted to have her again before I leave. Just one for the road.

"What?" she says, looking back at me weirdly. She doesn't like the way I peer at her, I can tell. It makes me smile.

"Please, don't hurt me, not anymore…"

Bitch, please—you haven't even met my friend *hurt* yet. Not even close.

But I must resist. Wanting to fuck her so badly is what created this potential cockup. I have responsibilities.

I stand. Cross my arms. Survey my prisoner.

I can't leave her to scream her head off when I don't know how well the basement hides the sound. The last thing I need is for a neighbour to hear her and truly fuck everything up.

I go upstairs. Find a dirty sock and some masking tape. Return to find Ava pulling on the chains.

"It won't work," I tell her. "But feel free to keep trying."

I try to open her mouth and she resists. I pinch her nose, and she's forced to open it, and I shove the sock in, then cover her mouth with my palm before she can spit it out. I fix the masking tape around the back of her head, letting it pull on her hair, then wrap it around her mouth, tightly, again and again, until I have wrapped it repeatedly around her head.

I stand back. She tries to shout. Tries to scream. She can barely make a sound.

Beautiful.

I take Ava's phone and I text Flora as I make my way out to the car.

Sup slut

Wots goin on

This is Ava

I know dude lol

Like ur in my phone

You ok

Hows your dad

Er totes annoyballs

I hates him

Like proper hates him

 iMessage

He duz my head in soooo much

Like get a grip ur a 40yroldman

Have you spoken to miss fletcher about it

No

I thought you was going to

What he's doin isn't right

Whatevs

Don't even care anyway rofl

iMessage

like this ass cant get a rich guy anywayz

wot do I even need him for

LOL

I still don't think its right

Like so over it

Change topic Flee

Like bout how i totes saw liam today

You did?

Where?

iMessage

He wunt let me say

Is he okay?

Yh

Listen

Im gna hang with him for a bit

He needs a friend

But you hate Liam

You said he was proper weird

Yh like he is

 iMessage

But I dnt want him to hurt himself or nuffin

Ok

Still seems a little weird though

I wnt be at schl tmrw now

Like we r goin 2 hang

Just want make sure he ok

You're not coming to school?

Ava you have an exam in two weeks

 iMessage

You said you were really worried

Like I cn revise where I am

Stop wurryin

Ull giv urself wrinkles

Ava im worried

This isn't like you

I mean wotevs

Uve known me 4 wot 5 mins

Sumtimes I just got 2 get away u no

 iMessage

I no

It's just

You don't like Liam

And you never cut class

I'm really confused

Stop tellin me wot I do n do not like

U dnt own me

I'm sorry

I dnt mean to make you feel like you can't talk 2 me

iMessage

Thn stop wurryin

Ill be fine

Just dnt tell anyone yh?

The last thing we need is someone makin a fuss

Fine

But please come back soon

I don't like having to hold onto these secrets

Dnt worry beatch

Like totes we will

iMessage

Gots to go tho

Chow 4 now

Bye xx

Xx

 iMessage

THIS IS WRONG

This is wrong.

    All of it. Everything. It just feels…

    Familiar.

    Like I'm being lied to.

    Like the way I was lied to before.

    Am I?

    Am I being taken advantage of? Teased? Misled?

    Is it even them texting?

    No. Stop it, Flora. Remember what Doctor Hawes said. That my trauma would do this. That it would take meaningless events and trap them in meaning that isn't there. That my head would want to solve enigmas; make puzzles out of ordinary incidents when the explanation is right in front of me. That if I'm not careful, my life will become nothing more than moments of fretting, and being unable to let a thought go.

    I'm not even making sense.

    But this doesn't make sense.

    Then I am wrong.

    I am not being lied to.

    Maybe I am, but probably not.

    Probably.

Doctor Hawes said that I would feel like other people are doing to me what he did. That it's an evolutionary instinct to guard myself from similar experiences occurring again.

Every time I like a boy, I wonder if I actually like him or whether I've been coerced into feeling like I can't escape.

Every time I have a friend, I imagine they are laughing at me behind my back.

Every time I am touched by a hand, I think it's to bend me over and fuck me until I cry, because crying is what happens when you get fucked.

This is wrong. I am wrong. Or am I wrong? Something's wrong.

Or maybe nothing is wrong.

It is trauma, dammit! It's exactly what Doctor Hawes said would happen. It is my paranoia.

I expect everyone to be like Gerald.

Oh God, I hope there's no one else like Gerald.

Because I hate him.

I hate him so much.

He's probably sitting there in his mansion with a whore on her knees and a body at his feet, thinking about how much he got away with and how much I still owe him. He probably thinks I am a missing possession, like a watch or a DVD or a book that's been lost, and he sits there, night after night, lamenting over that watch/DVD/book's departure.

No, lamenting isn't the right word. He doesn't lament.

He grieves over it.

He ruminates over it.

His aggression grows over it.

Until he grows furious at the audacity that his possession ever dared retaliate in the way I did.

Then he is wrong.

He was wrong to make me distrust every person I meet; to search for ulterior motives; to distrust every action; to question intentions.

Before, I may have been naïve in never believing people could be anything but kind, but at least I was happy in my blissful ignorance.

Liam could be messing with me. Ava could be messing with me. They could both be planning to make me say something or do something, and then show it to the entire sixth form in some kind of elaborate prank.

But they aren't doing that—that's me talking.

No, that's wrong. It's him talking.

It's always him.

And Doctor Hawes said I need to trust that it's not him.

But what about trusting myself?

If I should trust my judgement, **then Doctor Hawes is wrong.**

Then this isn't trauma. It isn't my mind protecting me. It isn't me making something out of nothing. And Liam is acting strangely.

But I don't know what strange is for him. I don't know him. I think I love him, yet I don't know him. I don't even know if I can love, yet I think I do. Oh God, how fucked up am I?

But Ava...

She was so determined that today would be the day—that she would finally tell her mother what her father had been doing to her —that she would finally tell him that he would never touch her again—that she would go to the police if she had to.

And she changed her mind and ran away.

It feels wrong.

It is wrong.

It's just wrong.

THIS IS WRONG.

And I don't know who to believe.

CHAPTER SEVENTEEN

GULLIBLE BITCH.

Honestly, I could probably tell her I'm a magical elf who's come to whisk Ava away on an adventure and she'd be like, "Oh, well if you're sure, have a lovely time, I'll say nothing because I'm a stupid fucking idiot."

I cannot wait for what I have in store for her after tonight.

I put Ava's phone in my pocket as I approach the gay bar. I pause. Brace myself for what I'm about to do. Convince myself that there's nothing wrong with my doing it—that, once again, there are masculine standards set in society that are not true, and that I need not adhere to.

Though I am masculine.

Masculine as *fuck*.

And this won't change it. Fuck off if you say it does.

I walk in. The music is louder. It feels like more of a club feel. I remember that it's Friday night, and people seek a different kind of night at the weekend.

Shane is already across the room, talking to a small guy with a moustache, leaning over him with eager come-ons that the man doesn't seem to reciprocate. He wears his tie and tank top and shirt and trousers from work—I wonder why he never brings a spare outfit. Especially for a night where people are wearing shirts and jeans; where people are dressed specifically for dancing, and he's dressed for fingerpainting and story time.

I pause at the bar. Put my hand up for the barman. I don't order a whisky—I crave one like hell, but it doesn't fit tonight's persona, so I have a vodka and tonic instead. The tonic is cheap, and the vodka is sticky, and it tastes like the cheap shit teenage girls drink in the park.

I watch Shane, hoping to catch his eye. I've never done this with a man before, and I imagine it must be easier than with a woman—not every woman wants to fuck, and the ones who do are often fussy about who they do fuck. A man, however, is always up for a fuck—especially this man.

It takes less than a minute for him to catch my eye. I hold it for a moment, then look down, too shy to hold his gaze. I make myself look nervous, fidgeting with the beer mat, like I'm a damsel in distress. I don't know how else to play this other than act like the kind of woman I usually seek to fuck and destroy. Does a gay guy look for the same things as a straight guy? Fuck me this LGBT shit is complicated.

I take another sip of the drink. It makes me want to puke. He appears at my side. I can smell a day's work on him. If he's always so desperate to pull, why doesn't he at least have a shower?

I answer my own question: because it's a man he's after, not a woman, and a man's taste is far simpler. You don't have to be interesting and funny and hard-to-get and strong yet sensitive and elusive yet certain and ready to rescue the damsel whilst also respecting that the damsel does not wish to be rescued—you just have to be weak and half-pretty and willing to entertain putting out.

"Hey," he says, leaning close so I can hear him above the music, and I recognise the smell on his breath as the same smell every teacher I had as a child had on theirs; a combination of coffee and old saliva.

"Hi," I say, bite my lip, look up at him, look down, look back up at him, look away and sip my drink.

"Are you on your own?" he asks.

"I guess."

"Me too."

"Really? You?" I wonder whether I'm supposed to say *really such a handsome brute like you,* but I leave it implied. I feel like Belle in *Beauty and the Beast.* I'm good-looking and in need of being convinced, and he's an ugly cunt with hair in his ears.

"So do you come here often?"

Jesus Christ, Shane, do people actually use that line nowadays?

"Once or twice. You?"

"You could say it's my regular spot."

I notice his wedding ring is still on. "Are you married?"

"Oh, no," he tells me, shaking his hand around. "He died a year ago, and I haven't had the heart to stop wearing it yet."

HAH! You insipid little liar.

"I'm sorry to hear that," I say, though I wouldn't give a shit even if this fake husband wasn't imaginary.

"It's okay. He was ill for a while, so we kind of saw it coming. I've made my peace with it."

I nod. Drink the rest of my drink to conceal any laughter.

"Hey, do you want another one?" he asks.

I look around. The place is starting to fill. Everyone here is so young and there are dudes kissing other dudes and I just want to get this over with.

"Maybe," I say. "Or there's a hotel around the corner. We could go there and talk or something, I don't know."

He grins like he's hit the jackpot. So he should, I'm an attractive sonofabitch.

"I'm up for that."

He finishes his drink and guides me to the door with a hand on my back and it's weird for me to be the one guided out—and is this how easy it is to pick up a man? Really?

I mean, with all the shit us guys have to do (I say *us guys* —I stopped doing it a few years ago when I discovered whores)—all the talking and chatting up and spending money on drinks and dinner—all it takes for you fucking women is a small chat and a hotel room and you can fuck a man just like that?

I don't like cock, but I'm tempted to see if I can convince myself to, especially if this is how easy life could be.

It's raining outside. He doesn't shelter me with a jacket, but I'm not sure if he's supposed to. What's the decorum here?

The hotel is only around the corner, and it only takes a minute to get there. He tells me to wait by the lift while he goes to the counter and sorts a room. I know money's not an issue for me, but even so, you don't even have to pay when a man pulls you. All those women complaining about their rights and all that shit need to look at how fucking good they have it.

After a few minutes, he's next to me and he's guiding me into the lift. He hits the button for floor five, and I catch a sight of myself in the lift's mirror (still handsome as ever, this guy's a lucky fucker), which is when I am accosted by Shane. He shoves me against the wall, interlocking his fingers in mine, and presses his lips so hard against mine that I can do nothing to stop his tongue from slithering between my lips. His tongue isn't dainty and curious like a woman's, it's ferocious and flappy like a thrashing eel. I feel smothered against the wall, just like every woman I've ever taken up a lift in a hotel probably has, and suddenly I'm regretting my remark about how good they have it.

I go to push him off and stop myself.

I remind myself that this is for Flora.

How this is part of the plan that I almost fucked up by abducting that stupid Ava girl.

Then Ava's bikini pictures float into my mind and it gives me a boner and he can feel it against his hip and he moans with delight, saying, "Oh someone's up for it," and trust me, Shane, that boner is not for you.

The lift door opens. He takes me by the hand and whisks me across the corridor. Most of his hook-ups might consider this a romantic gesture, but I see him keeping his gaze pointed toward the floor, and I know when someone is trying to stop CCTV from picking up his face—this man does not want *anyone* to know what he gets up to at night. Poor Mariam, she has no idea that her husband is leading a man—one she believes wishes to fuck a corpse—across this softly carpeted corridor to the cheapest hotel room an expensive hotel will provide.

Once we are inside his arms are around me again and his tongue is in my mouth and his hands are inside my top and slithering beneath my belt and I will NOT be going all the way with this, and even if I was, stop being so eager you desperate prick, this is not how you do it.

I grab his arms with my fist. I drop the dainty, delicate act; now it's time for me to take charge.

"What's up?" he asks. I have evidently disrupted his rhythm.

"Get on your knees."

"Excuse me?"

"I said get on your knees—and let *me* punish *you*."

Oh the excitement on his face—it's like a fucking child with a new doll. He gets on his knees and I drag him by the collar across the room until we are by the edge of the bed.

"Give me your tie," I tell him.

"Why am I—"

"Did I fucking stutter?" I grab his throat and look into his eyes. He's scared for a moment, then I give him a quick peck on the lips (bleurgh) and raise my eyebrows, and I've never seen a stronger look of arousal.

He takes off his tie and gives it to me. I use it to restrain his hands behind his back. I do a triple knot to make sure.

"Now close your eyes and keep them closed."

He closes them.

"I mean it—if you open those eyes, even for a second, then there will be no pleasure for you."

He nods eagerly. Like a dog waiting to be fed. Pathetic little man.

"Open your mouth."

I take out Liam's phone. I unlock it. I open the camera.

And, with his eyes closed and his hands restrained, I stand with my crotch inches from his open gob, direct the camera down at him, and begin filming.

"Now beg for my cock."

"Please… Please give me your cock…"

"Beg better."

"Please give me your cock I need it…"

"Who are you?"

"I am your silly little servant…"

I wonder whether to get him to say his name, worried that Flora won't recognise him with his face pressed against my crotch, but I needn't. Even if the camera doesn't catch sight of his face, his tank top is easily recognisable. She will know who this is.

With the camera in one hand, I loosen my belt with the other, and I take out my cock.

I guide it into his mouth.

And he sucks it.

And I film.

And I just let this happen.

I close my eyes and think of Ava and her bikini pictures. I remember she's in my basement and I wonder if maybe abducting her wasn't such a bad idea after all when I have such a delectable treat waiting for me.

He speeds up.

I've had my dick sucked many times, and I must say, he isn't bad. I'm not saying he'd replace a whore, but if I close my eyes and pretend it's someone else, then I can even take a little pleasure in it.

"Do you like my cock?" I ask him.

"Yes," he says, though it's muffled as his mouth is full.

"Do you love it?"

"Mmhm."

"Like Flora loves it?"

He pauses. Frowns.

That's when he opens his eyes.

And he sees me filming.

And his face fills the screen

"Hey!" he says, and he stands, and he tries to grab the phone but forgets his hands are bound and he tries to loosen them but dammit I can tie a good knot.

"Stop filming! Stop it! I didn't say that was okay!"

I barge into him and knock him to the floor and he flops around like a dying fish. He tries to get back to his knees, but I kick him in the back of the head and he falls back down.

I turn the camera off.

This part's just for me.

I lift him up by the collar and I bring my fist down against the side of his skull and his head impacts with the floor with such force it's a wonder his eyes are still open.

I lift my pristine leather shoes and bring my heel down upon his face, making his nose bleed.

I mount him. Squeeze his throat as he splutters and his face bleeds and he stares up at me with the same terror I saw in Pretend-Flora and the whore before her and the one before that.

"Do you know what the best part of this is?" I ask him,

though he's suffering too much to reply. "You're so desperate for no one to know what you were up to tonight that you'll lie without me telling you to."

I lean my face close to his.

"If you tell a cop, then your family will know what you are."

I stop squeezing his throat, as I fear he is about to pass out before I want him to.

"But I don't even need to worry, do I—because you won't dare tell a damn person, you cock-sucking adulterer."

His eyes widen. He's groggy, but I'm certain he understands me. I raise my fist and pound it against his skull again, and he's knocked out.

I consider killing him.

I really want to kill him.

But I must resist.

Not yet.

Not just yet.

But soon, though.

Soon.

CHAPTER EIGHTEEN

THAT WAS A STRANGE EXPERIENCE.

I wonder what you make of it.

Not that I give a shit what you think of it—but I am intrigued as to which 'camp' you will sit in.

Either you're in the first camp, and you will automatically accuse me of homosexuality despite my exclusive desire for tits and vaginas, simply because of the experience; perhaps you'll even consider me emasculated; in which case, grow the fuck up. Just because I let a guy put my cock in his mouth for two minutes doesn't mean any of that shit. It's part of a plan, and this is exactly what I'm getting at with this whole 'society taught you this' crap—you are thinking thoughts that the world you live in has given to you. I bet that, should you be in this camp, then you haven't had an original thought in your life that society hasn't ingrained on you since youth.

Or perhaps you are in the second camp, and you think it's very progressive of me. Oh, look at Gerald, the man who shags whores, the man who kills women, he doesn't discriminate, he shags and kills blokes too, he is so modern, doesn't concern himself with sexual inclination he just does what he wants, maybe he's even pansexual (which is just bisexual said in a more confusing way)—and if this is the camp you belong to then you can grow the fuck up too.

It was means to an end, you dickhead.

It was what I had to do to get results. It was an unfortunate action that gave me what I need.

A video to delight Flora with.

And, as I pull up to my house, I cannot wait to send it to her. I can picture her face and her little hands and her sad eyes as she looks at the foster-father she adores, sucking cock behind his wife's back.

Then I remember I have something even more exciting to deal with first, and that thing resides in my basement.

I enter the house and lock the front door. Turn off the lights. Practically dance to the basement stairs. I lock the basement door behind me (not that I am expecting intruders, but I take every precaution necessary—I can afford the best lawyers, and they can get me off almost anything, but being caught in the act is pretty difficult to fight), and I descend the steps, each one another wooden plank that sinks beneath my feet, until I reach the cold stone floor of the basement.

There is a distant dripping. Moisture has caused mould to grow along the edge of the ceiling. It is cold and clammy, and I would not like to spend a prolonged period of time in such conditions—I've made the basement in my mansion more comfortable, and I miss it. Even so, I don't care about the conditions right now—for there is a teenage girl on the brink of womanhood staring up at me with eyes so vulnerable it makes me want to skullfuck her.

Her arms still hang above her head from the restraints, and her wrists have gone a little purple. There is a damp patch on her tiny little sports shorts where she's evidently peed. Her cheeks are damp as if she's been crying.

I kneel before her and cup her face.

"Oh dear," I tell her. "You truly have had quite an ordeal since I've been gone. How about we fix you up, huh?"

I go upstairs and return to the basement five minutes later with a bucket of soapy water, a sponge, scissors, and a toolbox.

I begin with the scissors. I slice away her skirt, then cut her undershorts down the front and down the back. The flimsy nylon falls to the ground. I do the same with her top. She wears a red bra that matches the panties I removed earlier, and I pretend she wore them for me.

She's crying again. The gag muffles her sobs, but the tears still trickle down her cheeks. Her eyes look weak. Staring up at me like a child who's done something wrong.

I cut off her bra. Her tits are tiny and her nipples are hard. Her vagina is messy—the flaps are too big, and the hair is bushy, and it stinks. I take the sponge, dip it in the soapy water, and rub her labia with it. She flinches. The water is cold, and the soap probably stings. I don't care—I don't want a piss-stained hole, I want a glorious entrance. I rub harder, until it's spotless, then push the sponge up her and make sure she's clean inside too. She tries to scream through her gag, but I don't care if it stings—if she doesn't like this, then she shouldn't have pissed herself.

When I've finished, I stand and look down upon my prey. Goosebumps prickle on her arms. Her hair is matted. Her naked body is thin like a child's body, with little definition. She's lost weight since those bikini pictures, and she was already thin enough in them. I wonder if she has a problem with eating.

She makes noises. Like she's trying to speak to me. I cut through the masking tape around her mouth and pull it off, taking a few strands of hair with it. She spits the sock out.

"Please," she says, her voice cracked and broken. "Please let me go. I won't tell anyone, I swear, please just let me go."

Is that all she wanted to say? I thought it was going to be something profound. Exciting. She was so desperate to speak that I expected an amazing insight into this experience that would change my entire outlook on life. All I get is the same crap they all say. What a disappointment.

Ah well, I have things to do, best get to it.

I bring the toolbox closer and open it. I was disappointed I forgot to bring my torture kit with me, and I miss the incisors and scalpels and trocars and clamps and everything else I use to inflict beautiful pain upon my victims—but the previous owners left a toolbox under the sink and, as it turns out, it has everything I need.

I open it and survey the items, trying to decide which to start with.

"Why are you doing this?"

Oh yawn. Now come the questions. Soon she'll be trying to tell me about her family.

"Please, I have a family."

Oh, there it is. So predictable.

I start small. Take out the sandpaper. Rub its coarse edge against the back of my hand. It's rough. I look at her and decide which part of her I wish to sand off.

"Please stop! You don't need to do this, I'm a good person."

Her nipple stands out to me. The one on my right. It looks bigger than the other one, and it looks like it's taking up more of her breast than it should.

As I approach, she starts wriggling and fighting. Her bound hands stop her from running away, but she still backs up, trying to avoid my reach. I put my hand on the back of her neck and kneel on her legs to keep her still.

"Please! Please!"

I rub the sandpaper against her nipple. She cries.

"Stop it, it's hurting me!"

I snort back a laugh. That's kind of the point.

"Please, it hurts so much…"

I rub harder and harder, and faster and faster—fortunately, I spent my adolescence learning how to rub quickly with this hand—and her nipple gets redder. The skin around her nipple starts to redden too. Then her skin spots blood.

I keep going and she keeps crying and I go harder and she cries harder and it bleeds and it bleeds and it bleeds, blood trickling from the areola, until her nipple starts to shrink and I keep going until the entire nipple is flat and covered in sticky red goo.

She's not begging anymore. She's screaming. She's quite hysterical. I can barely decipher her words.

I return to the toolbox. Hmm. What else is there?

Pliers.

I pick them up. Look at her. Wonder what I could do with these.

I could pull off the other nipple, but I feel like I've already done the nipples.

I could pull off her fingernails, but I feel like there's something better.

Her teeth.

Ah yes, her teeth.

I approach her, and her wide eyes reflect mine—except hers are out of terror, and mine are out of glee. She tries to struggle again, tries to get away from me, and I sit on her legs and put my arm around her neck and hold her head still.

"Please stop you don't have to do this please stop I'm a good person my dad can pay he has money I mean it please stop please just stop."

She tries to close her mouth. Tries to keep her lips shut tight. I wrap my spare arm around her head and pinch her nose. She tries to resist, but she can't help it. She needs to breathe.

I put the plier on her right front tooth first. Get a good grip. Then I pull, and I can just imagine her pain, the loosening of the tooth, the agony as it wobbles. She screams as I pull, and it's really hard to yank off, but with a few tugs I manage, and I hold it high to show her, and she cries, and blood fills her mouth and drips down her lips.

Once I've pulled her other front tooth out, I look at her again, and she isn't so pretty anymore. In fact, she looks ridiculous. I wonder whether to do the other teeth, and then I think of the opportunity. I rarely put my dick in their mouth as I'm scared they might bite it; but if I remove all her teeth, it's no longer an option.

"Hold still," I say, and she struggles even more, but I have her in a good grip, and I go from the outside in, starting with the lateral incisors, then the canines, the molars, pulling each out as her mouth fills with more blood and she cries harder.

Eventually, she stops screaming, and she closes her eyes and takes it. All she can do is withstand the pain.

Once I've finished, I shove my dick in her toothless mouth and fuck her head without her being able to do fuckall about it. I've never skullfucked a woman without teeth before and it's actually quite good. I make a mental note to try a pensioner instead of a whore at some point.

I return to my toolbox as she sobs. Her loud, hysterical crying is reduced to miserable little weeps. I've destroyed her spirit. She's given up hope. I love this part.

The screwdriver. Hmm. I look at her. What can I do with the screwdriver?

Fuck it, I'll just stab her a little.

I swing the screwdriver at her chest. Her belly. Her leg.

Then I plunge it up her cunt, and I hold it there as she screams and her eyes widen and her mouth opens and her scream keeps going and going and I twist the screwdriver and she can't calm down, she can't return to her subdued cries as it hurts too damn much, she can't stop shrieking with pain, can't stop the need to writhe and weep.

I pull the screwdriver out and blood gushes over her thighs and I shove my dick inside of her and use the blood as a lubricant. I put my hand around her throat, not hard enough to choke her but hard enough to keep her obedient, and I fuck her and I stare into her eyes as I do.

She doesn't even beg anymore.

She just stares back at me with that meek gaze, the sorry child, the wounded animal, the woman who knows that this is the glorious end to her unremarkable life. The poor girl is barely conscious.

I cum quickly and I step back and I wipe the last dregs of semen across her cheek.

And I return to the toolbox.

And I get the hammer.

And I approach her.

She says something. A word. It comes out in a faint whimper, and I can't decipher it.

"What's that?" I ask.

She pushes the word out, and it turns out she was asking, "Why?"

I shrug. "Why not?"

And I strike her head with the hammer. She yelps, then she goes quiet, and doesn't make another sound as I strike her again, and again, and again.

Her body falls limp.

I don't stop yet. I want to make sure.

After a few more, there is a large indent in her skull and there is no more breath leaving her lips.

I check my watch. It's three in the morning. I have a few hours before Flora will get up—and I would love to be watching through her window as she awakes, checks her phone, and sees what I'm about to send her.

There is a hacksaw in the toolbox. I saw Ava's body apart,

sneak back to the farm where I took Liam, and feed the pigs. I return to the house to clean the basement—something I do on automatic; it's as routine to me by now as brushing your teeth is to you.

By the time I'm done, the sun is rising, and I drive to the Warner's house, eager for what comes next.

CHAPTER NINETEEN

I PARK my car amongst the early morning commotion, down the street from the Warner's house. My Mercedes doesn't look too out of place beside picket fences and grand family homes. This is where the people live when they have enough money to afford a nice house, but don't have enough money to call themselves rich.

I don't envy them.

They must get up early in the morning. They must leave the house by a certain time. They must do what a boss tells them all day. I couldn't do any of that. I inherited my business, and I employed the best businessmen to run them, and they grow my wealth for me. There is little I need to do except fire someone when my wealth isn't growing as exponentially as I wish it to.

But these people…

Men in suits with toothpaste on their collars dash from their house with briefcases in hand, reversing out of the drive with the tiredness that comes with being a parent.

Sometimes, women leave in an equal amount of rush, wearing outfits that aren't as smart as the men's suits but pass as okay. This is why I never hire women to run my businesses. The men wear suits and get the better promotions, then the women bitch about how they only got the promotion because they are a man whilst wearing fucking leggings to work.

I create a new email account on Ava's phone. I draft an email. I attach the video of Shane on his knees with my cock in his mouth. (I've since decided that those of you who thought I am progressive were right and not fucking idiots, and that it was very progressive of me—though don't get too cocky, I imagine you're still a fucking idiot in other aspects of your life.) I find Flora's email address on Ava's phone, type it into the draft email, then hit send with a large grin smacked across my face.

A light comes on through the upstairs window. Oh, I hope I haven't woken you, dear Flora. You saunter to the window, wearing baggy pyjamas that do not do your body justice. You lift your arms up, stretch, and open the window—it's a hot day, and you need to cool down. A woman walks by and shouts hello to you. You wave back. And you sit on the windowsill, a bay window that you've placed cushions and blankets on, in perfect view for me to watch, almost as if you intended it, and you pick up your phone.

Your face is blank and bored. You scan the usual monotony of Apps—I imagine you are checking text messages, seeing if Liam has messaged, if Ava has messaged... Then you open your emails. Oh, there's some junk mail for penis enlargements and another junk mail from a Nigerian prince—don't need them. But what's this? You don't know that email address. You are curious, and you open the email, and you play the video...

And then there's a little frown. It's cute. Your nose crumples up, and I can't tell you how much I look forward to destroying that face—first with my cock, then with a brick.

Then you stand. Cover your mouth. Look around, like you're going to find an answer in the solitary confines of your room. You even look out the window, like someone is watching you. I am, but you don't know that. Then you watch the video again.

You stare at it. Glare at it. Frown at it. Become puzzled by it.

You know who it is. You know what he's doing. You now know what he gets up to at night, and the fascinating part is, Flora, what you are going to do with this information.

Will you confront him? Tell Mariam? Or will you just hide it away?

You place the phone down. Think. Then you pick it up. Nurse it like a dying bird. Watch the video again.

It will not change the more you watch it, Flora, you dumb fuck.

You put the phone in your pocket, then pause, crossing your arms then biting your nail. The perplexities of the conundrum cross your face. You disappear from the window.

I wish I could watch the rest. It's like someone turning off my favourite movie halfway through. I don't have to wait long, though—you reappear through the dining-room window ten minutes later. You're now fully dressed, your hair in a ponytail, wearing a t-shirt with a picture of an alien's head on it and a pair of flared jeans. You carry a woolly jumper with you. It's boiling, but you want the comfort of knowing you can cover up at any time, don't you?

You sit at the breakfast table. You're in a trance. Mariam puts food in front of you. Bacon, eggs and fried tomato. Looks like a nice breakfast. But you don't eat it. You just stare at your lap, still biting that nail.

Claire sits beside you. The little girl you were pushing on the swing in the photos, eating her eggs like there's a shortage of them.

Shane enters. Sits opposite you. Says something. *How are you*, perhaps, or *good morning*.

You look up. Look down. Look away.

He says something else. *What's the matter* or *what is it* or *why are you looking away you dirty little toad* (probably not the last one, but I can't hear them, so I enjoy a bit of make believe).

You say nothing. Mariam joins you at the table. They talk to you, and you don't respond.

Are you going to tell them, Flora? Are you?

I wait longer. You don't move. They say something to you, and you finally sit up and eat—though you don't really eat, you just prod at the food, and occasionally put some in your mouth. You leave most of it.

Oh boy, Flora—if this is enough to put you off your appetite, just wait for what is coming.

When you finally give up on your breakfast, you scrape it into the bin before anyone else can see how much you left. Isabella appears at the front door and knocks on it. You leave with her, walking to school, and I wonder if you will say anything to her, but you don't.

You walk right on down that street in silence, barely saying a word.

I KNOW THAT BODY

I know I should be shocked by what Shane is doing in that video. I know I should. And I am. It's just the man he's with...

I know that body.

I know the shape of the legs and the way the hair thickens as it approaches his scrotum, like a forest growing darker as you reach the big bad wolf.

I know the mole on the inside of his thigh, shaped like rabbit's shit; it always rubbed against my ear when I gave him head.

I know the curve of the belly and the way it's toned like someone who carries around a lot of heavy bodies.

I know it all, and I know it well.

Which makes it even harder to convince myself I'm wrong.

It might not be him. It might not. It probably isn't. I mean, what are the chances?

Gerald is not gay, for a start. He demonstrated his toxic heterosexuality on my body day after day after day. Never once did he show any inclination that there was anything else he enjoyed wrecking beside the female form. He revelled in the destruction of a strong woman as he turned them into a shadow of their former selves—never men.

So I could be wrong.

I could be.

He wouldn't go this far. Not for me. Not for revenge.

Then again, how far did I go?

Pushing a corkscrew against the inner lining of my vagina was more than uncomfortable. I did it because I had to. If he sees this as something he has to do...

No, I don't know that body. I can't.

But I know the way he stands, legs always so wide apart, as if showing the world how much he loves his dick.

I know the way he expects the recipient to put his entire shaft in their mouth until it touches the back of their throat and forces them to gag, like prompting someone's gag reflex is something to take pleasure in.

And I know the kind of man who would film something so vile and send it to me.

And for a moment, a brief few seconds, I convince myself I'm right. It's him, and I need to brace myself for what's coming, and I need to tell my foster family the truth about what happened, and I need to protect myself and I need to protect them and I need to run as far away as I can to ensure he can never find me again.

That's when Dr Hawes' voice repeats itself.

You will see reasons why someone wants to hurt you everywhere you look.

You will find details of him in every man you see.

Your pain will talk to you, and when you don't listen it will shout, and when you still don't listen it will scream, until it's almost impossible not to listen to what it has to say.

That pain isn't real.

Ground yourself.

Put yourself back into reality and stop letting your trauma rule your perception.

I stop watching the video. I tell no one about it. I wouldn't do that to Shane. To Mariam. To Claire.

This could be anyone.

A child or a parent Shane pissed off; a client that resented Mari-

am's advice; an old feud from university Shane told no one about; someone after money; or notoriety; or just wishing to spread hate.

I know that body, but only because I see things that are familiar.

I can't know that body. I won't let myself know that body.

It's just tough when there are these small imperfections I know too well.

I need Ava. Isabella and Eleanor are fine, but they've never spoken deeply with me about anything. It's Ava who listens to me talk all evening on the phone, and I want her around again.

I try calling her.

I let the phone ring, and I replay the video in my mind as I do, and I am sure I recognise that body.

But I don't.

I do, but I don't.

So stop it.

I text Ava. I ask her to call me. I tell her I need her. Say that she doesn't need to tell me where she is, just to get in touch.

I don't receive a reply all morning. Not until I check my phone again at break time.

And that's when I have a text message back.

It is one line, and it reads: This is not Ava.

And I drop the phone.

Please call me

I need a friend

Things are really crumby

You don't need to tell me where you are

Just call

Ava?

Ava are you there?

Fine I got to go to school now

Please just text me

 iMessage

This isn't Ava

What?

What do you mean?

This isn't Ava

It's pretty self-explanatory

Then who is it?

It's Liam

On Ava's phone

She had to step away for a moment

 iMessage

Where's your phone?

It went dead

Forgot to bring a charger

What's up

Please just put Ava back on

She doesn't want to talk to you

What do you mean?

She said she doesn't want to talk to you

Can't be bothered with you anymore

 iMessage

> I don't believe you

> Put Ava on

She's peeing

> Fine when she gets back

Hang on she's coming back

Here she is now

Wots up beatch

> Ava can you ring me

Cant

Soz

 iMessage

Busy

Wots up

Really weird things are happening

I could do with a friend

Its not all about u hun

Sumtimes otha pple r allowed problems 2

What are you saying?

I sayin I cnt give u all this attention all the time

I mean GOD

iMessage

U r so needy

Why are you being so mean?

You know how hard it's been for me

Oh its always SO FRICKIN hard for U

It's always flora flora flora

Why are u bein like this?

I thought we're friends

YAWN

Ur just boring me Flee

iMessage

I want to spk to someone more interestin

He is well interestin

U r not

I don't understand this

I spoke to you for hours about what your father was doing the other day

For HOURS

And I now want some support u say no?

I wud NEVER say no to you

 iMessage

I wud NEVER say that you were boring me

I thought we were better friends than that

OMG FLEE

Just fking get a grip

Ur life aint that hard

Wot happened 2 u aint that hard

Wot happened 2 me was shit

An you did fk all to help

All that talking didn't help?

 iMessage

Talking?

I wnted the man DEAD

I wnted someone to help me make him DEAD

U just frickin talked

Great friend huh

So wot?

If I didn't kill your dad im not a good friend?

U said it

Not me

 iMessage

Ur acting really weird Ava

This isn't like you

You don't say things like this

Since I've known u we've never fallen out

Wots going on

Liam is wots going on

He said u were borin

That he was thinkin of dating u

But that hed prefer me

 iMessage

Why are you bein so mean?

Why are you bein so DULL

I sucked liam off yday

We had the time of our life

While u… wot?

Sat in your pyjamas

Wotchin tv with ur foster mum

The sex therapist

Wot's that got to do with anything?

iMessage

Face it Flee

U were fun for a few months

Now im done with u

Moved on

Got bored

Found some1 betta

Now leave me alone

Ava is this really u

OMG Flee u really are fked up aren't u

 iMessage

Now go fk off and die

U stupid slut

Ava is this u?

Tell me its u?

Tell me something only we know

Tell me something that means I know this is you and I'll leave you alone

Ava?

Ava?

Please

 iMessage

Ava?

Are you okay?

Ava?

CHAPTER TWENTY

OH, this is fun.

I can tell she's twigging. That something doesn't feel right. That something is off. I have little time left before her instinct will scream at her, and she can no longer ignore it.

Which means I must move onto Mariam, and I must find shit on her quickly.

Only, she seems to be perfect; what society would consider to be an upstanding citizen, even if such religious zealots would find her choice of vocation slightly taboo. (I despise religious judgements, and do not have any time to give such imbeciles even a smidgen of my thoughts—the only thing worse than someone who suppresses their nature is someone who suppresses their nature to obey a religion. You're one of trillions: even if there was a God, which there is not, you are not significant enough for Him to care whether you fuck someone before you get married; grow up.)

I digress.

I follow Mariam. She goes to the post office and collects a package. She drives to her office, and she always sticks to the speed limit. If a traffic light turns from green to amber, she doesn't speed through before it changes—she slows down and frustrates everyone behind her.

When she sees her clients, she smiles at them, welcomes them, and discusses their problems calmly and rationally. She never loses her cool. She is always calm. This is strange, and with most people I would hypothesise that this is restraint—but she seems to be naturally tranquil. A peaceful person. How disgusting.

She goes to the local independent sandwich shop for lunch, no doubt wishing to give a small business some trade. She asks what their vegan option is. She has a salad heavy sandwich on wholewheat bread with dairy alternative cheese. When she orders a latte, she asks for soya milk. I want to slap her round the face with bacon and tell her what she's missing. The only thing worse than spiritual people are spiritual vegans.

She calls Flora to see how she is when school ends. She calls Shane and asks what he would like for dinner tonight. She calls the child minder to check on Claire. She helps an old man carry his bags to his car. She is so fucking perfect and I HATE HER. Everything about her is repulsive and happy and grotesque and delightful and it just makes me want to grab her and shake her and demand her to tell me *what is it you're hiding?*

Maybe she isn't hiding anything. Maybe she is just good and pure. Maybe she is a nice person.

Fuck off. There is no such thing.

I stop following her and decide to see what I can find in her office.

I arrive and wait in the car for a few minutes. Make sure no one is looking out of their windows or hanging around on the street. I want no witnesses. When I'm sure, I enter the building, walk through the corridor, and reach her office. I try the door and it's locked, as I expected.

I check the nearby offices. They are empty. Lucky me. I

step back and charge at the office door, and it barges open on the first attempt. It is weak and small, just like Flora.

I sit behind the computer, move the mouse, and the screen comes to life. The computer is locked. I need a password. If she is as predictable as I expect, then this shouldn't take too long.

I try the self-descriptive words first:

vegan4ever

happyvegan

givemesalad

vegans

vegans12

No, this isn't right. She'll use her daughter's name. Of course she will. So I try it:

claire

Nothing. So I try it with different numbers, sighing at how tedious this is.

claire1

claire2

claire3

This gets tiresome quite fast, and I continue on automatic as my mind drifts off and thinks about Flora. I try to recall what she looks like naked. It's been a while, and she seems thinner. I've almost forgotten what it's like to be inside her. I truly cannot wait to wreck that body once again.

Ah, here we are! It appears that claire44 is the correct combination, and I am in.

I open her inbox on Outlook. There are messages with clients arranging appointments. Responses to bookings. Emails with her accountant about her tax forms. Nothing interesting.

I open *my computer*. Look through the files. Different clients have different files. I even have one—well, Tony does. I am curious, so I double click on it.

The file is password protected.

Oh, Mariam, you wily little minx, you really appreciate confidentiality, don't you?

I try claire44. It doesn't work, and I'm not prepared to go through further combinations in the hope that I find the right one just to satisfy a mild curiosity. Besides, I can already imagine what kind of nonsense it says.

I return to the emails. There is nothing suspicious. Nothing wrong. Nothing at all bizarre.

I open the internet browser. Look through the favourites. There is a link to an email inbox. It is for a Google Mail account.

I return to your emails in Outlook. This is a Yahoo Mail account.

You have another email account that you've chosen to keep away from your mailbox... Why on earth would you do that... Unless you wished to keep the contents discreet?

I open the email inbox.

The username for this email address is a combination of letters: j7rkfhk923490—nothing coherent that someone might guess. This is intentionally done—you are wishing to ensure the email address cannot be linked back to you. I even check what name you send your emails under: it is *Penelope Smith*. That is not your name, Mariam, oh no it is not.

The account only communicates with one recipient. Another jumbled email address, with the name *Kurt Salamander*. I have no doubt that is not Kurt's real name.

I open an email at random.

The content of the email reads as so:

Name: Clyde Wilcox.

Age: 40.

Family: Wife Lynda Wilcox (41), two daughters Kayleigh (7) and Sharon (15).

Malady: Compulsive sex prompts multiple marital affairs.

. . .

I remember this guy. Clyde was in the group meeting with us, and this was what he was telling us about.

Turns out you don't appreciate confidentiality at all, you little rascal.

There are multiple attachments to this email. I open a few. They are session notes.

Kurt Salamander has replied. There is no text in his emails, but there are pictures of Clyde with a woman. And another picture with another woman. And another.

Mariam, I cannot believe you.

You are a renowned sex therapist with a worldwide reputation and published work. You charge extortionate amounts for your services, then you earn more on the side.

You are conning these people, Mariam.

You are learning their deepest darkest secrets, then using it to blackmail your clients.

I can't help but laugh. Actually, it's more of a cackle. I feel like a villain in an action movie, chortling as my plans come together.

I look at more emails and their attachments, and holy moly, she isn't just giving information about her clients—she's fucking them. There is a video of her, on the very chair I sit on, straddling a man, grunting with a poorly faked orgasm as the webcam picks her up. I assume she couldn't get the evidence she needed on these particular clients, so this is what she resorts to; this is how she cons them.

The clip clop of high heels echo down the corridor, and I wait, feeling giddy. They slow down as they approach the broken door. I sit back in the chair and grin.

Mariam enters. Slowly. She sees me and is overtaken with rage.

"What the hell are you doing here?" she demands.

I just grin, wide and gleeful.

"Get off my computer!" she insists.

"Now, now," I tell her. "Considering what I've discovered, I'm not sure you're in the position to be giving any demands, are you?"

She goes to speak but doesn't. She's stumped. She's figuring out how to play this, but she doesn't have a clue.

"Why don't you have a seat," I tell her. "We have so much to talk about."

CHAPTER TWENTY-ONE

SHE SITS on the edge of the seat her clients would normally sit in. Tentative, cautious.

"What do you want?" she asks. "Money?"

"I have plenty of money."

"So what is it then? Gloating? I know things about you too, you know."

"What, that I only get turned on by corpses? I made that shit up, you dumb whore."

I kinda made it up; I can still get turned on by living women as well.

"Then what do you want?"

"I dunno. Maybe to see what the press thinks of this."

"No, please…"

I raise my eyebrows.

"It would ruin me," she insists. "I have a family. A life. A house. I'm a foster parent, I help a child with PTSD." I laugh. "This would destroy all of that."

"And remind me why I'm supposed to care?"

I can see tears. She's become emotional far quicker than I expected. "Please…"

She holds my gaze, beseeching me with her eyes. They are

wide, wearisome eyes, but they are far from innocent. Flora's eyes are child's eyes—these are experienced eyes, full of damage and regret.

"Let's take a drive," I say, walking toward the door.

"A drive? I don't want to go for a drive."

"I don't think you have a choice."

"So if I go for a drive with you, is that it?"

I pause in the doorway. She stands, edging toward me but keeping her distance.

"Let's put it this way," I say. "If you do everything I say for the next few hours, I won't tell anyone."

"Really?"

"Yes."

"So what is it you want me to do?"

"We start with a drive."

I stride down the corridor. I don't look back to see if she's following. Of course she is. There's too much on the line. In fact, I don't look at her until she's climbing into the passenger seat of my car next to me.

I turn on the ignition. The Mercedes revs into life. It's a beautiful car. It purrs like a cat. I grin at Mariam, waiting for a compliment over the vehicle. I don't get one. She just sits there, staring at me with forced innocence, tears moistening her cheeks, her hands on her lap, her body retracting in on herself. She's so self-involved.

"I've never seen you like this," I say as I drive. "You always walk around with such confidence. You hold yourself with such grace. Let me ask you something—do you actually believe in all this spiritual bullshit you preach?"

"Yes, of course."

"It's not part of an act?"

"No."

"And you're a vegan?"

"Yes."

I tut. Shake my head. "But it's natural. It's the order of

things. We fuck, we kill, we eat. It's what we are. Why do you deny that?"

"I just don't think we should own animals."

I slam my fist against the dashboard. It makes her entire body jolt. "It's not about ownership! We don't fucking own anything, we just think we do, nature has no ownership, but it has entitlement, and we are entitled to feed on the weak, and that means animals are food. If a lion saw us, we'd be weak. It's all crap, and you know it."

She says nothing. She still stares at me. Like she's waiting for me to suddenly announce I'm letting her go. There is hope behind the pain in her eyes. It's pissing me off.

"Say it," I tell her.

"Say what?"

"That you know all this vegan stuff is crap."

"Would it help you if I said it?"

"What the fuck do you mean, would it help me? What is this fucking psychobabble? I just want you to say it."

"Fine. It's crap."

"Mean it."

"I... it's crap."

She doesn't mean it. And she's trying to use her psychology tricks on me. I hate her even more. My arms are shaking, they are actually shaking, that's how gripped with rage I am, and I remind myself that I am not supposed to kill her yet.

"What are you going to make me do?" she asks.

"I don't know, Mariam. How far are you prepared to go to make sure no one hears about what you've been up to?"

She looks down. The first time she isn't staring at me. She shakes her head. Sniffs. She's crying again. Fuck me, does she ever stop? I don't get it. What does crying do? It serves no purpose. What, is it supposed to purge emotions? Because anyone who I've seen cry gets more emotional, not less. I don't get how bits of water coming out of your eyes are supposed to give you any kind of advantage in anything.

"I guess I'd be prepared to go quite far," she admits, her voice weak and quiet.

"Quite far?"

"If it's sex you want… Then… I'll do it, if I have to…"

"Sex? Well, that's a start."

I pull into an industrial estate. Only a few of the warehouses are operational, and most of them are empty as the working day has ended. I pull the car up outside a vacant warehouse.

"Get out," I tell her.

I collect a bag from the boot and march into the warehouse. She follows, taking tiny steps, fiddling with her fingers, her head dropped.

The warehouse itself is quite large. The vast open space is perfect. The floor is dusty, and it smells like damp. There are a few windows high above us, and some of them are smashed. Most of them are grey, covered in streaks of dirt. Mould grows on the walls. This place hasn't been used in a long time.

There are a few broken plastic chairs in the corner. I take one, place it in front of the far wall, and put my bag beside it. I sit on it and turn to Mariam, who fidgets at the entrance.

"Well?" I say.

She edges forward, so slowly it's annoying, until she's stood beside me.

"There," I tell her, pointing at the space between myself and the wall. She moves into it, standing like a child summoned to the front of the class to be punished. There is little I love more than watching a woman who claims to be strong and independent being brought down to a quivering wreck—we all show our weakness eventually, no matter how much we try to pretend we are strong.

"Take off your clothes," I tell her.

"Is that it? Once I take off my clothes, will you—"

I lurch to my feet and strike my fist into the side of her head. She retracts, covering her hair, turning away from me.

I sit back down again.

She looks back at me with more ugly tears on her cheeks.

"Once I give you the instruction, you carry out the instruction."

She vaguely nods. Puts her hands at the bottom of her stupid hippy top and lifts it over her head. It's hardly much of a sexy striptease, but I'd rather watch her suffer than get her to dance. She unhooks her skirt and lets it drop to her feet. She wears white pants and a black bra. Pubic hair pokes out from beneath her knickers. I can't help but laugh. I'd have thought a sex therapist would know how to make herself a bit more enticing.

She puts her arms around her body and looks at me expectantly. As if I want her to stop there.

"Continue."

She unhooks her bra and lets it drop, then slides her knickers to the floor. She has a slight podge in her belly—one that you'd expect from a woman her age who's had children. There is a stretch mark on her belly. Her thighs are large and rub against each other, but curve enough to keep me satisfied. Her breasts are large and sag a little, but not too much—she would be perfect for the *milf* category on any porn site.

"Are you going to have sex with me now?" she asks, her voice so quiet I can barely hear her.

"Turn around," I tell her.

She nods reluctantly, as if coming to terms with being fucked from behind, and turns around.

Spots lead across her buttocks to her arsehole, which sprouts a few hairs. No wonder her husband prefers cock.

I do not fuck her from behind, however. I can afford the most glorious whores in the world; I do not need to settle for such a woman.

Instead, I take a pair of handcuffs out of my bag. I place one around her right wrist.

"What are you doing?"

I smile at her. "Shut up, Mariam."

I put the handcuff around a pipe that runs across the wall above her head, then I fasten it around her left wrist.

I stand back and marvel at my work. I really enjoy what I do. I know you probably think this is sick and wrong and twisted and yada yada yada, but, honestly, don't knock it until you try it. I mean it. If you didn't deny your nature so vehemently, you'd probably have quite a good time. And don't give me that crap about *oh but I'll get caught*—I've already told you in chapter one how to get away with it. There's no excuse, really, unless you enjoy being one of the deplorable members of society who pretend they've never had a violent thought, and those people are the fucking worst. Don't be the worst, reader, please don't.

I open the bag. I take out a paddle. It's long and thick and wooden. I clutch the handle in my right hand. The instrument still retains flickers of crusted blood from a woman I abducted a few years ago.

"What are you doing?" she asks, looking over her shoulder. She sees the paddle and her eyes widen. "Please, no! Just fuck me, it's fine, I won't try to stop you, but not the paddle, not the–"

I strike her back with it. The impact with her flesh makes a beautiful sound that reverberates around the vast open space. Quite wonderfully, it's also made her shut up.

I strike again, aiming at the mark I've just created. I hit most of it.

I strike again, and her body flinches upon impact.

Another strike, and this time she shrieks as I do it. She tried to hold in her pain at first, I can tell, she didn't want to give me the satisfaction, but her skin is now burning and she cannot help it, and it's beautiful and miraculous and wonderful and exciting and I strike her again and it burns her some more and I love it.

Another strike and her skin tears again.

I step back. Pause for a moment.

"Please stop… Please stop…"

I take out my phone. Start the video recording. Rest it on the chair so it gets her entire body in.

"What are you doing? Are you recording me? Please, I'll cooperate, just don't–"

I strike her again and she cries out even harder, her agony filling the warehouse, her anguish making my dick tingle.

Her bare back reddens, disguising her pale flesh, and it's hard to tell where I've already hit her, so I just hit her anywhere and she doesn't stop shrieking, and her body won't stop shaking, and her fists can't stop clenching.

"Please! Please, just stop! I'll do anything."

I step toward her, until I'm over her shoulder, and I whisper into her ear, so close she feels my breath against her skin, "Spread your legs."

She spreads her legs. She's relieved. She thinks I'm just going to fuck her, and that the strikes will be over with.

Her body almost relaxes.

And that's when I launch the paddle against her dry, hairy cunt.

And oh, how she screams. Oh, how she hollers. Like the world is ending.

She closes her legs.

"Open them."

She shakes her head as she cries.

"I said open them."

"Please, no, just, no…"

"Open them or I tell everyone what you've done."

Her head drops and she weeps harder and she hesitates and reluctantly spreads her legs.

I strike again. And she screams. And I laugh. I just laugh and I laugh, and I can't seem to stop myself.

Another strike and the agony must be excruciating and it's just such a glorious sight.

I keep going until I lose track of time and I realise that her absence might end up raising her family's suspicion.

I uncuff her. Let her dress as I re-watch the video on the phone, then return to the car and drive back to her office. We stay in silence the whole time. She doesn't stare at me any longer—she watches the world go by out of the window, leaning forward so the seat doesn't make contact with her back, and keeping her legs open to ease the pain in her crotch.

I pull up beside her car.

"What are you going to tell your family about the marks?"

She doesn't look at me. "I'll think of something."

Silence.

"Can I go now?"

"I'm not stopping you."

She huffs, shoves the car door open, and she hobbles to her car, unable to walk properly.

Oh, my dear voyeurs, I really do love my life. It is, without doubt, quite fantastic, and I cannot wait to see what Flora does when she watches this video.

CHAPTER TWENTY-TWO

I REVEL IN MY GLORY, sitting across the street from Flora's window, in my car, playing the video over and over and over.

There are things I didn't notice the first time.

The way Mariam flinches upon each strike.

The way her body shakes harder the more it hurts.

The way she cries, and occasionally looks over her shoulder, as if to say something to me, as if to plead, to beg, before changing her mind and turning her tears back the other way.

And my laughter, so clear on the video, is echoed in the car.

It's just so very beautiful.

And this is what you miss out on, my dear reader, by fitting in with a world that condemns my actions!

Flora's bedroom light turns on. She's on her phone, sitting in her bay window. She seems to like it there. She curls up on the cushions and draws a blanket over her.

I open the anonymous email account. Draft a new message. Attach the video of Mariam and the most enticing paddle spanks I've ever experienced. Press send and wait for the inevitable reaction.

Her face doesn't change. She must still be scrolling down the same nonsense she's already scrolling down, articles about hair styles or teen quizzes to find out which celebrity she'd most like to fuck or something like that; I don't know what teenage girls like.

Then she frowns. She's seen it, I can tell. She taps the screen with her thumb, then watches. Her frown deepens, forming lines on her forehead.

The video lasts eight minutes and thirty-two seconds, and I time her so I will know when she's finished watching it. When it finishes, she's still staring at the screen. She taps something and stares some more. She's watching it again. How strange. I expected her to be horrified, and instead she's curious. The look on her face says disgust, but also intrigue. I don't quite understand.

I time it for a second time and when the time is up, she doesn't move. Just sits there. Glaring intently at the screen. Locusts swarm around her mind, each another nasty thought.

She puts the phone down. Leans her head back. Stares at nothing. Appearing contemplative.

What are you doing, Flora? What are you doing?

I expected the reaction you gave me for Shane's video. I expected detestation, horror, repulsion, revulsion, abhorrence, disgust — yet you have a face of pondering. I have provoked thought, not terror.

I haven't even done my video with Claire yet. The murder of an eight-year-old girl was going to be the finale that prompted the last stage of your breakdown.

But where is your breakdown, Flora?

Where is it?

Where. The Hell. Is it.

I pick up the phone and watch the video again, trying to understand. It's horrific, you should be scared, you should be alarmed, you should be–

Ah.

I see it.

FUCK.

How could I be so bloody stupid?

SHIT.

You idiot, Gerald! You damn fool! You're no less idiotic than she is! (Well, no actually, that's not true, as that would be quite a leap, even so, I've been very careless.) This was NOT part of the plan!

FUCKING GODDAMIT!

And what's the problem, dear reader? What am I losing my shit about so immensely?

It's my face, that's what it is.

My unblemished, perfect face.

Visible, just for a second, about two-thirds through the video. Glancing at the camera from the corner of the screen.

I meant to send you a video of torment, and instead I sent you my confession.

And now you are turning away from the window, and walking further into the house, out of sight.

Oh, fuck.

I CONFESS

It's him.

I know that laugh. I know that body. I know that suit, that swagger, that cocky strut.

And I know that face.

You made a mistake, Gerald. You turned around and glanced at the camera, and you didn't realise it, and you let it go on, and you sent it to me, and now I know I'm not being irrational.

I watched it twice for clarification.

It's you.

Which means you've found me.

My entire body tenses, and my arms shake, and I can't do anything but stare. I thought there would be tears, but I'm beyond upset; I'm mortified, and I struggle to move.

You know where I am. You know who I am with. Which means you have seen me. Maybe even followed me.

Are you watching me right now?

You might be. You might not. I don't take the risk. I stare at the wall, aware that I might be in your gaze. If I do anything to give away that I know, if I give even one unexpected movement, then you might see me, and you might realise—I know you're here.

What gave me away?

Shut up, Flora, you can ask those questions later.

Let's just figure out what to do.

I stare. Stare and stare. My thoughts a mess, my heart racing, my leg bouncing, agitated, nervous, scared.

You must be plotting something. You must be seething over what I did, planning something for me that's worse than death, and that must be the only reason I'm still alive.

I swivel around and place my feet on the carpet. I don't move quickly, not wanting to show any prying eyes that I am acting with urgency.

I step away from the window.

I walk downstairs and into the living room. Mariam and Shane watch television; a show where contestants are competing to bake something. I tell them I need to talk. They mute the television. They tell me to sit down. I don't.

I say I have something to confess.

And I tell them they must confess too.

And I tell them everything.

Gerald. Mum. Life with them. Being fucked. Being used. Being abducted. Being tied up. Hiding the corkscrew. Escaping.

I explain the trauma that I have yet to fully understand.

They sit with their jaws hanging low, and silence fills the space between us for so long that I can't stand it, so I fill it by confessing more. I confess what I've seen. And I show them the videos. And they watch them. Starting with Shane.

Mariam doesn't react. She watches coldly, her face stern, as if she expected it. Shane looks away. He cannot watch. He's not angry, he's disappointed. That's even worse.

Silence lingers after. Mariam is angry, I can tell, but it's not over.

I show them Mariam's video.

And the silence continues.

Until I tell them they need to confess.

Shane breaks the silence. He tells us he's bisexual. That he's been hooking up with men for months. That he's addicted to it. That he can't help it. That he needs help. He asks for Mariam's forgiveness.

Mariam says that he doesn't need her forgiveness—not until he's heard what she has to say.

And she confesses. Conning people. Blackmailing people. Fucking clients to force money out of them. She says that he was following his libido while she was following her ill intentions. Now she asks him for forgiveness.

And they hug. And we hug. And we cry. And we stay like this until I must ask the question I'm dreading to ask.

What do we do about Gerald?

Should we go to the police?

They look at each other. Then look at me.

They ask if I want to go to the police.

I say no. I say it will get worse. I say that any evidence is gone now and he's rich and it will just intensify the pain.

They say that I can go to the police if I wish, but that Mariam would be arrested and charged—that Gerald would hand over his evidence against her and she would be condemned to prison.

But there is still a problem.

Gerald is not going away. He will kill us. And he will torture us.

And then there is silence again.

It lasts a while. The television screen flickers in the background. Presenters conclude the program, end credits roll, and adverts follow, first for car insurance then Viagra then tampons.

It is Mariam who finally makes her suggestion.

She confesses she wants revenge. For what he did to her. To her husband. To her foster daughter. That she needs to make sure he stays silent. That she needs to make sure he doesn't attack, and that I am safe.

Shane is too nice. He is a gentle person. Too kind. Too sensitive.

Mariam is ruthless.

And she is the one who makes the suggestion.

And it is I who agrees.

And it is Shane who reluctantly nods.

And it is at that point that I pick up my phone, and I open my text messages, and we begin our own plan.

Claire sleeps soundly upstairs, a peaceful child in a silent slumber, unaware of what those she loves are about to do to another human being.

Liam?

Are you there?

I'm here

How is Ava doing?

Ava is fine

How are you?

I need to talk

What's up

I know

You know?

iMessage

You know what?

I just know

What, did Ava tell you?

She sucked me off

it's no big deal

Ava didn't suck you off

Er yes she did

No she didn't

She would never touch you

And how do you know

 iMessage

Because this isn't liam

Huh?

I know this is you

I know you sent me the videos

I know you're here

I know who this is

What videos?

What are you talking about?

Stop it now

iMessage

I know

Gerald

I know

Gerald?

Yes

Now do you want to stop this act

Or are you going to keep denying it

Hmmmmmmm

Was it my face in the video?

 iMessage

Yes

How disappointing

This needs to end

I want to meet

Ive had enough

You want to meet, do you?

How interesting

How so very unexpected

Yes

Gerald

iMessage

I do

I want to meet

Are you going to meet

Or are you going to carry on with your sick games

Fine

Let's meet

Shall I bring the corkscrew or should you

Fuckkkkk you

You little slut

 iMessage   🎤

Fuck you

Why couldn't you have left me alone

I was doing fine

I didn't say anything to anyone

You could have just left me alone

Why didn't you?

Did you say you wished to meet?

Or did you just want to have a boring little breakdown?

 iMessage 🎤

Yes I want to meet

Fine

Where?

When?

There's a café on Sanders Street

9am

And what exactly do you think is going to happen when we meet?

This is not going to go well for you

You just take care of yourself

 iMessage

You sick man

I hate you so much

Oh, Flora, please stop

It is not becoming of you to be so crass

And these are all things we can discuss in the morning

Fine

I do hope you have a good night's sleep tonight

You're going to need it

You really are

iMessage

CHAPTER TWENTY-THREE

IT IS AT THIS POINT, dear reader, my ever-present voyeur, that we should perhaps pause for breath.

Not for myself, but for you—I imagine this is quite full on for someone not used to witnessing such violent escapades. First Ava, then Mariam. If you are not at least a little perturbed, then I would be most surprised. The most I imagine you've endured is mild teasing whilst tied up, or a little light consensual spanking. Paddle-beating and skull-fucking and screwdrivers in cunts may just be a little too much for someone so restrained—for someone who so vehemently denies their nature.

And, before you say, *oh no, I don't deny my nature*, or *I don't want to do those things*, or *I could never hurt someone*, I would kindly tell you you're full of shit. Unless you are reading this from the confines of a prison cell, or unless you are hiding a very big secret, then you undoubtedly deny your nature.

Speaking of which, I have been meaning to ask you—why is it you deny it, out of curiosity?

Not that you can reply. This is a book and does not lend itself to a two-way dialogue. Besides, the last thing I want is to listen to your repugnant, misinformed opinion. I honestly don't give much of a shit about your answer—it would be wrong, anyway.

But, since I have you here, let *me* tell *you* why you deny your nature—and in turn I will inform you of the reason you are so bloody miserable.

Because, as I have repeatedly rammed down your throat (so much even I am finding it tiresome), you have been conditioned by a society who cannot cope with someone different from their expectations. Your need for conformity and the overwhelming power of conditioning one's beliefs in childhood are the most essential factors in determining your view of life, and your view of right and wrong.

Right and wrong.

HAH!

It is a concept that only repressed humans could ever be so foolish to create. And, once you liberate yourself of such concepts, you will see how free it makes you. You could be *you,* but a better *you,* and there would be no reason to conform to these bizarre moralistic concepts. A tiger never asks its prey if it's okay that he eats it; a monkey never asks another monkey if it's okay to fuck; and a wonderful specimen like myself never cares about what the world around him would have to say about his actions. When you cease considering what is right or wrong, you cease wondering whether you should or shouldn't do something, and you cease overthinking every decision. You don't worry, you just live.

Isn't that a lovely proposition?

No more ruminating or painful reflecting or losing sleep as you replay moments from your past.

You just accept that things happened as they did, and you behaved as your instinct told you, and that it happened in that way and there is no need to ponder on it any further.

But instead, you call me a psychopath. Why? Because it's the only way you can understand me—categorising me in such a way comforts you. It convinces you I am *different*. But I am not *different*. We are all brutal murderers, it's just that most of us don't release our bodies from the prison of restraint.

But the most painful part of this, my dear reader? The most excruciating, frustrating, annoying thought that seems most prevalent?

You. Still. Won't. Change.

You. Will. Still. Condemn. Me. And. My. Actions.

You. Will. Still. Continue. To. Be. Miserable.

Sure, you'll have moments. You'll read a self-help book and it will give you a new idea that you'll have forgotten by tomorrow, a new way of looking at things that doesn't make your life any better but makes it a little less painful. But it's fleeting. It's not permanent. It is never permanent because you are not being you.

You are being everyone's expectation of you.

I mean, there's no such thing as *you* anyway. Not in a literal sense, as you clearly exist, but in a metaphysical sense. You show a different side of yourself to your friends, to your boss, to your parents, to your partner (assuming you've found an insufferable wretch as insufferable as you, thus allowing you to suffer each other together). Let me ask you— which of these is the real you?

Again, I couldn't care less about your reply. I'm going to tell you the answer.

You are all of them and none of them.

Because your personality is interchangeable. Therefore, it does not exist. When describing your personality to others, you may articulate some of the traits that you perceive in yourself, as if these aspects are unique to you; but they are not. Oh, you wear your heart on your sleeve, yet often find it hard to express yourself? You have big ambitions such as writing a book or doing an art project, but find that life gets in the way? You have a soft inner core and a hard outer shell? You struggle to let people in, but when they are in, you are loyal to them? You find yourself feeling insecure with people you don't know very well? SO DOES EVERYONE. These are cold-reading statements. It's how psychics convince everyone of their bullshit. They are just generic statements that sound specific, yet apply to most idiots. None of these define your personality; they define everyone's.

So this begs the question: then who actually are you?

You are an animal.

If you've ever had a pet dog, you might notice that they cuddle you, love you, lick you—yet when you try to take food from them, they might bite you, or growl at you. Why? Because they can't deny their instincts; they cannot refute what they really are.

You can treat women with respect and stop making inappropriate comments in the office and stop staring at Sandra's tits. Doesn't mean you don't want to push her face into the floor as you fuck her from behind. Doesn't mean you'll be able to stop yourself from picturing it. You'll still stare at her tits, you'll just be more subtle about it.

You have three motivations: To eat. To fuck. To kill.

It is who you are. It is who I am. It is who we all are.

And, whilst this rant may be for you, it is for me as well.

I need to remember what I am.

So I can make sure that, when Flora walks through the door of that café, I am not swayed by her words, not manipulated by her deception. That I remember what I want from her.

I want to mutilate her. Then fuck her. Then kill her.

I want revenge.

I want it now. I want it so much that I can barely keep myself still. I want it so much that it makes my belly ache and my legs bounce and my arms shake and my brow sweat and my dick harden.

I had a plan.

Fuck that plan.

Everything changes now.

It's time for me to destroy that slutty little mind-fuck.

And now, as it is 8.59 a.m., I am afraid I must adjourn this life lesson I have imparted on you, dear reader. I have a prior engagement.

And shit is about to kick off.

CHAPTER TWENTY-FOUR

THE CAFÉ IS cheap and tacky, but I shouldn't have expected anything less. The plastic seat creaks with my every movement, the table is laminated, the menu is stained, the coffee tastes like grit, and the large window that takes up most of the wall does not reveal to me a beautiful view of hills or cityscape, but a shitty car park through which a hobo crosses, pausing to piss behind a bin.

The ambience of the place is just as detestable. Out-of-date pop music plays through a low-quality stereo, and children's shouts and moans are the only noise to overpower the tuneless melodies of one-hit wonders. My pristine leather shoes stick to the floor, and I hate this place so much that I almost think Flora chose it intentionally.

Even the waitress is dumpy. I'm used to young women with good skin and long hair and a happy disposition. This woman looks like she's named Gurt or Bertrude, her ankle fat spills over the top of her white trainers, and the apron that resides over her large belly is full of stains that I struggle to decipher.

"Can I get you any food?" she asks, then leans her weight onto one foot, tapping her pen expectantly against her pad.

I glance at the menu. I would like some waffles, but I'm worried about the hygiene standards in the kitchen.

"No. Not yet. Just coffee."

She huffs and struts away, then returns a few seconds later with a cheap mug of shitty black liquid. If I was not preoccupied with bigger things, I would smash her head to pieces with a sledgehammer for the impudence.

I watch the door, waiting for Flora. Every time someone enters the café, the bell over the door rings, and I don't understand the point of such an irritating noise. I observe another family enter, growing increasingly irritated that Flora is yet to arrive.

She's late.

Maybe she's not coming. Maybe it's a trick. Maybe police are mobilising right now, creating a perimeter, preparing to strike.

But the odds are in my favour. Yes, I may go to prison, but so would Mariam. I have enough on her to send her away for years. I doubt they would risk it.

I gaze out the window, ignoring the stains and smudges smeared across the glass. Across the street, a bus pulls up. A minute or so later, it departs, and a young, recognisable figure stands at the bus stop.

I'm unable to help a grin forming. What a wonderful day this is!

She looks both ways as she crosses the road, then strides across the car park. She walks uneasily, and her expression appears uncomfortable. She sees me through the window. I raise a hand, greeting her like an old friend, ensuring she sees my smirk. She doesn't respond. Just looks at me, then makes the doorbell ring as she enters.

Today, she is dressed differently to how she's dressed since I've been watching her. She always covers up, wearing t-shirts to avoid cleavage, wearing long shorts to cover her thighs, wearing jumpers so no one will notice the shape of her body. Not today. Today, she is wearing a vest, revealing a line between her small, perky breasts. She wears a skirt, short and flowy, and no tights, displaying her legs. They are smooth, and I am positive they have just been recently shaved.

I know why she's doing this.

She's using her sexuality. Honestly, it's the only weapon a woman has, and she's trying to take advantage of it. She knows about my high libido; she knows which parts of her body drive me crazy; and she knows how, despite everything, I would be quite keen to grab her by the hair and fuck her over this table.

She doesn't make eye contact with me as she enters. The waitress intercepts her as she approaches the table, and Flora orders a coffee as she sits down. She rests her chin on her fist and still doesn't look at me.

I am not so restrained. I can't help but stare at her. Sure, I've been watching her from afar, but the last time we were this close she was impaling my penis on a corkscrew she'd inserted inside her vaginal canal. Being in her presence is both invigorating and infuriating. It is glorious and terrible. It is magical and beautiful and rotten and sick.

She looks out of the window, and silence sits between us, settling like a third party to our meeting. I don't find silences awkward, though I know other people do. Flora doesn't seem bothered. She's happy looking anywhere but at my prying eyes.

The waitress brings her a coffee, and Flora thanks her, always so polite, despite the aggravated nature of this woman's demeanour. She asks Flora if she would like some food. Before Flora can reply, I answer for both of us.

"We'd like a plate of waffles," I say. "Each. With cream and chocolate sauce."

She writes something down on her pad, as if such an order is too difficult to simply remember, then walks away.

I continue to watch Flora, refusing to be the one to break the silence.

Eventually, she speaks.

"So how did you find me?" she asks, still staring out the window, still unable to shake my eager gaze.

"Hired a private investigator."

"Where?"

"The dark web."

"How much did he cost?"

"A lot."

"And how long did it take him?"

"A week."

"And what did he tell you?"

"Everything."

She shakes her head. She crumples the napkin in her fist, then huffs, gritting her teeth.

"He gave me pictures of you pushing your foster sister at the park. Pictures of your friend's social media accounts. Details of your therapist. Location. School. I knew exactly where to look." I reach a hand across the table and place it on hers. She flinches her hand away. "I will always find you, Flora."

"And my foster parents? You just had to involve them?"

"Naturally."

"You couldn't have just gone after me? You had to go after them?"

"Yes."

"At least you spared Claire, I guess."

"On the contrary, she would have been next."

She rips the napkin apart, then realises what she's doing, and sits back, trying to disguise her blatant agitation by curling her lip and folding her arms.

"I didn't know you enjoyed having men suck your cock," she says.

"I don't."

"So what was all that with Shane?"

"A means to an end."

"And Liam? Ava?"

"Yes?"

"What happened to them?"

"They are gone."

"And their bodies?"

"Gone, too."

"Why?"

"For you, Flora. It's all for you."

She shakes her head, a little at first, then it gets more vigorous. Her leg is bouncing. Her fingers dig into the bare skin of her arms. Her eyes are red and she's holding back tears.

"You didn't have to kill them," she says, and there is crying in her voice that she quickly attempts to disguise.

"Of course I did."

"You didn't. You were after me."

"It was all part of it. It was all because of you."

Now she turns and looks at me, and oh boy, the fury in her eyes, I tell you—hell truly hath no fury like a woman scorned as fuck. There is rage and there is pain and there is hate, and it's all there in her pupils, all there in the intense glare she finally directs my way.

She goes to speak again, but is interrupted by the arrival of our waffles. The waitress dumps them on our table like she's emptying the contents of a bin. She places cutlery down, wrapped in a cheap napkin, then stomps away without so much as a word.

Flora doesn't move. Her arms remain folded, her glare remains set on me, and the hatred intensifies.

I unwrap the cutlery. Cut off the corner of the waffle. Smother it in the chocolate sauce, scoop a bit of cream on top of it with the knife, then place it in my mouth.

It tastes shit, but I'm not eating for pleasure. I'm eating

because I know it will annoy her, and I hold her gaze and purposefully eat with my mouth open, allowing the slopping sounds to repulse her, to spark her animosity.

I want her angry; I want her full of rage; I want her hating me so much that she cannot think straight.

"You should really eat your waffles," I tell her. "You'll need your energy."

She shakes her head at me, like a headmaster telling off a wayward pupil. It's both patronising and hilarious.

"Why couldn't you have just left me alone?" she asks, her voice soft yet angry; honestly, she sounds a little demented. "I left you alone. I didn't go to the police, I didn't tell my foster parents, I didn't even tell my trauma therapist the truth—why couldn't you have held onto your side of the deal? Why couldn't we have just lived in peace, without needing to care about what the other is up to?"

"You seem to forget something."

"Oh, and what's that?"

I place another large scoop of waffle into my mouth and talk as I eat it. "You fucked up my dick. I had to pay a shit-load of money to get it fixed."

"Since when do you care about how much something costs?"

"I don't."

"Exactly, you don't. It isn't about money, it isn't even about what I did to you—it's about ego. I insulted your male pride, and you couldn't take it."

"Typical feminist, assuming our greatest fallacy is our self-image, and that the same doesn't apply to you."

"What are you on about?"

"You hurt me, Flora."

"And you hurt me! What about all those times you made me think it was love? All the time you kept me prisoner? All those times you raped me?"

She's getting a little aggressive, and people are aiming a

few cautious glances in our direction. Even so, I can't help but chuckle.

"I didn't rape you," I say.

"Excuse me?"

"You wanted it."

"I don't remember you asking for my consent."

"No one asks for consent—no fucking woman is turned on by a bloke stopping and asking if he has consent. It's implied."

"I don't remember implying it."

"Is that so?"

"You just took it."

"You know what, Flora, I don't give a shit. You were mine, and I took what was mine, and you thought you could get away from this."

She looks at my right hand and raises her eyebrows. I realise I am gesticulating toward her with the knife. People are turning to look, and I swear if they do not stop, I will jab this fork into every fucking eye that dares to look in our direction.

"What you going to do, Gerald? Are you going to kill me here?"

"Kill you?" I chuckle, and cut up another piece of waffle, not caring for how much force I place on the cutlery; so what if I scratch the plate, it's cheap as fuck and I don't care. "By the time I'm done, you'll be begging for me to just kill you."

She says nothing else. I finish the waffle, cutting each piece with force, chewing every mouthful with my eyes locked on hers, until I slam the cutlery down on the plate, push it away, and lean back. It was disgusting, but I was hungry. I take a swig of the coffee and struggle to understand how someone could get coffee so wrong. It's ground coffee beans, not dirt and shit, and I don't understand how it can taste so foul.

"So what now?" Flora asks.

I lean back, my arm draped over the chair next to me. There is a yellow stain on the back of it I avoid.

"What do you mean, what now?" I retort, willing myself to calm down.

"Where do we go from here?"

"Home."

"Home? Back to your mansion to put me in chains?"

"Something like that, yeah."

"And if I say no?"

I raise my eyebrows and lift my shoulders to convey the vast range of possibilities.

She looks down at her lap, then lifts her head again, returning her glare to mine.

"You're never going to stop, are you?"

"What are you on about?" I'm growing tired of this.

"You're never going to stop coming after my friends. My family. If I don't go with you now, you'll just kill every single person I love, won't you?"

"Pretty much."

She sighs. "Then I guess I must come with you."

The waitress comes over to collect our plates. I give her a twenty quid note and tell her to keep the change. I don't want to tip her, but we seem to have reached a resolution, and I am keen to leave.

I stand. She stands too.

"So where to now?" she asks.

"My car."

And, with her arms folded, and her head bowed, she follows me out, trudging across the car park, ready to enter the last few days of her life and the agony that it will bring.

CHAPTER TWENTY-FIVE

I STRIDE across the car park, my hand on Flora's back to force her to keep up.

I have to say, she has come quite willingly. I was expecting more resistance, but she evidently realises that she is not in a position to negotiate. She wishes to save her foster family and friends from the same fate as Liam and Ava. It's honourable, but pathetic. Who's to say I won't just kill them after I'm done with her? It's not like I owe her any loyalty, or that we've made a deal. And even if we had, so what—it's hardly like I'm constrained by society's obsession with trust and morality. I can say what I like, do whatever I wish, and there is not a damn thing she can do about it.

I open the door to my Mercedes for her.

"I assume you're not just going to run away as soon as I go to the driver's side?"

"And let you kill everyone I care about?"

I chuckle. "Poor child. There's no one that cares about you."

I indicate for her to get in. She climbs into the passenger seat. She stares straight ahead as I shut the door.

I get into the driver's seat and, just as she promised, she

has not tried to flee. She's right, of course—what would be the point? If she's trying to be all noble and save her foster family and that fat girl and nerdy girl she hangs around with, then running would hardly do her any good at this stage.

I drive away, leaving the car park and joining a dual carriageway. I stay on this for some time, and she remains stubborn with her averted gaze.

"You are a silly girl," I tell her.

She keeps staring out the window, leaning her chin on her fist as she watches the world go by.

"I offered you everything. A mansion to live in, money to spend, a dick to suck. And you gave it all up for, what, this? A life with a closeted primary school teacher and a corrupt sex therapist? Who would choose that?"

Without turning her head, she says, "I would rather be a gutter rat than your slave."

"Slave? You didn't have to be my slave. You could have been my queen!"

"A queen? Do you know what kings do to their queens?"

"They treat them like royalty. You'd be my Ann Boleyn."

"Ann Boleyn's king charged her with adultery, incest and treason then chopped her head off."

I snort back a laugh. "I thought you were doing drama at school, not history."

"Do you know what? It would make sense that you'd choose Ann Boleyn. You're a lot like Henry VIII in a way—narcissistic, egotistic, foolish, deluded—"

I slam on the brakes, bringing the car to a screeching halt, and cars behind us swerve to avoid us. I grab her chin, squeeze hard, and turn her face toward mine.

"Never, ever called me *deluded.* I am *not* deluded. I can see the world clearer than anyone else on this planet. It is the other seven billion fools who are deluded, thinking this is the life they must live—not me. *Never* me."

She frowns. She's holding back words, I can tell. She

wants to spit at me, tell me to fuck off, tell me I'm a piece of shit. She wants to unleash a tirade of insults that she knows will only make her suffering worse.

But she remains silent. Trying to be the calm, rational one, but forever being the mistaken hypocrite who can't tell her arse from her elbow.

I release her face, and I ignore the insufferable bastards honking their horns at me as they divert their cars into the fast lane to avoid a collision, and I press down on the accelerator again. We gain speed quickly—it's a bloody fast car—and we endure the next period of the journey in silence.

Eventually, I get off the dual carriageway and navigate to a country road. I prefer these roads. There are barely any other cars, and we are lost amongst the countryside. The air is different here. It's fresh. It isn't stained by the breath of ingrates.

My legs do start to cramp, however. They seem closer to my body than they normally are. I realise my seat is a little further forward than I normally have it—I usually arrange it all the way back, and it's strange that it is so far forward.

I go to move it back, but it won't budge.

Flora turns to look at me.

I try to move it back again, but it still won't reverse. There's something in the way, in the foot space of the backseat. I don't understand why, as I haven't put anything there.

It is at this moment of confusion, dear reader, that Flora leans forward in a movement so abrupt I don't catch it, grabs the steering wheel, and directs the car toward a tree. I shout something at her, and twist the steering wheel back, but there is movement behind me, and there is a figure in the backseat, and I see Shane's eyes in the rear-view mirror, then there is a rag over my nose and mouth.

We crash into the tree and the airbag goes off and I'm dizzy.

The rag smells sweet, and a little like disinfectant.

It's chloroform.

I struggle to get away, but I'm already feeling faint, and they are holding the rag with force.

Oh, Gerald, you fucking idiot.

Of course she would not go with you. Of course she wouldn't make it this easy.

Of course you were being misled.

How stupid could I have been?

My eyes close, I pass out, and the last thing I see is Flora's cocky, triumphant smirk.

CHAPTER TWENTY-SIX

I AWAKE to see their smug faces beaming down on me.

I'm tied up in a basement—a cliché I thought only I was capable of—and I'm naked. I'm on a wooden chair and splinters dig into my right buttock. My arms are bound behind me and tied to the chair with rope.

I try pulling on the rope, testing its strength. The rope is frayed; it is old, but only a little weak. The knots aren't as good as I can do—they wouldn't be, would they—but they are firm enough to stop an immediate escape.

"Well, well, well," I say, looking from one smug face to another. "I'm glad we could all be together like this. Been a while since I've been part of a family."

Shane stands to my left. His arms are folded, and he has a stern expression, but it's impossible to appear intimidating in a tank top. I wonder if he ever wears anything other than that outfit, and I wonder if he realises that he looks like a nonce.

Mariam is to my right. She's a little fiercer. A proud resolve in her grimace. Her arms are folded over a long purple dress with a white diagonal pattern on it. The base of the dress ends in a combination of blue and brown flowers. She's such a fucking hippy that it makes me sick; someone needs to tell her that the sixties have been and gone, and her attempt at looking spiritual makes her look like a frumpy, out-dated hag.

Flora stands between them, echoing their folded arms. She has this determined look on her face, like an Olympian who's won a silver medal but still craves the gold. She's excited, even though she'll tell herself this is a duty, not entertainment, but I recognise the look of anticipation; I've worn it myself many times.

"So what are we doing here, then?" I ask. "You all just going to stare at me naked or what?"

Flora looks down, her eyes descending to my penis. She grins. I feel rage glower inside of me. She knows what my penis looked like before the corkscrew incident, so she knows how different it is now. There is a scar running down its edge, and another one along its rim. The urethral opening is a little bigger than it should be, having had the twisting worm of the corkscrew down it, and it's still bright red despite all the time that's passed.

There is nothing wrong with my penis, I must insist—but it is not the repairs to the mangling she caused that amuses her; it is the fact that I had to have them. It is the wounds she has left on my toxic male pride. It is that I had to have surgery, and that whilst the resulting outcome is still a splendid specimen, it's not what it once was.

"I am going to fucking kill you," I growl, unable to help it, aware I'm not in a position to make any threats, but unable to help doing so.

Flora's silence just angers me more.

I look around the room. Searching for ways out. Looking for how I can escape. It is a brick-walled basement, with a few boxes against the far wall. A few nails stick out of the wall, crooked and skewed, and I wonder whether I could reach one of them to cut myself loose.

I press my weight down on the wooden chair and feel it

creak. It moves back and forth, but only slightly. It is breakable, but it will take a bit of force to break it, and I'm going to have to be patient.

In short, for now, I am fucked.

"So, what are you going to do to me?"

I'm still met with silence, and it enrages me that these people are just standing there, staring at me, whilst I'm demeaned and annoyed and cold and *how fucking dare they!*

"What the fuck are you doing, just staring me to death?"

Still nothing. I'm shaking. My whole body is shaking. The anger grips me so hard and so furiously that I find it too hard to contain—but there is nothing I can do with it.

"Stop fucking staring at me!"

My voice echoes around the basement.

There are footsteps above. Child's footsteps. Patting across the wooden flooring above my head. A small voice calls out.

I grin, and I hope they see it.

"Claire," Shane whispers to Mariam. I don't know why he's whispering; I can still hear him. "I'll go."

Shane walks up the feeble wooden steps and, with a sneer at me over his shoulder, he leaves the basement to see to his child.

"Just the ladies then. Threesome?"

I wait for Flora to have a burst of aggression, to grab a weapon and charge at me with it, to hit me, to punish me, to do something to me—but she doesn't. She's too restrained. She doesn't recognise the sport in this, only the outcome she wishes to achieve.

"So what's going on? Because I haven't got all day, and I'd love to know what–"

"Shut up," Flora says. "You talk too much."

"Finally. It speaks. So what's the plan?"

Flora looks over her shoulder at Mariam. Mariam nods at her. Flora steps forward and places a foot on the edge of the chair, in front of my reformed junk. She leans forward on that leg, blocking the single light bulb hanging from the centre of the ceiling and covering me in her shadow. She's so cute when she tries to be scary.

"We're not handing you in, if that's what you're wondering," she says.

"Never thought you would. So what, you're going to tease me to death?"

"We will kill you. But not yet."

"Not yet? Are we going to make out first?"

"First, we're going to put you through what you put us through. I want to make sure you know what it's like to be one of your victims."

"Lovely. How are you going to do that, then?"

She doesn't reply. She walks to Mariam and they whisper something to each other. I can't tell what they are saying. Shane returns to the basement, and they both turn to him.

"Well?" he says.

"Would you like to go first?" Mariam asks.

Shane looks at me, then looks back at them. "Yeah."

And so it begins—my night of torture.

It's not at all as fun as it sounds.

CHAPTER TWENTY-SEVEN

SHANE BEGINS, and I can't help but laugh. I know he's going to attempt to unleash excruciating pain on me, but it looks more like he's going to tell me off for getting my finger painting on his shirt.

I mean, his mean face looks like a child's cartoon character, like his name should be PC Plod and he should be waving a baton at some overzealous character. The more he narrows his eyebrows and furrows his brow, the more my cackles turn into hysterics.

I know I'm naked.

I know I'm restrained.

I know I'm not getting out any time soon.

But this is fucking hilarious.

"What's so funny?" Shane says. "Huh, punk?"

I burst out a loud *HAH*, elongated and high-pitched—it sounds like he's trying to do a Clint Eastwood impression! What's next, DeNiro in Taxi Driver? Is he going to ask if I'm looking at him? Oh, God, I actually have tears in my eyes I'm laughing so much.

I make eye contact with Flora, who sits in the corner, and raise my eyebrows as if to say *you cannot be serious*. Mariam has gone upstairs to deal with the brat, or something like that —who the hell cares?—and it's a shame she isn't here to witness her silly little husband standing over me, trying to act like a terrible villain from a shit action movie—I thought they were going to torture me, not entertain me.

"Stop laughing," he says, and he stomps his foot, and I can see why he became a primary school teacher; every mannerism is like an overgrown five-year-old having a tantrum.

Then he shouts, "Stop it!" and he slaps me—I mean, he slaps me—not punch, not strike, nothing like that—he slaps me with an open palm, and I've had five-foot anorexic bitches slap me harder than that. Again, it's hilarious, and I can't help but laugh. In his head, it's like he's at the Oscars standing up for his wife over an inoffensive no-hair joke, whereas in reality he's like a child trying to stroke an adult's face.

"You are pathetic…" I grumble.

"Shut up."

"You know, you should tell me when the torture is going to start."

"Stop it."

"Because this is the cheapest night's entertainment I've ever had!"

"I said stop it."

"I mean, you are one weak little boy, aren't you? No wonder Mariam fucks her clients for money."

He slaps me again. I guffaw. I need a drink; the laughing is making my throat go dry.

Shane looks over his shoulder at Flora. He says two simple words: "Get it."

Flora smiles, nods, and floats up the stairs, leaving us alone.

I shake my head, the laughter calming down, looking up at him with the clearest expression of *what are you doing you pansy* I can muster.

Flora returns a moment later with a bag, and something in it. Something large.

"What you got there?" I ask. "A glove to slap me with?"

"We told you," Shane says, reaching into that bag, "that we are going to do to you what you did to us."

"And what exactly are you going to—"

Holy shit.

That is the longest and thinnest cock I've ever seen.

I mean, I've seen dildos before, I've seen plenty—I've watched enough porn in my life, and once paid a whore to fuck another whore with a strap-on—but this… Even the most prolific back alley hooker wouldn't fit all of that up their vagina.

Shane smiles, enjoying my astonishment.

"You like?" he asks.

"Hey, whatever you want to get up to…"

He takes something else out of the bag. A washing peg. What the hell is that for?

"This is taking the piss now," I say, looking around. "I mean, I'm bored, are you—"

He marches toward me and puts the peg on my nose, so tight that I can no longer breathe through my nostrils.

"How many women have you done this to?" he asks.

"What, put a peg on their nose?" I retort, my voice sounding nasal.

"Not quite."

He brings the dildo toward my mouth. He's got to be kidding; it's as big as my throat. I turn my head away, and Flora appears behind me and holds me still, but she doesn't have enough strength, and she shouts for Mariam, and she comes down and she helps hold me still, and even though I can still wriggle a little, they manage to limit my movements enough to get the dildo between my lips. I try to close my mouth but, just as I have forced such a reaction from many sluts before, my inability to breathe forces my teeth to part and allows the prosthetic cock into my gob.

Though not all of it.

Just enough to reach my tonsils.

Shane pulls it out but leaves the tip by my teeth, and I try clamping down on it but it makes no difference, my teeth just scrape along the edge as he reinserts it, and inserts it again, penetrating my face with this ridiculous thing.

This is not torture. This is a farce. This is pathetic. What do they expect me to—

Oh fuck.

He goes a little too far, and it reaches the back of my throat, and the gagging reflex kicks in, and whilst Shane has a face of concentration, I can hear Flora and Mariam giggling behind me—it is a reflex they are apparently familiar with, and they know just how horrible it feels.

I want to object. I try speaking. It comes out muffled. Of course it does. But if a woman were to object to the presence of my cock in their mouth, I'd just stuff it in harder, and that is exactly what Shane does; he keeps going, keeps hitting the back of my throat, and I gag, and I feel vomit get ready to lurch up, and I protest but it's muffled and he shoves harder and I gag and he shoves it again and I can't help it, I can't, I puke, everywhere, but he doesn't take the dick out of my mouth and it spills over the edges and down my chin and down my throat and down my chest and onto my lap, until my penis is coated in thick lumps of regurgitated food.

I try to breathe, try to take in air, and surely they'll let me, they don't want me dead yet, and Shane takes the prosthetic out of my mouth for a second, enough for a breath, then he's plunging it back in again and I'm making the noise I've forced so many women to make and Flora is cackling and Mariam is giggling and I've done this to Flora over and over and she must be FUCKING LOVING THIS.

He shoves it harder and it penetrates me harder and I feel

sick again and I don't think there's much left to bring up, but there is, and bits of waffle spill out over the edge of the dick, along with blood and bile and liquid I can't decipher, and he finally takes the dick out of my mouth and I suck in air, wheezing on it, choking on it. He wipes the cock against my chest, smothering my skin in the last dregs of vomit.

Now it is *them* who laugh at *me*.

"Very good…" I grumble. "Very good… Do to me what I did to you… You fucking prick…"

"What? Me, a fucking prick?"

"What do you want, a medal?"

"No." Shane looks at his family. "I want lunch."

And they have lunch.

Mariam makes sandwiches and brings them down and they sit around an upturned box in the corner of the room, eating almond cheese in brown bread with salad on the side, and I am forced to watch them.

I feel a little sick, but mostly, I feel hungry. There is nothing left in my stomach; it's all over my stained body, drying, stiffening against my skin as I watch them play happy families, talking about future plans and what to see at the cinema this weekend and whether Flora has had any offers back from UCAS yet. All to shove it in my face. All to show that I have not damaged them beyond repair.

Just wait.

Just you all fucking wait.

I curtail the rage as much as I can. I am going to need to endure more before it's over. I glance at the nails sticking out of the far wall. I tug on the rope around my wrists. I feel the softness of the chair.

I'll get out of here, I swear it.

They won't be able to go as far as they want. They all have a conscience. They will struggle to kill me. I know they will.

Meanwhile, I must sit here in filth, feeling stickiness on my skin, wishing I was wearing one of my Armani suits, or scrubbing away the filth in a bathtub of hot water and restorative bath salts.

Once they've finished lunch, Mariam saunters toward me and bends over as patronisingly as she can, her hair dangling over my face. It's itchy.

"It's my turn now."

She turns around and collects something from the other side of the room.

It's a paddle.

I laugh. How predictable.

But it's not an ordinary paddle. The closer she gets, the bigger it becomes, and it's odd that a paddle is quite this long and quite this thick.

Is everything fucking bigger here?

I close my eyes. Clench my face. Grit my teeth. Wait for impact.

And wait.

And wait.

It doesn't come. So I open my eyes.

That's when she strikes me with it—when I'm least prepared, the insensitive slut.

She strikes it across my chest, and it's a sharp pain, like getting smacked with a tree branch, like a hot poker slapping my skin.

She strikes me again, and I go to cry out but refuse to release my voice. My skin is already splitting. Bruises appear on my pectorals. I'm not bothered about the marks; I hope that she scars me; I like scars—scars show character. It is how long I'm going to have to wait to get back at this bitch that troubles me the most.

She strikes me again. She doesn't wait for the pain to subside, or the swelling to lessen. She strikes me repeatedly, in the same spot, again and again until I cry out, unable to contain the anguish, and she laughs, finally getting the response she wants.

"All right! All right, I get it!"

"I don't think you do…"

"I hit you with the paddle, you hit me back, fine, we're done!"

"Done? You didn't just hit my torso…"

I frown, not quite understanding what she means. Then I realise. And my eyes widen. And the paddle strikes downwards this time, aimed at my most precious possession, squashing it against the chair, and it hurts far beyond what I expected, like there's something red and hot burning inside the shaft, and that's only the first thrash and it's already throbbing.

"Okay, okay, stop!"

She strikes again, and the pain intensifies, and it's shooting up and down my cock and I wonder if I'll ever be able to get an erection again.

"Please, stop!"

She strikes again. It's worse pain than I could ever convey to you in these wretched, paltry words.

"Please!"

"Oh my God," Flora says, chuckling. "He's begging… He's actually begging…"

And now my pride throbs too, my ego swelling under the strain of the humiliation, and I scowl at Mariam with the biggest scowl a face contorted with agony can muster.

"Stop…"

She strikes me again, and I worry I might pass out, and she strikes again, and now I do get a little groggy, my head lulling, my chin rolling against my shoulder.

And then she stops.

And finally—fucking finally — I hear her drop the paddle to the floor.

I go to thank her, but stop myself. I thank no one. But I appreciate it, I do, so much.

But it's not over. I hear snaps of metal. Clangs of a utensil.

They have all reached into the bag, and they are all stepping toward me, all with something behind their backs...

Snapping metal...

Over and over...

Tiny clangs...

"What is that..."

Please, no, don't let it be...

"No..."

Oh God...

"Keep them away from me!"

Flora takes hers from behind her back first, the twisting end of the corkscrew pointing toward me. The room seems to have gone dark but there's light on her face and her hands and she's grinning and I'm fighting it, but I feel it again, what it was like, the pain–

—I thrust inside of her, expecting pleasure, expecting a warm, tight canal of bliss, to find a searing discomfort fire up my urethra as the corkscrew embeds itself down my shaft—

"No, I—"

—then Mariam is holding one. Next to Flora. And so is Shane. And they are grinning so manically and so sadistically and their heads seem to have grown and their bodies seem to have grown and they are towering over me and all I can see is the damn corkscrews—

—those corkscrews—

—those corkscrews—

—those corkscrews—

—I feel the urge to run, but I can't, so I freeze, keeping my body stiff in the hope that staying still will somehow liberate me—

—then I am looking down at my body from above as they approach, watching myself whimper and weep, not caring how pathetic I look, only caring for what they are doing with those weapons those weapons those fucking weapons KEEP THEM THE FUCK AWAY FROM ME but they aren't THEY

KEEP COMING oh shit they keep coming and I'm waking up in hospital and there's a problem with my dick and I'm phoning private healthcare and they are operating and I'm awake for it as they won't give me anaesthetic and I don't know why and it's not even numb and they are attaching bits and sewing bits and my scrotum is covered in blood and it's everywhere and ohmygodwillIloseit, they tell me no, no, no, they'll recreate it if they have to, there will still be something there, there will still be something I can work with, I will get to fuck again but what if I don't what if I don't what if I don't, what if she's taken everything from me after I gave her the world—

—and I'm back in that field again—

—and I'm sliding myself inside of her, and she's up for it in a way that I don't even register as suspicious, and my penis moves between her labia and it's in slow motion, her eyes looking down at me, sultry and seductive, all an act, all a performance, and I'm entering her and this happened quickly yet now it's happening slowly, so slowly, and now it's quick again and I'm shoving myself inside of her and it's unbearable and the pain is shooting up and down and I'm back in the basement again—

—and they stand over me.

With corkscrews.

And my heart is racing too fast, and my breathing is too quick, I'm sweating, and I'm panting, and I'm wheezing, and it's all going fuzzy, and it's all disappearing, and they have won, and I have lost, and I am passing out.

I'm passing out.

I'm passing out.

I'm passing.

Out.

CHAPTER TWENTY-EIGHT

WHEN I AWAKE, I have no idea how long I've been out, whether it's minutes or hours, but I do know one thing—I had what a psychiatrist might refer to as a post-traumatic episode—and I am furious with myself for it.

How could I sink to the level of an ordinary human? How could I allow the fallacies of mankind to become my fallacies? How could I be as pathetic as you?

I do not suffer from such maladies. I am better than that. I am above it. And not only am I irritated with my own actions, I am FURIOUS with Flora and those abominable cretins for bringing out something within me that should NEVER have been there.

The image of the corkscrews returns to my mind, and it makes my body shake. I tell myself to stop it, and I refuse to be tainted by the same wretched misjudgements that exist in a mind that society has so successfully tainted. I am above trauma; I am above sadness; I am above any kind of detriment to my cognitive abilities, and I refute that such an episode even took place at all.

I want to kill them.

Oh, how I want to kill them.

I want to destroy them and murder them and mutilate them and I want it to be painful and slow and I want them to know that no one—and I mean NO ONE—forces Gerald Brittle to relive such disturbing events in a way that makes him pass out.

I do not pass out. I do not suffer episodes. I DO NOT SUFFER FROM THE HUMAN CONDITION.

I am a magnificent specimen that acts in defiance of the constraints by enforced by societal suppression, and I refuse to acknowledge that such an event occurred.

The light is off. There are no windows. I am in pitch black.

But I hear voices.

They are quiet and hushed, coming from the other side of the door at the top of the steps, but if I listen carefully, I can just about make out the conversation.

"What are we going to do with him?"

"We can't let him live."

"We can't carry on tormenting him. We are better than that."

I scoff. *Better than that.* Better than me, you mean? Oh, how I look forward to grinding them up into ash. Just as the thought enters my mind, so do the corkscrews, and my heart races and I'm panting again, and things are going fuzzy, and I am wary about passing out for a second time, not just at the detriment of losing my senses, but for suffering another moment of weakness that should only be exhibited by you stupid lemmings.

"So we kill him."

"Now?"

"Not now. Not with Claire in the house."

"She's asleep. She won't hear him scream."

"I just don't feel comfortable with her being in the house when we do it."

"Fine. We do it in the morning. When Claire has left for school."

"How do we do it?"

"A knife, I guess. The ones in the kitchen are pretty sharp."

"Is that a humane way to kill him?"

"Do you think he cares about whether he kills people humanely?"

"No. But we need to be better than him."

Better than him?

Really?

Better?

You are NOT better.

You will NEVER be better.

You are beneath me. Scum. Shit on the shoe. Vagabonds. Insufferable slaves to ethics I refuse to succumb to.

I feel myself getting worked up again, and I go dizzy, and the world fades, and I need to stop, my mind feels fragile, I need to stay conscious…

"So what now?"

"We go to bed."

"What about him?"

"He's tied up and passed out. He's not going anywhere."

"I can't sleep with him here."

"Take a sleeping pill."

"You know I don't like those pills."

"Look—it's just one night. One night, then tomorrow morning, this will all be over."

"I know. I'm surprised, though."

"At what?"

"I didn't realise how easily he would crumble. I mean, did you see how he reacted? All we did was hold corkscrews."

"I know. He's a sad, silly little man. The world won't miss him."

Sad?

Silly?

LITTLE?

Oh, you just wait, you just wait you arrogant pricks, I will show you just how little I am, just how… Just how… Little…

No… Too much energy…

I'm getting too worked up…

Don't pass out again…

Don't pass…

Don't…

Fuck's sake…

CHAPTER TWENTY-NINE

WHEN I WAKE UP AGAIN, the house is quiet, and I'm trying not to think about how I passed out for a second time.

This time, however, my anger wakes me like a bucket of icy water. I feel too powerful to pass out again. Too energised. Refreshed. Ready.

I mean, what they did wasn't even that bad. A few smacks. A bit of choking. Albeit, the strikes against my dick hurt like a motherfucker, but I've done far worse to many people, and they've endured it.

And it's quite obvious just how amateurish these people are.

Yes, they left me in darkness. But they also left me on a fragile chair, with splinters and a nail in the wall, completely unguarded.

If they are going to leave me in such flimsy restraints, they should at least have someone keeping watch. But no, I bet they are all upstairs, sleeping the night away, dead to the world.

Soon, I will give them a new meaning to being *dead to the world*.

I pull on the rope. It's not as tight as the knots I can tie, but it's still not loose enough to unravel. I move my hands up and down the chair, feeling for splinters. I find one. It's small, and might not have any effect, but it's worth a try.

I rub the rope against it. It breaks the splinter off, and the tiny shard of wood taps on the floor. Plan A hasn't worked, but there are plenty of other options.

I stand, taking the chair with me. That's when I realise they have bound my feet while I was unconscious. Attached them to the legs of the chair. An extra precaution, I assume. If it makes them feel safer, fine—it doesn't make any difference to me. I'm still able to lift myself into a crouched position, with the chair waving in the air behind me.

I test the chair first. Tap it against the floor. Feel it for weakness. It wobbles upon impact. It's not at all sturdy. In fact, it's quite fragile. Maybe they didn't want to get one of their best chairs all bloody. Another rookie move.

Right. This is going to make some noise, so I'm going to have to be ready if someone hears it—but there's no way I can do this without smashing the chair.

I lean forward. Get as much purchase as I can, brace my body for impact, then throw myself backwards.

The chair wobbles, but it remains intact, and I fall to my side.

I wait for footsteps. Talking. The door opening. Anything.

Nothing.

Right, this time it's happening. I need more force. I need to remain unfazed by the noise it makes.

I roll myself onto my front, bring my knees as far toward my chest as they can go, and use my toes to bring me to my feet, balancing the chair on my back as best as I can.

This time I lean further forward, hover on my toes, readying myself, push myself as high as I can, then throw myself onto my back.

The chair smashes, each leg breaking away from the seat,

and the back of the chair shattering into pieces until I'm laid on just a pile of wood.

I pause again. Listen. Waiting for a reaction.

Waiting.

And waiting.

Nothing comes. I've gotten away with it.

Idiots.

I take my ankles out of the rope. My hands, however, are still bound behind my back. It's pitch black, and I do not know exactly where the nail is that I spotted earlier—but I know it's against the far wall.

I hobble over, my legs aching. My dick throbs too, still in pain from the strikes inflicted by that stupid slut, but I remind myself that it is not long until I can have my payback.

The nail was about neck height, so I crouch a little and rub my cheek up and down the wall, then across it, feeling for the nail. I find it, skewwhiff and broken, but conveniently sticking out.

I bend over so my arms stick upwards. They don't quite reach the nail, so I bend over further, as much as I can, elevating my wrists, and eventually I find the nail, and I place the rope upon it, and rub.

It hurts my muscles. I'm stretching in ways I don't usually stretch, but I am a magnificent specimen with enough muscle and finesse to endure such discomfort.

It takes a few minutes, but I wear away most of the rope, which was already pretty frayed (another rookie error), until it's broken enough that I can pull it apart and liberate my hands.

I stand. Feel my wrists. Stretch my arms. Stretch my back.

I am free.

And they are all peacefully unaware.

I tiptoe to the steps, as if it makes a difference, and ascend them, each slab of wood sinking beneath my bare feet, and I place my hand on the door handle.

I expect a lock. That I will have to barge the door open. Yet I turn the handle and it just creaks into the hallway, and these people truly do not have a clue.

They are too nice.

Nice never gets you anywhere, as I am so blissfully proving.

I'm aware that I'm still naked. Not that it bothers me; I have a toned chest and a glorious body. My dick isn't what it once was, but its girth is still enough to impress anyone. Still, I know what I wish to do next, and I need to be clothed for this.

I sneak through the hallway, into the kitchen. My eyes adjust to the small amount of moonlight that sneaks between a crack in the curtains. There is a clothes horse with laundry on it. I feel the material, and it seems to be dry. I despise the thought of wearing any of Shane's attire, but I do not have a choice; I will cover it in his blood soon, so at least there is a positive.

There is a polo shirt. Yellow and cheap. I put it on, and the material is coarse against my skin. Cheap clothing truly is a displeasure to wear. There is also underwear—I'm a boxers man, but there are only briefs, so I skip it. Not like I need it. And I find a pair of beige trousers, equally disgusting, but after understandable hesitation, I put them on.

I consider, for a moment, whether I should run. Get out. Leave. Recuperate and come back stronger.

But I cannot.

My thirst for revenge is stronger than it's ever been. And it's not just Flora anymore—it's all of them. The parents. Even the child who sleeps soundly, unaware.

The child…

Eight-year-old Claire…

A grin alights my face as I recall what I plan to do.

I sneak upstairs and pause in the hallway. Her bedroom isn't difficult to find. The name *Claire* is attached to the door, with Disney princesses around the lettering. How sad it is that we teach little girls to aspire to be Disney princesses. They are feeble characters with unhealthily tiny waists who require a prince to save them. It teaches girls to be weak and subservient.

Still, that's how I like them.

I pass the other bedrooms in silence, push open the door to Claire's room, enter, and close it behind me.

CHAPTER THIRTY

HER BEDROOM MAKES ME SICK. It screams *weak little girl*, and I bet the family isn't even aware of it.

The décor is fine, I guess, for a child's bedroom. It's lit by a nightlight with the freakishly large face of a cartoon character on it. The walls are a light purple, the carpet a light brown, and there is a white wardrobe with a frame that curls at the end, as if attempting to be fancy. There are various components of the bedroom, however, that strike me as particularly repulsive: the heart-shaped mirror above the bed; the duvet with some Disney princess in a long blue dress on it; the pillows with big faces of Disney princesses; photos of princesses in pink frames; and pale pink curtains with multiple pictures of Beauty and the Beast printed in a repetitive pattern.

This girl will grow up (if I let her grow up) to base every relationship she has on the perfect romance portrayed in these movies. She will seek a man to save her like a prince, whilst claiming she's powerful and independent, as that's what a modern woman is supposed to say. She will base her ideal size and weight on the unrealistic waist of Disney princesses. Ultimately, conditioning the child into typically female interests will teach her to conform to unhealthy gender stereotypes, and will impair her ability to secure an identity that will make her happy. She is going to grow up feeling confused about what it is to be a woman, and will become yet another confused feminist who can't decide which bits of equality they wish to keep or disregard.

Anyway, I digress. The little girl sleeps soundly beneath the duvet, her long blond hair spread across the overzealous face of Princess Jasmine on her pillow. Her pyjamas are pink and make me feel sick.

She does not stir as I enter the room.

I take a chair from the corner of the room, shove the item of clothing that's placed upon it to the floor (a fancy-dress outfit I'm sure imitates one of these princesses), and place the chair next to her sleeping head. It is a child-sized chair, and I sit on it awkwardly, perched on the end with my knees at my shoulders.

And I watch her sleep.

She doesn't snore, but she breathes deeply. She lies so still that, if it weren't for the faint puffs of air from between her tiny lips, one might mistake her for being dead.

I run my hand down her hair with affection, hoping not to startle her as she wakes up.

"Claire," I whisper. "Claire, I'm here."

Her mouth slops. Her head twitches.

"Claire, it's okay, don't be afraid."

Her eyes open faintly. She looks alarmed at first, but I speak before she can scream: "It's okay, I'm not a baddie. I'm here to help you."

She looks around. Frowns. Looks back at me.

"My name is Gerald," I tell her. "I'm what's called a monster hunter. Do you know what that is?"

She shakes her head.

"Well, your daddy hired me. He's a very sensible man, your daddy, isn't he?"

She nods.

"And I imagine you love him a lot."

She nods again.

"Well, he cares a lot about you as well, and he told me you were worried about there being monsters in your cupboard. Is that right?"

She nods.

That was a lucky stab in the dark.

"Well, I'm a monster hunter—it is my job to make sure that all the monsters in your cupboard have been scared away. Is it all right if I do that?"

Her alarm fades, and she seems to relax as she nods eagerly.

"Good girl. You are such a sweet girl, aren't you?"

She smiles widely and nods. Her fear has gone, replaced by happiness. How easy was that?

"You're a princess, aren't you? Like in the movies?"

She nods. "I have a princess costume."

"You do?"

"I have two."

"Wow!"

She looks at the cupboard. "Are there any monsters in there now?"

"I don't know, there might be. Shall I check for you?"

"Yes, please."

I stand. Peer at the cupboard. Step toward it with feigned trepidation.

I place a hand on the door handle, pause, then open it. I look inside, searching every corner. I look behind the ridiculously bright outfits on the clothes hangers, and beneath the pile of tiny knickers on the bottom of the cupboard. Once I have completed a thorough search, I turn back to Claire.

"It's clear. Would you like me to check under your bed for you?"

"Yes, please."

"Good idea. That's another place they often hide."

I lower myself to my knees, then look under the bed. I look from one side to the other, ensuring that she sees me being thorough, then I lean back up again.

"We are okay under there. Is there anywhere else they might be?"

"I don't think so."

"What about under the duvet? Quite often, they sneak in at the end of the bed, and they make their way up your body and smother you in your sleep. Shall I check?"

"Yes, please."

"Okay." I lift back the duvet. Look underneath. "We seem to be okay." I check the clock. It's half-past five. "We still have a few hours until we need to get up. Daddy suggested I stay here to make sure no monsters come. Would you like that?"

"Yes."

"Shall I get under the duvet with you to make sure no monsters sneak in?"

"Yes."

"Move over then."

She shuffles across, and I squeeze myself into the other side of her single bed and pull the duvet back around us. I put my arm around her waist, pull her in close, and smell her hair. It smells like innocence.

"Go back to sleep then," I whisper in her ear.

"Okay. Thank you, Mr Monster Hunter."

"You're welcome."

She closes her eyes and, almost instantly, she is breathing deeply again, returning to a sound slumber as she lays beneath my arm, her body fitting perfectly in the curve of mine.

TODAY IS THE DAY

I sleep better than I thought I would, I wake sooner than I normally do, and I'm in a better mood than I thought I'd be.

Today is the day it ends.

Today is the day where I don't have to hide anymore.

Today is the day I no longer have to look over my shoulder on every street and in every classroom and in every café. I will no longer have to avoid leaving an online trail and I don't have to lie about who I am. It's almost over.

I don't feel happy about killing Gerald. I truly don't. But I don't feel sad either. I am painlessly numb. I am ready, and I am keen to get it over with.

I tried to avoid this happening. I tried to just leave, to let Gerald get on with his life, for us to live apart. And he came back. He hunted me and the only way to end this is to end him.

I wish there was another way. I truly do. I wish we could let him go knowing that he wouldn't search for me, that he wouldn't taunt my foster parents, that he wouldn't abduct my friends—but I can't.

Today is the day, and it's the only solution.

I get up. Leave my bedroom and pause as I pass through the hallway. It's quiet. I thought he'd be screaming or something. Maybe he's still unconscious. Or maybe he refuses to 'lower' himself to such actions. God, I hate him and his stupid arrogance. When he's gone, everyone will be safer; killing him is a duty I owe to any more potential victims, and I need to keep reminding myself of that.

The sun is shining through the frosted glass of the window as I enter the bathroom. It's hard not to feel positive when the weather is lighting up my life in such a way. I wash my hair in the sink. I'll wait to have a shower until it's done; I'll probably need to scrub his blood off my body. Then again, am I going to be the one who does it? Or will Shane or Mariam want to avoid burdening me with the memory of committing his murder?

These are things we need to discuss.

I rinse the shampoo out of my hair and look down at my body. For the first time, I feel like it's mine. It's a stupid thing to say, and I feel sad for even thinking it, but for as long as Gerald has been free, I've always felt like it belongs to him. Not that I give it willingly, but I know he feels no hesitation in taking it.

Now he cannot take it. Now it is mine, and only mine, and I can do what I want with it.

What a silly thought. It should sound profound, but I just sound damaged. But I don't mind. Today, I will be liberated.

Today is the day I can stop checking the faces of strangers for his likeness; I can stop scanning every room I enter to make sure he's not there.

Today is the day I can begin to heal; I can walk around knowing that I control who touches my body, and no one has the right to take it.

Today is the day my fear dies.

I step out of the bathroom, and there is a noise from the kitchen. The hiss of bacon in a frying pan, the grinding of the coffee beans, the laughter of Claire. She sounds so happy and excited. Is she helping to make breakfast? How sweet. It's a lovely image. Mariam and Shane stood at the stove, and Claire getting in the way with the best intentions, trying her best to help. I'll be glad to have a big breakfast; I need the energy today.

I return to my bedroom. I want to wear something smart,

knowing how important this day is—but I also know I'll need to destroy what I wear for fear of leaving incriminating evidence.

In the end, I choose to wear an old pair of dungarees over a white t-shirt.

Then again, should I be wearing white?

Screw it, who cares? I'll throw it out after. Or burn it. Whatever.

I put my hair into pigtails. I want to look childish for him. It's silly, but I feel like it will make him think I'm weak—and the image of weakness juxtaposed with my actions of strength will be a contradiction his mind can't fathom.

Is it strength? Killing someone?

I don't consider Gerald strong.

But this isn't a narcissistic serial killer's rampage. This is a means to an end. This is ending what needs to end.

Today is the day my life begins.

It's today.

Today.

How wonderful.

I leave my bedroom. The sound of Claire's laughter and of breakfast being made continues, and it makes me smile.

I walk past Mariam and Shane's room on the way to the stairs, and pause as I notice Mariam still in the bedroom, doing her hair. How strange. Normally it's her who makes breakfast.

Then Shane walks out of their ensuite.

I frown.

"Guys?" I say.

"Yes?" Mariam replies.

"I thought you were making breakfast."

"We thought you were…"

"But… Surely Claire's not down there on her own…"

I feel my eyes widen. Mariam drops her hair clips and Shane quickly does up his belt and I race to the stairs, gallop down them two at a time, followed by my foster parents, and we speed across the hallway and the dining room and into the kitchen, where we come to a sudden halt in the doorway.

"What are you doing?" I cry.

Gerald turns around and smiles. He's got the frying pan handle in one hand and a large kitchen knife in the other.

"Don't you–" Shane says, charging forward, but stops when Gerald puts the knife next to Claire's throat.

Claire is standing at the counter with her back to us, already dressed for school, completely unaware, chopping tomatoes, singing her favourite Disney song, "For the first time in forever…"

"What are you doing?" I repeat with even more urgency.

"I'm making you all breakfast," Gerald says. "Claire is helping me. She's a delight."

"Don't you dare–"

He holds his knife behind Claire's head again and instructs us: "Sit down."

We do as he says, sitting at the places he's laid out for us. We each have a knife and fork and a freshly poured glass of orange juice, and there's a hot pot a coffee in front of us beside a pot of sugar and a jug of milk.

Claire places a pile of napkins on the table. Shane tries to grab her, but Gerald moves the knife toward his daughter and Shane stops.

"Good morning," she says, then adds, "thank you for getting someone to scare the monsters away, Daddy. It's really kind of you."

She returns to the tomatoes as Gerald turns around and says, "Yeah, thanks Daddy," then winks, that gloating smile spreading from cheek to cheek—the same one he would wear as he grabbed me when I arrived home from school and shoved me over the kitchen counter to be fucked.

Today is the day it ends.

Only, I'm not sure who it will be the end of.

CHAPTER THIRTY-ONE

I PLACE a plate in front of each of them. Two rashers of bacon, a sausage, two halves of a fried tomato, fried mushrooms, beans on the side. They all stare at their meal like it's toxic.

"I haven't poisoned it," I tell them. "Trust me, that would be far too easy."

I place two plates of food in my seat. I sit down, and I guide Claire to my lap, where she sits and eats, blissfully unaware of the glares her family is giving me.

I grin back at them. They hate this. I knew they would, and they don't disappoint. They want to call her to them, but they see the knife in my hand as I hold it by my side, tapping it against the side of my chair to make its presence known, and they know what I'm capable of, and they do not dare object to what I'm doing.

I must pause for a moment to advise you, dear reader, that I am not a nonce. I find such fiends deplorable. Given, it is only in the past century that we find it deplorable, but still, it is not where my attraction lies. Not because it is taboo, I would be quite happy to act on wherever my sex drive takes me, but I do not find a lack of womanly form appealing—a child has no hips, no curves, no tits—what is there to arouse me? Nature intended us to be aroused by a body that shows evidence it can bear a child, and anyone who is attracted to a body that does not is completely against the natural order—they are defuncts of nature—and should I ever knowingly meet a man who is so inclined, I would remove his genitals with a cheese grater—in fact, I have an old, rusty appliance saved for such an occasion.

If nature does not attend it to be appealing, then I do not find it appealing, and deplore those who do.

What I find appealing, however, is that these people do not know that I am not so inclined, and probably believe that I am gaining some form of sordid pleasure from this, and it is destroying them, and I LOVE watching them squirm.

"Why aren't you eating, Daddy?" Claire asks. "I cut the tomatoes myself, aren't you going to try them?"

Shane stares at her. He can't move. He does not know what to do, and I relish every minute.

"Perhaps you should try one, Daddy," I add. "And be careful not to choke."

He frowns at the reference, and it makes me snigger. He tried torturing me, yet referring to the event makes him feel uncomfortable, not me. These fucking suburban charlatans, I hate them, they are hypocrites, displaying a perfect image and hiding away their sexuality and the true intricacies of how they make money. I have exposed the hideosity behind the perfect mask, and it sparks such glee within me that I feel like dancing on the table.

But I don't.

Instead, I watch as Shane tentatively lifts his fork, sticks it into the tomato, and places it in his mouth. He eats it slowly, staring at his daughter, gulps it down, then takes a swig of orange juice.

"Perfect," he whispers.

He can barely talk.

He doesn't know what to say.

Oh, this is such fun!

"Mummy? Flora? What about you?"

I tuck my arms around Claire's waist and lean my head on her shoulder as I smile at them and say, "Yeah, what about you guys?"

They both stick their forks in a tomato—with such caution it's as if they are cutting wires on a bomb—and place it in their mouths. They chew, gulp, and stare back at us.

"Yay!" I say, clapping my hands, and Claire claps her hands too, and she turns to me and smiles and giggles and I lean forward and give her a little Eskimo kiss and Shane coughs and fuuuuuuuuuuuck this shit is funny.

"So what now?" Shane asks, trying to sound all manly. He has another tank top on today. It's lime green. Where does he buy this crap?

"Right now, we eat breakfast."

"Then what?"

"Then I think it's time for Claire to go to school."

"And she's going to be allowed?"

I put on a playful frown, and Claire looks at me and echoes it.

"Of course, silly," Claire says. "Of course I'm going to school."

"Of course she's going to school, Daddy," I add.

Shane drops his cutlery. Runs his hands through his hair.

"Can we just—like—I don't know—stop this for a second?" he says.

"Stop what, Daddy?" I ask.

He slams his fist on the table. "Stop calling me Daddy!"

I know this was meant to be an action of male dominance, but not a single person jumped at his outburst.

I say nothing. Just let him simmer. Watching me with that intense glare.

"What's the matter, Daddy?" Claire asks. "Don't you like the monster hunter? You got him for me!"

"No, I didn't, Claire."

"What do you mean?"

"Claire, I need you to listen to me very carefully. This man is going to—"

I lift the knife and hover it behind her throat. I grip the handle, ready to plunge it through her windpipe. All he needs to do is finish that sentence.

But he doesn't.

He falls silent.

"Eat your breakfast, Daddy," I say.

"Yeah, eat it, Daddy, I helped make it!"

"You certainly did."

I bounce her on my knee and she giggles. She picks up a sausage in both hands and chews on the end.

"Shouldn't you be using a knife and fork, darling?" Shane asks, and it's a strange thing to ask at such a time, but I guess he's just unable to help nagging. That, or it's the only thing he can control, and he's clinging desperately to the last dregs of parental authority he can find.

"She's all right with her hands," I say. "Nothing wrong with using your hands. Is there, Daddy?"

Claire giggles at this.

"What is wrong with you?" Mariam asks.

Oh, I guess it's her turn. I grin at Flora as I turn my gaze to Mariam. Flora turns away and stares at the floor. To be fair, she's responsible for this—if it weren't for her being so elusive, this wouldn't be happening. In fact, I wouldn't ever have met these people.

This is all her fault, and I think she knows it.

"Whatever do you mean?" I ask.

"I'm interested," says Mariam, "have you ever had a formal diagnosis?"

"Are you going all sex therapist on me?"

"I mean a diagnosis by a regular therapist."

"I tend to scare therapists."

"I'm just curious what they'd say. A personality disorder, maybe? Psychopathy? I have no doubt you have narcissistic tendencies, that's for sure."

"These are all big words for little minds, Mummy. Just because I'm the one who's different to you, doesn't mean I'm not the one who's normal."

Claire picks up a streak of bacon, holds it above her head, then lowers it into her mouth. She chews it with her mouth open, slopping away.

"This is wrong," Mariam says. "Can you not see that? It is really wro—"

I slam my fist on the table. This time, it makes everyone jump.

"We are having a nice breakfast, Mummy," I say. "Claire, tell Mummy we're having a nice breakfast."

"We're having a nice breakfast, Mummy," she says, too engrossed in her food to care.

"Tell Mummy she should eat, and stop being so nasty."

"You should eat, Mummy, and stop being so nasty."

"This is my *daughter*," Mariam persists, and I can't help leaning my head back and heaving out a big sigh.

"And what about you?" I say, turning to Flora. "Have you nothing to say? No attempts to rationalise with me?"

"There is no rationalising with someone like you."

"Really? Because I tried rationalising with *you*. I tried to give you a home, a place in my mansion, and you wouldn't listen. Now this is all because of you."

"No, it's not," Mariam interjects.

"Excuse me?"

"I said no, it is not."

"I don't understand what you mean."

"This is not because of Flora. Flora did not bring you into our lives, this isn't happening because of her, this isn't anything to do with her. This is all because of you, because of how—"

I swing the knife upwards, and halt it just next to Claire's throat, and Mariam abruptly stops speaking, gasps, and covers her mouth.

"I thought Claire told you to be nice."

Shane sniffs. He's crying.

"Oh, Daddy, please don't be so silly," I say.

Claire reaches out a hand and places it on Shane's. "What's the matter, Daddy?" she asks.

I ensure the knife is visible.

"Nothing, darling. I'm just not feeling well today."

"Do you think you are ill?"

"Maybe, darling. Maybe."

Oh, isn't this wonderful?

I have their child on my lap, and none of them will dare make a wrong move.

This is power.

Politicians can debate, and priests can preach, and bosses can boss, and husbands can beat their wives, and police can beat up the poor—but none of them will ever know power like this.

There is a knock on the front door.

All their heads lift.

"That will be Teresa," Claire says, and leaps off my lap.

"I'll see her out," I say to the family as I follow her into the hallway. "You stay there."

She takes her school bag and puts it over her shoulders.

"Will you be here when I get home?" she asks as we approach the front door.

"Probably not," I say. "But who knows?"

"Thank you for keeping the monsters away."

"It's my pleasure."

She opens the door, shouts hello to her friend, and scarpers out.

I shut the door behind her. Bolt it. Lock it. Take the key and put it in my pocket. (Hey, that rhymes!) Then I return to the dining room but, just as I expected, they aren't there—they have moved to the kitchen and are searching through the cutlery draws for knives. (Unlike them, I am not an amateur, and they will not find a single knife anywhere.)

I grab Flora as I enter, put my knife to her throat, and they all stop what they are doing.

"You think I'm that stupid?"

"Where's Claire? Did you let her go?"

"She's on her way to school. Hopefully, I won't have to intercept her. If you all cooperate, then all she will be is leverage. If you don't, then she will be dead."

"You think we won't get to her before you?"

"Think it would matter? I found Flora; you think I wouldn't find the rest of you?"

They know I'm right, and their silence is their confirmation.

"Now take your seats at the dining table," I say, shoving Flora into her chair.

Shane and Mariam do as I instruct.

"Put your hands on the table in front of you. Spread your fingers."

They obey.

"Lovely. Now I'm going to be your teacher. Let's start with lesson one—how to successfully detain and torture a prisoner. Seeing as you are all so lousy at it, it might be a good idea for me to demonstrate." I indicate the predicament they are in by waving my hand over them. "Do you see how easy it is?"

No reply.

"*Do you?*"

They mumble affirmative answers.

"Good. That means we can skip the next lesson—how to avoid being such fucking idiots."

I remain behind Flora and fiddle with her pigtails. I know she did those just for me.

"And we can move onto the final lesson," I say. "How to make revenge as sweet as it can be."

CHAPTER THIRTY-TWO

I STROLL around the outside of the table in circles, tapping the blade of the knife against the palm of my hand.

I want them to see the knife.

I want them to see the reminder; to know what will happen should they choose to dissent.

"Let's start with you, Mariam. The sex therapist. The one who knows how to deepen our connection with sex. You know you are full of shit, right?"

She watches me. Her tongue moves around her mouth. She curtails her reaction, though I know she'd love to give me a nice big *fuck you*.

"How can you possibly say that you know how to improve the sex lives of others, when your own husband is so sexually unsatisfied that he must run around, behind your back, having casual sex with other men?"

She glares at me in that way a woman does when she realises she is not, in fact, strong and independent, but is a hypocritical little bitch.

"You may reply," I tell her. "But be wary of the consequences of a wrong answer."

"What exactly would you like me to say?"

"I would like to know how you think you have any kind of authority on the subject of healthy sex lives?"

"My husband is bisexual. That isn't because of our sex life —it's because he is bisexual."

I imitate a buzzer sound and add, "Wrong!"

"Why don't you tell me exactly why, then? You seem to have the answer."

Oh, the scorn in her voice; it's palpable, it's tasty.

"Because you fucked a load of guys in your late teens and early twenties, and it made you feel good; meaning that how to cum is the only thing you left university being good at. And you weren't good enough to become a real psychiatrist, were you? And acting like you know all about sex makes you feel good, doesn't it?"

She shakes her head and looks away from me. I lean on the table and place my face next to hers.

"You think being a slut gives you knowledge, and isn't just you being a slut."

"A woman can have sex with as many men as they wish, and without your judgement."

"Can they? Because everyone judges everyone for everything—why should this be any different?"

"A woman can be as promiscuous as she likes—"

"But you never did it for sexual freedom, did you? You did it for insecurity. Because it made you feel better about your inadequate appearance. If a man wants you, then you must be attractive. You never realised you were just a hole to aim at."

"Not all men are like you, Gerald," Flora interjects.

"And oh, look who pipes up!" I hold my arms out grandly. I feel like a game-show host on the best game-show ever. "Little Miss Hidesaway 2022. Did you really think you could stay hidden?"

She looks the calmest. She quells her glare, knowing how much satisfaction it gives me. Oh, how well she knows me.

"Answer me," I tell her.

"Yes," she says. "Yes, I did, actually. I thought you would just leave me alone. That, if I didn't tell anyone, you would just let me be happy."

"Happy?"

"Yes. Happy."

"Flora, my love, my life, my everything—you could never be happy."

"I could, if it weren't for you."

"You will never be happy so long as you are in your own head. Tell me, how were you feeling about killing me today?"

She shrugs. "Fine."

"And you think that makes you any different from me?"

"I was killing for a purpose."

"And I am not?"

She doesn't reply. The question hangs there like a noose.

I leave Flora for now, wanting to save her for last, and turn to Shane, who scowls at me. He looks sassy. I like it.

"And you, Shane. How do you call yourself a man?"

"What, because I'm bisexual?"

"I don't give a shit if you're bisexual—which you're not, by the way, stop kidding yourself; you're *gay*. Either way, I am not saying that putting another man's cock in your mouth makes you less of a man. But do you know what does make a man?"

"I'm sure you're going to tell me."

"Less of the remarks, Shane, you don't want to upset Mr Knifey here." I place my hand on his shoulder. "A man is a provider. And that is not just society's decision, believe me, it is nature—look at cavemen. At animals."

"Actually, recent studies have found that cavemen and women were a team, rather than—"

I scrape the tip of the knife down his back. He cries out and shuts up.

"Wrong answers will be punished," I remind him.

He leans forward, weeping. I didn't even hurt him that badly.

"You do nothing meaningful for your family. Your wife earns more than you do. You spend evenings at gay clubs instead of with your daughter. You teach children who don't respect you. And you–"

"Enough!" he bursts out. "Enough, please enough!"

I stand back, affronted.

Has he dared to interrupt me?

I thought I made myself clear.

"What makes you so perfect, huh?" he says. Finally, there is some aggression to his voice, some hostility—I'm starting to see the Shane that should have been there all along, and it's delighting me. "What gives you the right to judge us? What the hell do you do?"

"Calm down, Shane."

"I will not calm down! I'm fed up with this! Are you going to kill us or talk us to death? I will not have you stand there and demean my family any longer!"

"You won't, won't you?"

"No. I will not. And it's time you leave."

"Time I left? Shane, you brought me here."

"Yes, and now I'm telling you to go. Please, just go. Because if I must endure any more of your self-righteous crap, then I will—"

I don't hear what he would do, and I don't care to. The knife ceases his rant, and blood fills his mouth.

Mariam and Flora jump up from their seats and back away.

Again, I gave explicit instructions to sit down. Do these people not listen?

I will deal with them in a moment. For now, I pull the knife out of Shane's neck, then launch it back in again, this time plunging it into another part of his throat, and his muscle gives me a bit of resistance, so I push the knife further, and I feel it penetrate something, and it must be his windpipe as he appears to become unable to breathe.

His wife and foster child run out of the room, screaming.

Is there no such thing as loyalty these days?

I withdraw the knife and plunge it into yet another part of his neck. I pull it out and blood sprays over the uneaten breakfast.

What a shame—Claire and I put a lot of effort into those meals.

Shane's face slams against his plate, and his body spasms as he endures the last few moments of his life. I wonder what he's thinking, whether his life is flashing before his eyes, whether he sees a white light, or, as I expect, whether he simply feels a lot of pain and then, suddenly, nothing.

His body remains slumped over the table as I turn to the doorway and pursue Flora and Mariam.

I've disposed of one, now I must turn my attention to the other two.

CHAPTER THIRTY-THREE

MARIAM AND FLORA flee like two little girls, scared that Daddy is home.

They try the front door, unlatching the bolt but finding they can't open it, and oh, what's happened to the keys, they were supposed to be on the table beside the door...

They are in my hand, you stupid cunts. I'm standing in the kitchen doorway, dangling them from my finger.

They scream and charge through the house, toward the garden door. Their garden is quite nice, I must say, with a birdbath, a neatly mowed lawn, and a water feature at the end. Unfortunately for them, I have those keys too. They scream and continue running through the house, and I chase them through the living room to the study to the dining room to the kitchen, then back through the living room again. It takes a few laps until it grows tiresome. We're just going in circles, and this isn't getting us anywhere.

I stop chasing them, and try running the opposite way toward them, trying to fool them, but they see me coming and scream and turn back and it's all just so tedious.

I mean, do they think I can't keep this up?

Eventually, they seem to realise they can't do this forever, and they direct themselves to the stairs. A silly decision, really, considering they are trapping themselves along a corridor with a dead end.

As soon as I realise which way they are going, I surge forward, sprinting harder, and Flora is halfway up the stairs with Mariam trailing behind her when I dive, my arms outstretched, and grab Mariam's ankle, forcing her to fall on her chest.

Flora turns back to her foster mother, forever the heroine.

"No, go! Just go!" Mariam insists.

Mariam kicks at me, even clocks me on the chin (I'll get her back for that, don't you worry), and scrambles back to her knees.

Flora's face appears hopeful.

Then I lift the knife above my head and bring it down, hard and fast, into the back of her ankle.

She screams like a bitch and tries to kick her other foot, but I stick the knife into that ankle too, cutting through muscle and scraping bone. She cries out again.

"Run!" she insists to Flora.

Flora hovers, not knowing what to do.

"Please, just run!" Mariam cries, and her voice is so assertive that Flora can't help but obey; she flees upstairs, her feet pounding across the hallway.

I place my wrists around her ankles and pull her down the stairs until her ageing, sweaty, stinky body (the furore has created quite the stench of body odour) is directly beneath me.

She puts up one hell of a fight. She throws her arms at me with no discernible plan to her flailing limbs, no sense of strategy; she just swings them in my direction, hoping they will hit me.

I grab her by the hair. Lift her head. Stick the knife into the base of her spinal cord. It meets resistance, so I shove harder on the handle, and it sinks further, and I sever her spine and her limbs suddenly aren't flailing anymore.

And oh, dear reader, her eyes in this moment—how I wish you could see them—if there ever was a moment of true, dreaded fear encapsulated in a look, it is this, and I find myself drooling over her terrified expression.

I wish I could savour this, I really do—but with my prized possession upstairs, I need to make the torture quick: if Shane was bronze, then Mariam is silver, and I am determined to get my gold.

So I disembowel her.

Not like they did in the olden days—back then, they would cut you open and pull out your intestines whilst you watch, and it would take some time for you to bleed out. Unfortunately, I do not have several hours, and I will need to make it quicker. But I do have a minute, as I am positive that Flora will waste time thrashing around the various rooms, trying desperately to open all the windows that I ensured were locked. (I am aware she might try to smash a window, and I listen out for such an eventuality in case I need to intervene.) For now, I slice open Mariam's dress and expose her frail, bare body. It's as anticlimactic as I recall it—her hairy crotch and her sagging boobs and her stretch marks and baby weight she never lost, it's all there, and whilst I usually find the marks of a woman's life well-lived highly arousing (I don't want to be a typical man and speak in such a derogatory manner about a woman's naturally ageing body, of course)—I can think only of Flora's youthful hips, and those are far more enticing than any other woman could ever be.

So I begin the end of Mariam's life.

I place my knife into the top of her pubic mound, sink it into her skin until blood oozes out, and drag it upwards, pass her navel, and shove it beneath her rib cage. I withdraw the knife, shove it back in above her left hip, and pull it across her belly until it reaches her other hip. Then I peel the skin away and look at what we have here.

She moves her eyes. She's trying to see what I'm doing. Trying to move the only thing she can move. She even tries to speak, but there's too much blood leaking out of her mouth and she can only gurgle.

I push aside her kidney and her spleen and her pancreas, and I reach past the colon and squeeze her large intestines. They feel thick and gooey, like something slimy sliding between my hands. Apparently, if you unravel a large intestine, it can measure up to six feet, and the small intestine can measure up to twenty-two feet. Biology is fascinating.

You may wonder how I have such an extensive knowledge of human anatomy. It isn't simply because my education probably costs more than your house; it's because I know what I need to know—much like I learned about disposing of a body via pigs, I know enough about human anatomy to do what I wish with whatever part of a cadaver I wish to do it to. Honestly, dear reader, I'm telling you—until you have fucked a human heart—I mean, actually shoved your dick into the vena cava, or cut open a hole in the ventricle to insert your pleasure-stick—then you cannot state that you have truly known ecstasy.

Mariam is truly terrified, her expression a constant contortion of discomfort. I show her the intestines so I can see the shock on her face. But she is also fading. Her energy is depleting, and this is growing tiresome, and I wish to proceed to the main event.

So I reach further in with both hands, push my fists beneath her ribs, force my hands upwards until my arms are painted in blood, and grip her lungs — one in each hand. I grin at her and maintain eye contact as I take hold of these lungs and pull.

They are really in there, and I have to keep tugging. I eventually manage to dislodge them, but I am embarrassed to admit that I am still unable to fully remove them. So I yank again. Harder. And again, harder, until I'm able to pull them away from whatever they are attached to and discard them on the floor.

I stand. My clothes and my arms and my chin and my neck are covered in a mixture of bright red and dark red. It glistens in the light.

It's my warrior paint, and I love it.

Mariam's face has stopped moving. She's done now. Enough of her.

I climb upstairs, stomping so I'm heard, and call out, "Flora, I'm ready for you."

I cannot wait to see what kind of fight she puts up.

I DID THIS

I did this.

I brought him here.

I could have gone anywhere.

I could have hidden in the wilderness. Bought a tent and disappeared. I could have left the country. Gone to a convent. Hell, I could have even gone to the police.

But instead I did this.

I thought I could have a life.

That we could keep him in the basement without him escaping.

That I wasn't compromising everyone by bringing him here.

But I cannot sit around and think about it. I can't. I must leave my thoughts downstairs with my foster parents. Should I survive, then I will give them the sadness they deserve. I will grieve and apologise to their graves until my voice is hoarse—but I cannot do that now.

He is coming for me.

I run from one room to the next. To Shane and Mariam's bedroom—the one they will never share again—stop it Flora, not now—then to Claire's room—the one where he entered whilst we were asleep, thinking we were safe, thinking that a bit of rope would be enough to contain a monster.

Dammit Flora. Stop it.

I did this I did this I did this I did this.

I stop and fall to my knees and break down and there is a voice, deep inside my mind, begging me to get up—but there is another one telling me that this is all my fault.

I drag myself to my feet, ignoring the sounds of chopping coming from downstairs.

Mariam isn't screaming. Is she already dead?

I go to my room. Shut the door. Lock it. It's a flimsy lock—just a small bolt from the door to the wall, but it's something, and I press up against it, panting, and I try not to think.

—I did this they are dead because of me I did this—

STOP IT.

For Christ's sake, Flora, stop it.

I search for a weapon. I ate tea in here yesterday with a knife and fork. What did I do with them?

I search under the chair in the corner. That's where I normally put my dirty crockery. But it's not there. Mariam must have collected it.

—Claire's still alive—

What?

—Claire's still alive—she's at school—she doesn't know—

Oh, God, she doesn't know.

I try the window. Why haven't I tried the window yet?

Be calm, Flora, organise your thoughts, you're being reckless.

Of course I'm being reckless! I brought him here! I did this, you idiot, I DID THIS!

I try the window. It won't open. I try lifting it harder. It's locked. I didn't even know it could lock. I don't have a key. When did he have time to lock the windows?

When I was asleep.

Which means he was in my bedroom when I was asleep.

He could have killed me then.

But he chose to wait.

I don't know what's sicker—that he was in here, watching me, or that he waited for an opportunity to make my death worse.

I pause. I'm panting. I will my breathing to calm, but it won't.

I have no choice.

I'm going to have to let him catch me.

I'm going to have to rely on my wits, and my contingency plan, and my determination, and my—

"Flora, I'm ready for you."

If I hadn't registered the words he'd spoken, then the inflections of his singsong voice could easily be saying Flora dinner is ready *or* Flora it's time to go to school.

But it's not. It's the omen of death. The prayer that begins Even though I walk through the shadow of the valley of death, I fear no evil, for You are with me—*but You are not with me; You have NEVER been with me.*

I press myself up against the wall. His footsteps grow closer. Heavy. Intentionally so. He wants me to know he's close. He wants me to know it's imminent.

He turns the door handle. Slowly. All a big tease; all a big game. It won't open. So he barges against the door and the flimsy lock flies away, and he stands there, filling the frame, and my God he is covered neck to foot in blood. The knife in his hand drips with it. It runs down his arms. His clothes have completely lost their colour. He is just a demented creature bathed in the misery of others, come to collect me for my death.

And he's just standing there, watching me, consuming every moment of my fear.

"Is she dead?"

I'm not even aware I'm saying it. My voice is faint, distant, like it's coming from somewhere else.

"What do you think, Flora?" he says. "This is what you do. You're like a disease. You bring death to everyone you love because you just won't obey me." He clenches his fist and curls his lip. "I hate it when you don't obey me."

I shake my head and go to object, but what's the point? When has begging ever changed this man's mind? If anything, it spurs him on. Therefore, I vow to give him silence.

And he steps toward me.

"You did this," he tells me.

But he needn't tell me.

I know I did this.

"This is all your fault."

I did this.

"If you hadn't run away, if you had just stayed, then none of these would have happened."

I did this.

I did this I did this I did this and oh I know I did this.

I fall to my knees. I'm crying. Not because of what he's going to do, but because of what he's done. Because of what I've done.

Because of what I'll do.

He steps forward. Kneels in front of me. Runs a hand down my hair like he did when I was not old enough for him to fuck me yet.

"Did it really have to come to this?" he says. "My little Flora, all grown up and so full of hate."

That's a good question, Gerald. A very good question.

Has it really come to this?

I hide my scowl.

Must I really do this?

Of course I must. I never had a choice.

He stops rubbing my hair, and instead takes a clump in his fist, pulls my head back, and slams it against the wall.

I feel dizzy. He's trying to knock me out.

I don't resist.

I close my eyes and allow the fogginess to take over, sinking further into my mind, a blank haze consuming me.

One way or another, this is going to end, Gerald.

And when it ends, and I have done what I truly did not want to do, I hope you remember—I did this.

CHAPTER THIRTY-FOUR

I CARRY her limp body to the basement. Seeing as this was the scene of my degradation, it makes sense that it is also the scene of hers.

I remove all her clothes. Slowly. So I can enjoy it. Pulling off her dungarees, then lifting off her t-shirt, then unclasping her bra, then pulling her pathetic purple knickers slowly down her legs like I'm unveiling a grand prize.

She looks much the same, except thinner. She's not been eating well, and her body is a little bonier, and has less shape than it did. Her breasts are still pert and perky, and her buttocks still wobble when slapped, and overall, I guess I'm satisfied.

I place her on her front and straighten her arms and legs. I collect the rope that they used to tie up my ankles. I place her hands over her arse, bind her wrists, and leave plenty of rope spare. I tie her wrists again, then pull the rope downwards, lift her feet up, secure them, then fix the two together until I have a beautiful, young, vivacious woman hogtied on the dusty, solid floor of the basement.

The box of implements they used to torment me still sits at the corner of the basement. As I wait for the humiliation of the backstabbing slut to begin (I don't want to start until she's both conscious and aware enough to understand what is happening), I open the box and peruse the items.

The paddle is there. The large dildo with remains of my puke. I quell my anger at the sight of them—I'm in charge now, and there is no need to let fury cloud my enjoyment of what is coming. There's also a small pot of liquid in there, labelled *Alkalis*. No idea what that's for. And the last items are a douche, more rope, and pepper spray. I can't help laughing. This is a poor excuse for a torture kit compared to my utensils.

There is sniffing from behind me. A moan. A cry.

She's awake.

Ooh, how lovely.

I lean against the wall and watch as she regains her senses. She looks around, realises where she is, and tries to move her limbs only to realise they are bound together. She peers around the room, scanning the area lit by the single light bulb before searching the shadows. She looks over her shoulder, sees me, and there is rank disappointment painted across her face.

Not that much fear, though. She seems numb to it. That will have to change.

"Hello, Flora," I say, my voice calm and low.

She huffs and turns away from me. She even rolls her eyes.

Does she not realise the extent of the situation she is in?

I have the power now. I am in charge. She is my little bitch, awaiting several nights of torture before her much anticipated death—and she dares to roll her eyes?

She needs to know who's in charge.

She needs to know it *now*.

I place my knife on top of the box, saunter toward her in a manner I intend to be infuriatingly casual, and crouch over her.

I lift her chin, and she pulls her head away.

I grab her chin, squeeze her cheeks together, and force her to look at me.

"Do you realise what's happening?" I ask.

Oh, my, she looks so full of spite. Poor girl. Fury doesn't look good on such a pretty face.

"I have you. It's over. You are mine, and I am going to bring forth a long, painful end to your life."

She spits at me.

She fucking spits at me.

The bitch fucking spits at me.

I can't believe it. Does she not realise that for every defiant action she takes, I will inflict further agony?

I punch her in the side of the head—not too hard; I want her conscious—and kneel over her.

"I think I need to show you who's in charge here," I tell her, and I turn her around, and I spread her legs.

Her shiny little cunt winks back at me. Her labia, coated in sweat, is tidy and neat. I can smell it. It's delightfully grotesque.

But I'm not an idiot. I will not make the same mistake again. I will not thrust myself inside of her to find another corkscrew lodged in her vaginal canal.

I shove my hand in first. And I don't just mean my fingers —I mean my entire fist. I push it harder, and force it in, and she whimpers and cries and does her best to hold in the pain, but I know it hurts—whilst I do not have a vagina myself, I can still imagine how uncomfortable receiving fisting in an unlubricated vagina will be.

I move my fist around (as much as I can, it's hardly like there's a huge amount of room), and it feels warm and soft, and I'm sure I feel a diaphragm, and whilst I feel angry at the possibility that she's using contraception because she wishes to share her body with someone else (the little slut), I can say

295

with absolute certainty that there is not a corkscrew in there—and that is the most important thing.

I pull my fist out and hold it beneath my nose, taking in big deep whiffs. It smells like her natural scent, but stronger, like the source of her odour emanates from her genitalia.

"I am going to fucking love this, you stupid little girl."

I take off my trousers. My boxers. I don't remove my top, as I am aware how strange a man looks with just a top on, and I want her to be repulsed by me. I spread her legs wide, forcing them against the pressure of the rope, and my dick is as hard as a fucking rock. I rest my bellend against her opening and I press my body against hers, forcing her breasts against the cold, hard floor, making it as uncomfortable as I can.

She doesn't cry, the little trooper. She barely flinches. She just stares ahead, her expression vacant. She almost looks like she's waiting for something. Silly girl.

I start slowly, easing my way in, just the tip first, then a bit more, then I move my mouth to her ear, and whisper so she'll feel the heat of my breath against her auricle, "Tell me when it hurts."

And I thrust. Hard. I go in as far as I can go.

And I feel something.

Something strange. Like a plastic surface. Is that the diaphragm? I thought it was, but it doesn't feel like one. It feels more like a balloon. It's squidgy at first, then I penetrate it, and it breaks, and then FUCK, oh SHIT—there is a sudden searing pain down my cock, and it hurts LIKE FUCK.

She flinches. Her face contorts into an image of pain and distress, but one that she appears prepared for.

I pull out of her immediately, stand back, and look down at my dick.

At first, I don't recognise it. It doesn't look like a dick. It's purply black, and it's burning—it feels like smoke should come off it—and I don't understand why it looks like that.

I rush around, trying to find something, and I pick up my underwear and rub it against my prized possession, trying desperately to wipe off whatever is on it, but it's overly sensitive and hurts to touch.

What the fuck has she done?

Whatever it is, it won't go.

And it burns more and more, pain shooting up and down the shaft, and the skin turns blacker and blacker, and I can't understand what is happening, what has she done, oh god what has she done, it scalds, and there are blisters forming and the skin is flaking and the pain is still firing and my penis is still shrinking and reddening and blackening and reddening and it looks like the end of a volcano, spewing molten lava, and can I smell smoke or am I imagining it?

I fall on the floor and writhe around—the only thing I can do to fight the excruciating pain—but it does nothing, and I'm just a flapping fish grabbing his own junk, wishing the pain would just stop.

In all the commotion, I hadn't even noticed Flora wiggle her way across the floor and take my knife. I stare helplessly at her as she finishes releasing her hands and wrists. She stands and searches through the box of crappy torture utensils. She's flinching, like she's also in pain, her face scrunching up and her breathing erratic. She is enduring agony too, but she seems to be taking it better. She removes the pot from the box labelled *Alkalis,* then takes out the douche. She puts the douche in the pot and allows it to soak up the liquid. Then she sticks that douche inside of herself, twists it around, and she does this for a while, before taking the douche out.

Then she puts her fingers inside of her, reaches high, and removes the broken plastic of a burst balloon. She puts the douche back in the pot, allows it to soak up the alkali solution, then places it inside of herself again, twists it, then removes it.

She leans against the wall, and her pain seems to subside as mine seems to grow bigger.

FUCK IT HURTS.

And it's getting worse, and I'm scared I'll pass out—please not again—but it's just too much for me to handle because in case I didn't mention FUCK IT HURTS.

"Do you think…" Flora says between pants, leaning against the wall, evidently waiting for the last bits of pain to leave her body. "That I wouldn't have a contingency plan?"

I try to retort, but I can't form the words; I am clinging to some semblance of control that's already gone.

"I suppose you want to know what's happening?"

She looks at my cock. She's still in discomfort but can't help smiling. I hate her. I want to grab her by the throat and choke her to death, but every time I move the pain gets worse. I even try lying still, but my cock is still red and black and still burns like fuck.

She lifts the pot labelled *Alkalis* and says, "Sodium hydroxide, potassium hydroxide, and ammonium hydroxide. Alkalis that neutralise acid. The only thing that can stop your cock from withering away."

A solution? A cure?

I reach for it.

As if she'd give it to me.

That's just how desperate I am right now.

And the pain only intensifies as I watch her turn the pot upside down and pour the contents onto the floor.

"No…"

"Do you think I'm a fucking idiot, Gerald?"

She straightens her back. It's still hurting her, but the satisfaction she's taking from this is overcoming any pain she still feels.

She steps toward me. Slowly. Her naked body that enticed me so much only moments ago, the one I wished to violate over and over, is now an omen of doom casting me in shadow.

"I... Will... Murder... You..." I gasp.

She chuckles at my mutters, the only few syllables I'm able to produce.

Is she going to kill me?

Burning dick or not, I will give her a fight, and I will wait for her to come closer to me, and I will get that knife and I will gut her and—

And she gives me a sympathetic smile. Like she pities me. She backs away, to the stairs, keeping her eyes on me until the last moment, then leaves the basement and makes her break for freedom.

The pain becomes a constant feature of my body, and I stop writhing, and I lay on the floor hoping that now she has gone, I can pass out, and hopefully wake up when it doesn't hurt quite so much.

After a few minutes, I hear the front door open and shut.

She's gone.

And I close my eyes and wait for the darkness to take me.

YOU NEVER LEARN

It was inside of me before we even met at the café.

We hoped to take our revenge, and we hoped to kill you, and we hoped it would be easy.

Our hoping was naïve. We were stupid.

And you thought you'd won.

But you never learn, Gerald. You never, ever learn.

I knew you were watching me when I stepped off the bus. I hid my discomfort, I tried not to wince, and I grew used to it. I'd lined the inside of the balloon with polypropylene to make sure the acid stayed there, waiting for you. It remained lodged beneath my cervix overnight, and I had to wash my hair in the sink as I was worried the shower would loosen it.

Still, I thought we could finish you without having to use it. It was a backup plan, Gerald, and I'd hoped that was how it would stay. But once you'd caught me, I knew I no longer had a choice— and I just had to wait for you to do what you do.

You never learn about the consequences, do you?

It hurt me too.

Of course it did.

I had acid dripping down the inside of my vagina, for fuck's sake. It burnt.

But it's hardly like I need to keep my vagina functional, is it? It's hardly like I will ever desire sex after what you did. I could never let someone make love to me without feeling the terror I associate with it.

Besides, the pain was temporary. That's what the alkali solution was for. I made the sacrifice of momentary pain, and now it only tinges a little, and I expect it to repair itself in time. But you had no such luck, did you?

Oh, Gerald, I can't believe you were so stupid yet again...

You never learn that a woman's intuition is far wiser than a man's aggression.

You never learn that the thing you want to take from me is the thing that will destroy you.

You never learn that I am smarter than you in every possible way.

I wanted to kill you. I did. I wanted to end it and make sure it wouldn't happen again. Make sure you wouldn't hunt me. I considered taking your knife and slitting your throat before I left, but your face, despite the pain you were in, was still stern, and you were still ready for battle.

So I left you to your pain, hoping the after effects will be a constant reminder of what happens when you try to take down a woman with strength you cannot contend with.

I am strong, Gerald, and my strength is all thanks to you.

I've left now, Gerald, and I will not make the same mistakes again. This time, I will put no one else at risk. There will be no way to find me. No school or UCAS forms. No foster parents or friends. No record of my whereabouts.

It's over.

Please, please, say that it's over.

Don't hunt me.

This is what happens.

But you never learn, do you? You never learn when it's time to leave me alone.

I feel guilt for the lives you've taken.

You did that, yet I am responsible.

I hate it.

I hate it so much.

But it's over, Gerald. It's over. It's done. We're done.

For all the things you never learned, I hope you learn these few things:

I am better than you.

I am fiercer than you.

I will never let you take anything from me again.

You never learn, but this time, I hope you do.

I sincerely hope you do.

You insufferable wretch

You think this is it?

You think this is over?

You think I'm not going to come after you after this?

You've made it worse

You've made EVERYTHING worse

I am NOT going to stop hunting you

EVER

Flora do you understand

 iMessage

You are DEAD

FUCKING DEAD

Calm down Gerald you'll give yourself a coronary

How's the penis btw?

Fuck you

You ugly retched disgusting little slut

Wow, you actually managed a three syllable word there

Bravo

Do you think you're funny?

 iMessage

I think I'm hilarious

I make great jokes

For instance

Just look at your dick

You will pay for what you did

You will pay

Gerald please

Surely you realise

Surely it's clear now

This is over

We are over

OVER

It's done

It's never over

You've hurt so many people

I would ask if you ever feel bad about it

But I think it would be a silly question

I will give you this option once Flora

And only once

 iMessage

Give yourself up

Let me have you

And I will spare anyone
else you care about

No

DON'T YOU FUCKING
SEE YOU STUPID
LITTLE CHILD

YOU ARE MINE

AND I WILL NOT STOP

I WILL NEVER STOP

Did you accidentally hit
caps lock or something?

iMessage

Ooh Flora

You are making things worse

So much worse

Look down

See what I did

And tell me how it could get worse

I gave you this chance Flora

I gave you this chance

Remember that

 iMessage

And I give you this chance

To leave me alone

Once and for all

It will never happen

Then that is your decision Gerald

But for me

I am out

And this time it's done

It is never done

It is never done Flora

[Your message could not be delivered]

Have you blocked this number?

[Your message could not be delivered]

Are you kidding me Flora?

[Your message could not be delivered]

You just wait

[Your message could not be delivered]

 iFakeTextMessage.com

You just fucking wait

[Your message could not be delivered]

I will gut you for this

[Your message could not be delivered]

I will GUT YOU

[Your message could not be delivered]

CHAPTER THIRTY-FIVE

WELL FUCK ME, I didn't see that one coming.

Which is fairly stupid, isn't it?

It's exactly what she did to me before—except this time, with acid instead of a corkscrew.

My dick is ruined—AGAIN.

So thanks a fucking bunch, Flora.

Thanks.

You unbelievable megacunt.

CHAPTER THIRTY-SIX

BUT IT'S NEVER QUITE good enough to end it there, is it?

You want a resolution. You want a climax, even if the balloon of acid burst before I could have one.

I'll be honest—I expected police cars to be waiting outside the house when I woke up. I expected to walk up the steps to flashing blue lights through the windows and dickheads in uniform barking instructions.

But I didn't.

I woke up, contacted the same man who repaired my penis last time, and arranged an immediate appointment. He was hesitant, as he had a night at the theatre with his family to go to, but I offered him enough money to feed his family for a year, and he finally acquiesced to my request.

So what do you need resolved, my ever-present voyeurs, my glorious readers, my nosy fuckers with nothing better to do than read about a psychopath getting his dick blown off?

I imagine it is this:

1/ My dick (first and most important).

2/ Flora (second and almost as infuriating).

3/ What the fuck I'm doing now.

Well, seeing as you are so insistent, I shall go through the list one by one (but only because if you've enjoyed witnessing the sordid acts I have carried out in this book, then you are halfway to being as bad as me, and I admire that).

1/ My penis.

The surgeon calls it a penile fracture. I call it a fucking catastrophe. The skin was mostly red and extremely sensitive to the touch, whilst also black in places. The bellend (or 'glans penis' for those of you who have the audacity to not understand British slang—which is ridiculous, as we invented the language, and you all should follow our colloquialisms instead of making up your stupid words—I mean, don't get me started —fannies are vaginas, not arses; a trailer is not a caravan, it is a teaser for a movie; and we put petrol in our cars, not gas) was particularly mangled and coated in wounds. Not only this, but most of the penis had eroded away, and something much smaller and less impressive had been left in its place.

They started with the urethra—and anyone who has had something put down the urethra will know how uncomfortable it is—and he repaired this from the inside, telling me he was using soothing alkalis and cream and shit that I honestly didn't listen to. Next was something called the tunica albuginea, and he repaired this, telling me what he was doing, and at that point I told him to shut the fuck up, concentrate, and give me painkillers or a sedative.

They went with a sedative.

When I woke up, they had grafted skin from my buttocks to make up some of the lost skin. They say the wounds will heal and my penis will be usable again, but it will hurt for quite some time, and I should not use it for at least twelve months.

Twelve months, dear reader, TWELVE MONTHS, without so much as a wank (for non-British: this means masturbate. Learn the fucking language). And even after that, it may still hurt to have sex. And I will have to go back periodically for more repairs as the wounds start to heal.

They say I can expect to have normal intercourse again, with minor pain, in several years. I am fucking livid about what that little bitch has done to me.

Which leads me onto:

2/ Flora.

Oh, Flora.

I have no words left. I have called you every hyperbolic adjective I know, and now my anger has gone beyond the realms of description.

You were once the object of my hate and my desire, and are now the object of my obsessive rage.

I swore I would hunt you last time you fucked up my dick. I highlighted the vehemence with which I would pursue you. I emphasised the fury which would power my search. I accentuated and underlined the raw wrath that would allow me to FIND YOU.

Now, it seems, I must remind you of this; but I won't, as I still am yet to find words harsh enough to describe my feelings toward you.

How dare you, you insufferable psychotic monster.

You will pay for this. You truly will.

And finally:

3/ What the fuck I'm doing now.

In story-telling terms, the above is known as Resolution, and this part is known as Return to Ordinary World.

But there is no world I wish to inhabit that would be considered ordinary.

So I did what you expect me to do.

I gave notice on the house I rented to pursue Flora and returned to my mansion. I continue to pick up whores, only now I make them fuck themselves for my entertainment before I kill them. I bring the shutters down around my home to trap them in, giving me sport in hunting them, seeing as I can't have sport in fucking them.

And in the moments where I am in solitude, the intervals between murders, I sit in one of my many living rooms by the light of nothing but a dim lamp. My chin rests on my fist and my elbow rests on the windowsill. I watch my driveway and admire my cars and adore my gardens and wonder what it is all for if I cannot have that which I truly crave.

And I seethe. And I suffer. But I go on.

Because Flora gives me purpose to go on.

My resolve has been renewed. My temper has been exacerbated. My determination has been strengthened considerably.

And I will not be deterred.

So I scour the internet. Hire private investigators. Scour the dark web for seedy men in seedy bars who can offer a solution for a generous fee.

I pursue her.

Pursue her like I've never pursued before.

Just as you, dear reader, are about to return to your ordinary life—that, after the next page or two, you will place the book down, consider its competence at entertaining you, possibly write an Amazon review if you think your opinion is so important that everyone else should care, then continue with your day as if it didn't really matter—I must do the same.

Perhaps you will feed your kids, take them to school, or put them to bed.

Perhaps you will give your husband a blowjob, or fuck your wife, or scroll through dating apps in desperate search of someone who isn't as much of a bastard as everyone you've dated so far.

Perhaps you will sit alone in your room and cry because you just can't handle the anxiety that life induces, or go to work and try to pretend you can tolerate being there.

These are all things you do. Parts of your lives. Often, they are what your life is based on.

And as central as these things are to your life, murder is as central to mine.

So I continue. Life goes on, much as it did before, except I must wait to use my dick again.

Because nothing ever changes, dear reader. We are an insignificant blip that's here for a short time, and nothing we do impacts anything else in the world. We are quickly gone and forgotten, and there is no afterlife to welcome our souls once our bodies are cremated or left to decay.

I suppose you could choose to find such a thought depressing.

But I don't.

I find it liberating.

Nothing I do matters. Therefore, I can do anything.

I am free to be who I am, never deny my nature, and treat people as I wish.

There are no morals holding me down, no promise of heaven after I'm done, and no god that I must obey.

There is this.

Existing.

Killing.

Fucking.

And once you realise that, my ever-present voyeur, you will understand that nothing I've done in this book needs repenting.

I free you, my friend.

I free you of this life.

And I hope you take your revenge on those who have oppressed you.

I will certainly be seeking mine.

JOIN RICK WOOD'S READER'S GROUP...

And get **Roses Are Red So Is Your Blood** for free!

Join at **www.rickwoodwriter.com/sign-up**

AVAILABLE IN THE BLOOD SPLATTER BOOKS SERIES...

Psycho B*tches
Shutter House
This Book is Full of Bodies
This Book is Full of More Bodies
Haunted House
Home Invasion
Woman Scorned
Sex Blood
He Eats Children

BLOOD SPLATTER BOOKS

18+

WOMAN SCORNED

RICK WOOD

BLOOD SPLATTER BOOKS

18+

SEX
BLOOD

Rick Wood

BLOOD SPLATTER BOOKS

18+

HOME INVASION

RICK WOOD

BLOOD SPLATTER BOOKS

18+

SHUTTER HOUSE

RICK WOOD

BLOOD SPLATTER BOOKS

18+

PSYCHO B*TCHES

RICK WOOD

BLOOD SPLATTER BOOKS

18+

HAUNTED HOUSE

RICK WOOD

BLOOD SPLATTER BOOKS

18+

HE EATS CHILDREN

RICK WOOD

ALSO BY RICK WOOD...

BOOK ONE IN THE SENSITIVES SERIES

THE
SENSITIVES

RICK WOOD

RICK WOOD

CIA ROSE BOOK ONE

WHEN THE WORLD HAS ENDED

Printed in Great Britain
by Amazon

84540251R00202